one
gun

one
gun

VINNIE HANSEN

LEVEL
BEST BOOKS

Author Photo Credit: Daniel Friedman

Second edition

ISBN: 978-1-68512-730-5

Cover art by Level Best Designs

This book was professionally typeset on Reedsy.
Find out more at reedsy.com

Praise for One Gun

"Vinnie Hansen's *One Gun* unspools a long, exquisite crescendo of foreboding and dread as clouds gather for a chilling, unexpected climax. Top-notch writing, sensitive touch, and heart-wrenching choices. Hansen is an author to watch."—James W. Ziskin, Anthony, Barry, and Macavity award-winning author

"A riveting book that will tear at your heart as the impact from one gun ricochets through a close-knit community. Hansen's commanding voice weaves a compassionate tale that rings true and clear. You won't be able to look away."—Edgar-nominated author Susan Bickford

"In *One Gun*, Vinnie Hansen weaves a spell with a modern-day tale of suspense, pulling the reader into a riveting quest to see if justice will be served. When a gun used in a burglary falls into the wrong hands, a chase begins to find the gun before it and its owner can cause more mayhem. But of course things never go as planned when a gun is involved. The beautifully described setting is the central coast of California, where hidden forces drive the have-nots to desperate measures, and the criminal justice system is often on trial along with the criminals. A bravura outing by the author of the popular Carol Sabala mysteries."—G.M. Malliet, Agatha Award-winning author of the St. Just, Max Tudor, and Augusta Hawke mysteries

"One gun. One moment in time. Vinnie Hansen's tense crime novel, *One Gun,* explores the consequences of a single act in thought-provoking and taut detail. Thoroughly researched and smartly written, the book twists its way toward a heart-wrenching conclusion that will leave a reader breathless."—Peggy Townsend, author of Amazon Editors' mystery/suspense pick, *The Beautiful and The Wild*.

"The weapon casts a gripping Chekhov-ian shadow over Hansen's tense stand-alone thriller."—*Kirkus Reviews*

"...a compelling cat-and-mouse game as perp, victims, and those caught in-between find themselves on different roads to obtaining or concealing evidence and the truth."—D. Donovan, Senior Reviewer, *Midwest Book Review*

"Vinnie Hansen's standalone novel, *One Gun*, takes a simple concept—a couple disturbs a burglary in progress in their home—and crafts an unusual story where a gun becomes an inert, silent protagonist on a fateful journey that profoundly affects several lives. No one is the same once the gun's journey comes to a close. Although there are many characters in this novel, the voice of each character is distinct and finely drawn, rooting the reader in their role of the gun's journey. I highly recommend this book."—Claire M. Johnson, author of *Fog City*.

Chapter One: Burglary

WEDNESDAY BEFORE THANKSGIVING

Above a display of Brussels sprouts, Vivi struggled to get her wedding ring back on. She'd taken it off because the diamond rolled and bit into her skin during downward dog. Now she risked the ring dropping and disappearing into the vegetables. Next to her, a produce worker rolled his cartful of boxes back and forth as though he'd like to bump her out of the way.

A mellow baritone voice said her name. As Vivi turned, warmth crept up her face. "You've escaped the yoga room."

Dimples edged Winn's smile. "Yogis have to eat."

"That's why I'd better shop." She made a slight bow.

"Wait a sec." Winn grazed her arm with the tip of his finger. They'd both come from yoga class where Winn adjusted poses. A palm on the back to straighten a spine. Fingers on ankles to coax heels toward the floor. These things had never caused a spark like this.

She glanced toward her husband Ben, waiting at the meat counter to pick up their turkey.

"Are you considering the retreat?" Winn said lightly. "Mexico. In December."

"It's tempting." *Way too tempting.* "I've gotta go," she said. "Luna—my cat—has been outside all morning." She scuttled away.

Ben hefted the boxed turkey into their cart. "Who was that?"

"Yoga teacher." She plopped a bag of asparagus atop the other items.

"He definitely checked you out."

Vivi looked over her shoulder, but Winn had disappeared.

"He's ten years younger than I am." She didn't know if that was true. He wound his hair in a man-bun, but gray shot through the dark strands. Vivi reviewed their shopping list. "I think that's everything."

They stepped from the store into a brisk California Central Coast day, the sun having chased the morning gloom out to sea. On their way home, Ben outlined his new strategy for roasting the turkey, an ever-evolving process that included setting the bird on fire. In the past, she'd looked forward to their just-the-two-of-them tradition, a welcome respite during a hectic school year. Now that she was retired, it loomed as a lonely event.

She thought about the retreat. Would it be too much? She'd barely finished dealing with the books, papers, and records of her thirty-year teaching career when her mother had died.

A white Lexus pulled out in front of them. Ben hit the brakes. Her body lurched, then slammed back against the seat. The Lexus driver putted along, head down, seemingly oblivious.

"Did you see that guy! He didn't even look. No obstruction to his sightlines." A retired traffic engineer, Ben noticed that kind of thing. "He had his head down checking his phone."

He closed the distance between their SUV and the Lexus. "He's probably old. They're the worst at using phones while driving."

"Let it go," she said. "It would be ironic to have an accident while obsessing about someone else's distracted driving."

Ben blasted the horn.

"Oh, for crying out loud. What's the purpose of that?"

"I want him to get off his phone."

The driver raised his head, white hair visible. The Lexus picked up speed. It wasn't fair that Ben was right when he was so wrong.

Breathe in, breathe out. Practice yoga. As Winn would say, "The real work begins when you leave the mat." Then he'd smile with those damn dimples.

CHAPTER ONE: BURGLARY

* * *

Ben turned onto their street, the last outpost of a residential neighborhood, three houses on one side and Oak Tree Elementary sprawling along the other side—long, low concrete-block buildings with brightly painted doors. Down the street, the school had arranged for a gate that blocked through traffic on Beverly Lane, dividing the street into two cul-de-sacs, one of the things he liked about their home's location.

He halted in their driveway—the SUV rocking to a stop. While lifting the boxed turkey from the back, he covertly watched Vivi with the bag of groceries, buttoned-up lips conveying her annoyance just because he'd given the old guy in the Lexus the horn. It had made him wake up and drive right. It amazed Ben how passive people in Playa Maria were. They'd risk a rear-end collision before honking a driver parked at a green light.

Calling for Luna, he hurried up the walkway, Vivi behind him. At least with Vivi, he understood. She'd grown up in a town without stoplights, where passing drivers greeted each other with the lift of a finger from the steering wheel and only used the horn to blast cows off the road. In Philly, where he'd grown up, people used their finger in a different way.

A *clump* came from inside their house. Too heavy to be Luna. And, they'd left her outside. He dropped the turkey on the porch, unlocked the door, and flung it open.

A backpack flying behind a dark jacket flashed toward the rear door. Ben sprinted across the entryway and through the kitchen. Pea gravel in the back yard crunched under a fleeing figure.

"Call 9-1-1!" Heart hammering, Ben thumped down the back steps.

The punk jumped on top of their hot tub cover and leapt toward the fence, hands clasping the top ledge. He struggled to chin himself.

Ben circled the tub. "What the fuck were you doing in our house?" Legs spun like helicopter blades, one shoe slamming into Ben's temple. Dazed by the impact, he pulled back, off balance. An athletic shoe kicked toward his face again. Ben bobbed down, a blurry sole swinging in front of his eyes.

The thief dropped, landing in a crouch, and sprinted toward the locked

3

backyard gate, much lower than the fence.

Ben scrambled after him. Tendrils of jasmine vine tangled his foot. He stumbled as the burglar heaved himself toward the top of the gate.

Yanking free, Ben rushed through the house, passing Vivi, standing stunned in the kitchen instead of calling 9-1-1. She followed him. He bounded down the front steps, angling across the yard to cut off the thief's escape route.

Vivi threaded between the planter boxes that filled the front yard. The man's eyes shifted between them like a trapped animal's. He rushed toward the sidewalk, so close the air flapped Ben's flannel shirt. The thief reached the asphalt.

Crows fluttered up and cawed as the two men pounded down the empty street.

* * *

In the front yard, when the guy bolted toward Ben, the case for Ben's drum tuner flew from the blue backpack. That galvanized Vivi. This stranger had been in her home.

"Call 9-1-1!" Ben shouted again.

Where was the cell phone? She ran for the front door.

The thief sprinted down Beverly Lane, and Ben, fit from regular workouts, launched after him.

Inside the house, the air felt wrong, as though it had been put in a blender. Vivi grabbed the kitchen phone.

The dispatcher asked her name. She added her usual, "Two V's like vivid." If she didn't say that, people invariably thought she'd pronounced some name they knew, like Deedee.

"My husband and I found a burglar in our house." Her voice sounded steady. All those years of teaching had taught her to remain calm, or at least to appear calm, when they had an earthquake, or a lockdown, or a kid fainted. Inside, her stomach flipped like a landed fish.

Carrying the phone, she raced back to the sidewalk. "My husband is chasing him down Beverly Lane toward Sixth Avenue." Fear gripped her belly. What would Ben do if he caught up to the guy? Would he tackle him? Would they fight? And how would that end?

"Can you describe the suspect?"

Two houses down, a neighbor, cellphone in hand, stood in front of his rental and farther down, past the gate, where the neighborhood gave way to industry, Big Al paced in front of his forge, phone to his ear. A chain of reaction, like breadcrumbs, followed the pursuit, but Ben had disappeared.

"Light-skinned African-American," she said. "Twenty to twenty-five. Medium build. Dark pants. A jacket? Dark blue backpack."

"And your husband?"

"Five-eight. Sixty-three. Wearing shorts. Athletic shoes. Flannel shirt."

"Is he fit?"

"Yes, very. But so is the kid he's chasing."

* * *

Ben chased the thief down Beverly Lane, their shoes smacking the pavement. With the school closed for the holiday, the neighborhood was deserted. Dumpsters lined up like reinforcements along the gate that bisected the street. The thief's athletic shoes skidded on the asphalt. He whirled around, holding a gun, arms extended. "Back off. I'll shoot you."

Ben stopped and threw his arms in the air, his heart banging in his chest, a whooshing inside his head.

The shithead pivoted and swung around the end of the metal gate. He dashed down the continuation of the street toward a stretch of industrial buildings.

He can't shoot while running. Ben pursued him. His heart pumped every day to the idea of justice. Now the idea had been doused with adrenaline and lit on fire. He shouted to the neighborhood: "Burglar! Thief!" He wasn't going to let this punk get away with breaking into his house and threatening him with a gun.

The thief turned off Beverly Lane into a parking lot that cut through to

Scenic Drive, a thoroughfare. Ben wasn't closing the gap, but he wasn't losing ground, either.

The apprentice from Big Al's Iron Works pounded the blacktop behind him, the beat a four-on-the-floor like Ben's kick drum. *Bam bam bam bam.*

At the end of the long parking lot, the burglar reeled around. The weapon pointed at Ben.

The apprentice shouted, "Whoa. Gun!" as though Ben couldn't see. Shoes thumped a retreat.

It was just him and the thief. And a gun.

Chest heaving, the burglar trained the weapon on Ben's heart. In back of the thief, traffic was light on the four-lane Scenic Drive. No one seemed to glance toward them. And if they did, they would only see the guy's back. They wouldn't see the weapon.

"I'm warning you, man. Stop chasing me," the kid panted. "I'll kill you." Both hands clutched the grip like he meant business.

Is this it? Would this punk kill him? Ben's vision tunneled. Was his life about to be sucked down that tiny black hole? Would he die here in a stupid parking lot with Vivi thinking he was a jerk? No farewell. No chance to mend fences with his son? Ben's heart hammered and ached with loss. He curled protectively around his center.

* * *

In front of Dwayne, the man cowered, breathing hard. Sirens shrieked, coming in their direction. Dwayne's heart pounded like a jackhammer. Options pinballed through his head as he kept the gun trained on the old man. What would be gained? If he shot this crazy mofo and got caught? His hands shook. He needed to ditch the weight and jam.

Jerking the pack from his shoulder, he dumped the contents onto the asphalt. The watch, camera, drum tuner, his screwdriver, and Slim Jim all hit the parking lot, bouncing and rolling. Maybe now the stupid fuck would stop chasing him. The man stayed frozen, bent over, his forearms up in front of his face.

Sirens wailed louder, and a tow truck turned toward them. Dwayne stuffed the gun in his pocket and raced across the empty lot of an auto parts store, closed early for Thanksgiving. Another watch that had caught on the pack's fabric jounced loose and skittered on the pavement. Cruisers from the Sheriff's Department would be coming straight down Scenic. He had to get off the thoroughfare.

Next to the parts store, a driveway ran back in front of an auto repair joint. It was still open. Dwayne strolled past the bays. An old Mexican grease monkey in a jumpsuit watched him.

At the back of the narrow lot, Dwayne glided to the fence, planted his hands on top of the wood, and jackknifed up and over. As soon as he dropped onto the other side, he ripped off his jacket. Sweat glazed his forehead. He needed to look different.

There wasn't much chance of that, walking while black in Playa Maria.

He stuffed the semi-automatic into his pack.

His grammy claimed to pray for him every day; he hoped she was praying for him now.

This back lot was barren, offering only one hiding spot. He stuffed the jacket and pack into it. Cutting through rear parking lots of other businesses, he threaded his way back to Scenic Drive. A sheriff's vehicle turned off onto a side street. Keeping an eye out for other cruisers, he loped across the thoroughfare toward an undeveloped ravine. Once out of sight of passing cars, he darted down a dirt fire road into the wild.

Chapter Two: Suspicion

WEDNESDAY

Vivi remained rooted to the sidewalk. She clenched her hands and willed Ben to return, willed a squad car to turn onto Beverly Lane, willed Ben to know she loved him even if he'd acted like a jerk. That Lexus had almost clipped them, and all Ben had done was honk. What if something happened and that was their last interaction?

Her eyes stung. Sirens screamed around the neighborhood. A cruiser flashed down La Paz, their cross street, but it didn't turn onto Beverly Lane.

Two houses down, from the balcony of his studio apartment, the neighbor leaned around his surfboard and waved to her. She absently waved back. She didn't know this new renter who'd taken the over-the-garage unit. She waved to Big Al at the end of the block, too. Big Al signaled that he saw her. He was a solid, honest man, and she wished he would come over to her, but he returned to his shop. He couldn't walk out on a customer or on irons literally in the fire.

Staring down the street wasn't going to make anything happen. She picked up the turkey from the porch and put it in the refrigerator. The cold air revived her. Closing the door, she drew a deep breath, thinking of the Sanskrit word *so,* meaning "I am." She exhaled slowly to an inner *hum,* meaning "all that is." A simple mantra: *I am all that is.* After only one breath, *chitta,* her mind, interfered. "Oh, so you're that turkey. You're going to eat yourself."

From the back door, bits of mud tracked across the kitchen tile. She followed them down the maple floor of the hallway toward their bedroom. Even though the thief was gone, she peeked into the hall bathroom and spare bedroom to make sure they were empty.

The top drawers of the dresser—Ben's side—hung open. Vivi's heart plummeted. *The money.* Ben had negotiated a cash discount with their contractors and stashed an envelope in his drawer with hundreds—maybe a couple thousand—dollars. Without touching anything, she examined the contents of the drawer.

The envelope was gone.

What else? When he was fleeing, the thief had dropped the empty drum-tuner case, which was odd. Maybe he'd taken the drum tuner out to see what it was? He'd stolen Ben's watches.

The photo album of Arthur, Ben's son, lay splayed on the floor, open to Art's thirteenth birthday photos, his eyes sparkling. *Such a beautiful boy.* "Life of a party," Ben had said. She picked up the album, closed it, and pressed it to her chest. It was heartbreaking to view innocent Art, a life of promise hanging before him, and to think of the coked-out man he'd become. She slipped the album back into the drawer, but left the rest of the crime scene as she'd found it.

She turned to the closet. The closed door. She listened for breathing. For rustling clothes. She yanked open the door. Two bars of silent shirts and dresses, a litter of undisturbed shoes below them. She exhaled.

At the end of the walk-in closet, her cedar chest was undisturbed. She perched on top of it. Thank God for small favors, for the thief not rummaging there, for her being young before the internet. Nowadays, a lot of people would find the nude modeling a colorful chapter of her life— nothing more. Ben did. He could barely refrain from bragging about it. But then, he didn't know all that had happened.

Hanging clothes hedged her in. Despite the cool dimness of the closet, sweat beaded on her forehead.

Taking a deep breath, she bounded up and peered into the bedroom. It was ridiculous to think anyone remained in the house, yet the burglar's aura

9

hung in the air like a contrail. The unfamiliarity of her own bedroom, the sense of disorientation, tossed her back to a humid morning in Hollywood. She squelched the memory and pushed herself back to an inspection of the crime scene. No mud tracked from the bedroom to the office. The desk drawers remained closed. The Mac desktop computer rested in its usual position. It seemed to her that a burglar would have started with this room, looking for digital stuff. But the burglar had gone directly to the bedroom. She followed the hallway trail of mud back to the glass kitchen door and down the steps into the back yard.

Twittering house finches attacked the bird feeder as though nothing had disturbed their universe. It was weird how life went calmly on while Ben was out there—somewhere—chasing someone who'd had the audacity to break into their home to paw through their most personal belongings.

She crunched over the gravel past a sculpture they'd bought from Big Al. The corner of the hot tub cover sparkled. Her Kindle. She snatched up the device. Nothing else looked disturbed. Jasmine crawled up the side fence. The gate to the front yard remained closed and padlocked. Anxiety about Ben percolated up again. She passed back through the kitchen, setting the device on the butcher-block table, returning to pace the sidewalk.

The new renter, hefty and blond, strolled toward her. He introduced himself, but Vivi couldn't focus on anything he was saying. His voice garbled like when her brothers used to drag their fingers on playing records so the singing would warp into a sound like hollering down a well.

"Did you see where they went?" she asked the renter.

"Once they ran past the gate, I lost sight of them."

"Welcome to the neighborhood," she said sardonically.

They shook hands. He asked a couple of questions about the burglary and then, like an apparition, floated back to his rental over the garage, and she couldn't even remember the name he'd given.

A girl coasted by on a pink cruiser bike, circled in front of the school, and pedaled back to Vivi.

"What's happening?" The girl, wearing UGGs and a ruffled skirt, straddled the bike in the middle of the street.

Vivi eyed the heavy make-up. The girl was pale, petite, and skinny, but not really a kid. Maybe twenty. Raven-black hair. It seemed odd she would ask—a bit nosy—even if Vivi was standing on the sidewalk and gazing down the street, even if the cacophony of sirens in the distance was only beginning to calm down.

"Someone broke into our house."

"Just now?"

Vivi nodded.

"Did he take a lot?"

"Stuffed his backpack."

"Whoa. You know, I saw a suspicious car around the corner on La Paz."

"What do you mean?"

"When I rode by, the guy in it ducked down. Like he was trying to hide. You know, like an accomplice."

"Uh-huh. The thief went that way." Vivi pointed. "If there was a car waiting, seems like he would have run to it." She spun around and started up the walkway. She didn't want to talk to anyone right now except Ben or the police.

From the corner of her eye, Vivi glimpsed the thin figure pumping her bike down Beverly Lane like she was off to check out the action. When she disappeared, Vivi returned to the sidewalk. She jittered with the urge to go, too, but the dispatcher had told her to "stay put." She hurried the short distance to the intersection and peered down La Paz. Unlike Beverly Lane, it was an old two-lane county road, small homes on big lots with heritage pines and almost leafless liquid ambers pushing up what little sidewalk existed. Vehicles crowded the street all the way to where it dead-ended into Del Amo. No way did she stand a chance of spotting the girl's *suspicious* car. Worried she might miss a callback, Vivi hustled to the house.

Finally, a sheriff's vehicle turned the corner and rolled up to the curb. Ben hopped from the passenger's seat. Her jaw and shoulders relaxed. Her legs regained solidity. She expected the deputy to follow Ben, but the car sped off so fast the tires squealed. It swept in a U-turn at the gate, zoomed back toward them, and ran the stop sign. "What happened?" she asked.

Ben moved through their front door. Vivi took up a position against the kitchen counter as he paced in front of her, back and forth like a caged animal. The air between them vibrated with his nervous energy. It emanated from him, struck up against the refrigerator and gas stove, and then rebounded back at her.

He recounted the chase, talking so fast he tripped over his words. She tried to follow his story. "The thief pulled a gun and threatened to kill me. But when he started running, I chased him. Then he pulled the gun again and dumped the loot in the parking lot. I stopped chasing then."

"I would hope so!"

"A tow truck driver turned into the parking lot from Scenic Drive. I was yelling 'thief.'" Ben's eyes widened around his dark irises. Sweat trickled from his temple. He swiped at it with a cuff, then tugged off his flannel shirt and slung it over a stool, the tee underneath reeking of nervous sweat.

"The tow truck driver held up his radio to show he was calling in. That was good, but he was between me and the burglar. That's when I lost sight of the shithead."

"Thank God he didn't shoot you."

"After a few minutes, a sheriff pulled up. He had my other watch."

"How did he get that?" she asked.

"A mechanic from one of those auto shops on Scenic gave it to him."

"Was that the deputy who drove you home?"

"Yeah," Ben said.

"Did he take a report?"

"No. Right now they're busy trying to get the guy."

She hesitated before saying what was on her mind. "I think the burglar might be someone related to the bathroom project." She pointed at the mud trail on the floor. "Those go right back to the drawer where you had the money—no stopping at the office or anything."

Ben followed the mud up the hall, pausing in the bedroom to take in the disarray. He returned to the kitchen without saying a word.

"You know who I'm suspicious of?" she asked.

"Who?"

"Brenden, the tile guy's new helper. He's young. Maybe he told a friend. I've heard of this kind of thing. A person gets his house worked on; two days later it's broken into."

Ben nodded.

"Let me show you where I found the Kindle." She motioned for Ben to follow.

"Don't touch the door handle."

"Good thinking," she said, even though she had already touched it, probably destroying their best chance of prints.

As soon as their shoes hit the gravel, birds swooshed from the feeder and disappeared into the photinia trees. Vivi passed their sculpture made by Big Al. Twisted vines of metal rose, wrapped around a globe-like ball of welded triangles, and then soared to the sky as leaves. She pointed to the far end of the hot tub cover.

"He must have lost it when he leapt for the fence," Ben said. "I didn't even notice."

They seemed to have the same thought at the same time. Ben aimed his finger at the hot tub cover. "Shoe prints."

Two large tracks ran over the top of the chocolate-colored vinyl.

"The fence was too high." Her gaze ran up the side fence, a solid eight feet topped with jasmine vines, and the back fence, a towering ten-foot wall. "So that's why he came over the gate to the front." A mere five-foot barrier.

"No doubt the way he went in," Ben said. "When he fled, he knew the gate was locked."

So much for the usefulness of locking the gate. "The cops should lift prints," she said.

"They're too busy with the chase," Ben said.

"The sexy part of their job." Bitterness edged into her voice.

Ben marched back toward the house. Vivi hustled after him, ground-feeding crowned sparrows whirring up in front of their advance. He crossed the kitchen to the phone.

"Who are you calling?"

"Frank."

The tile guy. "Why?"

But he had already pressed the auto-dial, and the seven-beep melody sounded into the silence. Jumping to her defense without question while she questioned everything, even honking at a car.

Frank answered on the first ring. As Ben told Frank what had happened, Vivi's gut fluttered—a person couldn't be sure. She hated the insinuation. Even if Ben were calling, she'd set the response in motion. Frozen, she listened to Ben's side of the conversation.

"We like you," he told Frank. "We want you to finish the job. But you have to respect our feelings here. We don't want Brenden in our house again. Ever."

* * *

Kneeling on his pads, Frank pocketed his cell phone and stared at the half-finished tile floor of today's project. The owner was a techie from Silicon Valley, converting a small house into a sprawl with a kitchen the size of an Olympic swimming pool.

This was a load of crap. Frank liked Vivi and Ben, but he could do without the small-potato job in their minuscule master bathroom. He could barely turn around inside it.

Holding a freshly cut tile, Brenden waited for direction, scowling toward the pocket where Frank had stuck his phone. "What was that about?"

Brenden wasn't a talkative guy and remained a bit of a mystery, even though Frank had known him since he was in grade school. As he'd told Ben, Brenden came from a good family. He was big and strong and basically a decent worker, although he was not too swift at thinking on his own or anticipating the next step.

"This sucks," Frank said aloud. He rocked back on the soles of his boots into a squat. He was going to have to tell Brenden the whole story. What else could he do? Brenden had come in from using the tile saw as he was asking Ben, "Don't you know Brenden lives around the block from you—on Del Amo? You might see him around whether you like it or not."

Frank stood up to relieve his knees and gave Brenden the lowdown about the robbery and Ben and Vivi's suspicion.

"That's messed up." Brenden's dark features drew together like that big solid exterior of his could blow up—shoot out a million deadly pieces of shrapnel.

"Look, man, I don't think you did anything," Frank said.

"I didn't. I was right here with you. And I didn't talk to nobody about the job or the money or anything." He rolled meaty shoulders and flexed his fingers like someone who wanted to fight. "Why would I get involved in that kind of thing?"

"Hey!" Frank said. "Just cool down. Do you need a break?"

Why *would* anyone do that kind of thing? Frank wondered. According to Ben, the thief had leaped over their gate. With that kind of strength, he could be carrying and cutting tiles like Brenden and earning eighteen dollars an hour. "You were right here when I was on my phone," Frank continued. "You heard me tell Ben that any thief would go to the dresser. That's the number-one target."

"Right. Lots of people keep valuable stuff in their dressers." Brenden handed him the tile.

Frank kneeled on his padded work blanket. "Hand me some spacers." The kid still looked sullen as he scooped up the white plastic crosses from a box.

Focusing on the floor project, Frank raised a cupped hand for the spacers. "Ben said the thief didn't get the money, though."

"He didn't?"

Chapter Three: Doubt & Certainty

V ivi drummed her fingers on the kitchen counter. "I could be wrong," she said when Ben hung up the phone.

He clicked a pen in and out in rapid succession. "Well, good thing I moved the money."

"That's a relief." They could have absorbed the loss, but with only pensions now, everything was budgeted. "Why didn't you tell me?"

"I don't know." He jabbed the pen into a mug holding a bouquet of writing implements. "Everything is whirling around now. It's hard to think straight."

"When did you move it?"

"Yesterday."

"Yesterday everything wasn't *whirling around*." Annoyed, she followed him into the office. Ben opened the file drawer and extracted the bulging envelope. The day before, he'd pulled it from the dresser drawer and counted bills into Frank's grout-splotched hands, payment for the first half of the job. Sometimes paying cash meant a better deal. The money had to be on hand, though. Contractors didn't want to cool their heels while you ran to the bank.

Ben returned the envelope to its new spot.

"If the burglar had come to the office," she said, "which seems like the logical place to me, he would have found the money." The fact firmed her suspicion of an inside job. "Why did you move it? Did you suspect someone

16

would do this?"

"No." With his leg, Ben nudged shut the file drawer. "I just thought they'd seen its hiding place, and I didn't want to leave any temptation."

The doorbell chimed. Ben rushed down the hall. She followed close, stepping on the back of his shoe and giving it a flat tire.

A county sheriff's deputy stood on the porch. Behind him, traffic clogged Beverly Lane—parents headed to a driveway that wrapped behind the regular school to a charter school. The White School, Vivi called it.

"I'm Deputy Hashimoto." His uniform was crisp and his hair cropped close to his skull. "We've apprehended a suspect in your burglary. We need you to make a field identification."

Over Ben's shoulder, she asked, "You arrested someone?"

"We're holding a person of interest."

Ben stooped to fix the back lip of his shoe. "Do you want both of us to come?"

"Just you."

The closing door puffed an old, familiar feeling around Vivi, one of staying with her mother while her father and her five brothers piled into the pick-up. Even if the guys were headed toward a grunt job like hauling fence posts, they bumped against each other and, loudly joking, jockeyed for who got to ride shotgun. Her brothers could be crude and mean, and yet, as the truck trundled down the driveway, spitting gravel, Vivi felt left behind. Left out.

As much as she treasured those quiet times with her mother—making jam or walking to the library—she envied the men rolling off in that pick-up, moving into the world, connecting with all that energy and force.

* * *

Inside the sheriff's cruiser, Ben's heart thumped with excitement and anxiety. He hoped they'd nabbed the right guy. *It has to be him.*

As soon as Deputy Hashimoto turned from Beverly Lane onto La Paz, he slapped a little card on his dash and rattled off a statement to Ben: "You are going to be shown an individual. This may or may not be the person who committed the crime, so you should not feel compelled to make an identification. It is just as important to clear innocent people as it is to identify possible perpetrators."

Other than the deputy droning on with the canned policy speech, the cruiser was eerily quiet, and Ben realized the deputy had turned off the radio. The little computer-like screen on the dash was a dead gray-black, too. To avoid prejudicing him, Ben supposed.

He couldn't concentrate on Hashimoto's words. If they had picked up someone, it was the shithead who felt entitled to invade his home, who'd pointed a gun at his head, who'd threatened to kill him. *Twice!*

Deputy Hashimoto turned onto Scenic Drive, a meandering corridor that corralled the communities of Playa Maria County against the Pacific. The inland side of the road quickly rose into parched foothills and, beyond that, forested mountains.

Hashimoto looked too young to have had encounters with Ben's son Art before he got straight and moved away. Ben was glad of that. Sunshine beat through the cruiser's windshield. The inside of the car was stifling.

Ben tapped a rhythm on the seat, trying to focus on the here and now. Despite everything with Art, he'd never been inside a cruiser. He pointed at the rifle beside him. "I didn't know you guys had weapons like this."

"That's an AR-15," Hashimoto said. "We take those out for stops with weapons involved. If they have a weapon, we want to have a bigger one."

Good luck with that.

As a former traffic engineer, Ben knew this long sloping stretch of Scenic Drive intimately, had, in fact, designed parts of it, but he felt like he'd never seen the section of highway before. Staring past Hashimoto's profile, he scanned the commercial buildings on the developed side for places the burglar might have hidden. How had he lost sight of him so quickly?

Ben twisted in his seat. A riparian corridor, a wooded ravine, dipped down on the other side of the road. The thief must have escaped across Scenic Drive and disappeared into the brush.

"Kind of interesting," Hashimoto said as if uncomfortable with the silence. "The scene of the crime—your house—is county, but by the time the thief started dumping your things, he'd reached city limits. It's a long, spread-out crime scene."

Two agencies could only complicate matters. In his work for the county, Ben had coordinated road projects with the city, and if you wanted a real nightmare, throw in the state, too. "Will that have an impact on the arrest?"

"Let's just see if the person we're talking to has anything to do with the burglary," Hashimoto said.

They'd traveled down the long slope of Scenic Drive and up the hill. Ben's body thrummed with adrenaline. Hashimoto turned right into a residential neighborhood spreading toward the foothills.

The image of the black gun barrel rose up before Ben, the tiny hole ready to swallow his life. His breath stopped.

As though inside his thoughts, the deputy said, "The gun is the big deal. Without it, we may be looking at catch and release."

"Catch and release? He could go free?"

The deputy clamped his lips like he'd said too much. He made another turn onto a tree-lined street that ran parallel to the freeway. He drove to a collection of patrol cars, two dark-green county sheriff's vehicles facing one way, a California Highway Patrol car across the street, and two Playa Maria police cruisers behind that.

So much manpower expended for one shithead. His head pounded and acid roiled in his empty gut.

Hashimoto stopped behind the CHP car and spoke into his radio. "We're ready." He cracked his car door, and Ben started to open his. "Stay put."

Crisp air flowed into the cruiser, reviving him. The accompanying growl of freeway noise marred the image of a quiet tree-lined street.

Hashimoto stood outside his open door. A heavy-set deputy climbed from the front sheriff's vehicle, opened the back door, and pulled out a handcuffed man who landed awkwardly on his feet and shrugged away from the deputy. The officer nudged him forward.

Hashimoto leaned into the car toward Ben. "Is this the guy?"

He took in the sweaty young man—not wearing the jacket or the pack. "That's him."

"How certain are you?"

"One hundred percent."

The thief stared at him. A trace of a smile flicked his lips.

The insolence, so like Art's. The beefy deputy clasped the suspect's bicep and spun him back toward his vehicle. The young man's head swiveled as though he had something to say, but before he could think of anything creative, the deputy pressed him back down into the cruiser.

Hashimoto climbed into the patrol car.

"I don't know if you're allowed to say," Ben said, "but do you know the suspect?"

"We're familiar with him." Hashimoto executed a tight U-turn.

On the trip back, the deputy asked, "Could you describe the gun?"

"Black and silver. Not very big. No spinning chamber. The kind where you load a magazine."

"A semi-automatic?"

"Yeah. A semi-automatic."

"Did it have an orange tip?"

He searched Hashimoto's profile, the high cheekbones and unblinking eyes. It was hard to concentrate on that moment when he thought he'd die. "No. I've never seen a gun with an orange tip. What does that mean?"

The deputy shook his head. He'd said all he was going to say.

Chapter Four: The Injustice of It All

WEDNESDAY - a little earlier

They cornered him in a back yard. Dwayne shot his hands high. He didn't want to end up another Trayvon Martin or Tamir Rice. This may be Playa Maria, but he was black, they were police, and he didn't want to die.

A deputy yanked his arms down and cuffed him. A police officer opened the gate for him to walk through to the front. Not locked like the one at that stupid, fucking house on Beverly. The deputy frog-marched him to a sheriff's vehicle.

Anger prickled his skin. Inside the cruiser, he wrestled with the cuffs behind his back, though it was useless. What was wrong with that dude chasing him? He could have shot the fucker. Should have shot him. But he'd never shot anyone before.

Dwayne butted the divider with his forehead. The deputy in the front had turned off the screen and radio. Dwayne couldn't see or hear what was going on.

He banged the divider again. "What am I being charged with?"

The deputy waggled his head. A no. He wasn't going to say.

"I wanna know the charge." He hadn't been Mirandized. He was asking for the info. The deputy could tell him if he wanted to. "Robbery?" That'd mean they found the gun.

His question woke the popo from his fantasy of glazed donuts. He turned a bit. "I don't know."

Dwayne snorted.

"But since you're asking." The deputy slid a creased cheat sheet from his uniform pocket and read him his rights. Dwayne looked out the window, the possibility of learning what they'd found disappearing with the words.

When the deputy asked if he understood, Dwayne grunted. He could recite the thing by heart, better than the deputy. At the rumble of an arriving car, Dwayne twisted around. The vehicle behind them jammed his view. The fat-ass deputy got out of the car, opened the back door, and hoisted him to his feet, pushing him toward the newly-arrived cruiser.

Seated beside a deputy, the dude who had chased him gawked through the windshield. The deputy got out and said something back through the door. The guy nodded his head.

Dwayne cut him with his eyes. Sucked his teeth. How had this shrimpy old motherfucker been able to keep up with him? What a stupid bust. There hadn't even been any good shit, not what he expected—no cash—not even good Apple picking. Then their cat had leaped onto the top of the gate, like it had suddenly decided to come home. It had sized him up through the bedroom window. Next thing he knew, the cat was being called, the owner stepping on to the porch.

Now the old guy cracked the cruiser's door like he was coming for him.

The fat-ass deputy spun Dwayne around. Dwayne glanced back over his shoulder, wanting to laugh. *Seriously, dude?*

The deputy stuffed him back onto the hard-plastic bench seat, started the vehicle, and gunned it. Dwayne shrugged his shoulders, working the collar seam of his shirt into his mouth. He gnawed on it. There was something about the way the officers were acting that made him think they didn't find the gun. They weren't quite cocky enough.

The ride didn't take even five minutes. The deputy pulled into a short driveway blocked by a wide gate and spoke into an intercom. "County Sheriff, one male."

The gate doors folded open like accordions. The cruiser rolled through to a sally port big enough to hold a fleet of vehicles.

County jail. Three hots and a cot.

The deputy yanked him roughly from the back seat.

"Hey, police brutality." The cold of the concrete garage, heady with diesel exhaust, swirled around Dwayne. The officer prodded him toward a table against the wall covered with stacks of forms and pushed him down into a white plastic chair.

"Sit there and behave yourself."

"Must need a donut fix," Dwayne muttered. "You like the ones with little sprinkles?"

An intake officer peeked from a door. "Need any help?"

"Nah. He's not going anywhere." The deputy returned his attention to a form.

Dwayne felt like jumping up and ramming his head under the deputy's white pasty face. He already faced a burglary charge, a possible gun charge, a resisting arrest charge. What difference would assault make? *Right now, The Restraint Chair.* That holy hell had been invented by some sick motherfucker. Who sat around coming up with a black molded seat all isolated in its own dark little room? That was some medieval shit.

"Let's go."

When the sheriff's deputy tried to raise him by the bicep, Dwayne shrugged away. He knew the drill. He entered the padded intake room. It stank of nervous sweat and vomit. Facing the wall, he spread his legs. The sheriff removed his cuffs.

The intake officer snapped on gloves and emptied Dwayne's pockets— breath mints and his mom's expired Sears card, leftover from better days. He'd returned to their old 'hood, the gray concrete buildings of Oak Tree Elementary School spilling out memories, random bits like the alphabet in cursive above a whiteboard.

The deputy patted him down. "Shoes and belt."

Dwayne didn't want to get The Chair. Last time he'd spent two hours there with his shoulders, arms, and legs in restraints.

He lifted his Raiders tee shirt so the guy could see he didn't have a belt to hang himself with. He untied his high-tops and toed them off, leaving them on the floor for the officer to pick up.

The officer ticked off items on a clipboard. "Hepatitis?"

"No." At least not that he knew of.

"HIV?"

Dwayne rolled his eyes. "No."

A correctional officer met him on the other side of the intake room.

Dwayne turned toward a holding cell.

"Dream on, buddy." The officer guided him directly through the metal detector to the computer for fingerprints. Then he pointed at the camera. "Time for your photo op."

Dwayne twisted strands of his goatee. No opportunity to call Espie, maybe get an assist. Once inside, his calls would be monitored. At the twinge of disappointment, an inner voice snarled at him, "Man up." That voice always sounded like his brother Wesley.

The officer escorted him to a closet-sized room where a Mexican dude grinned at them both—glad to have a job, Dwayne guessed—sized up his build and selected an orange top and bottom for him. The man scanned Dwayne's stocking feet. "Size ten?" Without waiting for an answer, he added jail sandals to the bundle.

As they continued down a glossy hallway, Grammy Rice came sneaking into Dwayne's thoughts. She resided in a soft spot under his left ribs, like a bruise to touch if you wanted to feel something. "Count your blessings, son," she told him.

I sure as shit will, Grammy, if I can think of any.

Well, no cavity search. He smirked.

Still, Grammy Rice's praying had latched onto him like head lice. You had to resist those easy answers. What was there to call a *blessing*? His dad had been shot in Utah. "Execution style," his mom said, pointing an acrylic nail at a yellow newspaper article. His dad was white, probably the reason he'd never done time, but he'd been living the thug life, no doubt. "Oh, yeah, baby," his mom would say, tapping the article, "But ask any of the Williams family, and I led their precious boy astray."

He'd pray, right now, though, if it'd get that sweet little Kel-tec off the street. If found, the gun would be straight-up plus ten. A blade of cold knifed his gut.

Chapter Five: The Stash

WEDNESDAY - a short time later

Marshall bolted from the collection of portable buildings that made up Vision Charter School. He cut across athletic fields his school shared with Oak Tree Elementary, went through the back gate to Del Amo Street, and hid behind a bush to jump the little rat-faced bastard Finn.

Students trickled around the corner. Moms in minivans rolled by. At least the sirens had stopped. Cops no longer swarmed the neighborhood.

Normal schools were off the day before Thanksgiving, but Vision Charter always tried to prove it was different. Marshall toed the dirt, waiting, thinking about his brother James. After the school bell had rung, Marshall had found him in his deserted classroom, hunched at his desk. On the back of James' neck was LAMES in jerky black pen strokes.

He knew Finn did it. The little bastard had been harassing James and calling him Lames since the start of the school year.

Now as Finn rounded the corner with a buddy, Marshall stepped in front of him. Finn froze. The friend stared wide-eyed at Marshall and then at Finn, waiting for Finn to react.

Pulling back his shoulders, Finn squinted up at Marshall. "Whadda you want?" Arms folded over his scrawny chest, popping small biceps.

The kid has balls. Marshall would give him that. James was two inches taller and fifteen pounds heavier than this freckled runt, should have been able to kick his ass. But James…well. Marshall's heart dropped.

Marshall poked Finn's sternum hard enough to back him up, off balance. "You touch my brother again, I'll pound the piss outta you."

An SUV turned the corner. Finn spread his arms to his sides like a gunslinger and smirked at him. "Ooohh. Aren't you tough? An eighth grader who can beat up a fifth grader."

The friend plucked at Finn's shirt. "Hey, we should go." Finn allowed himself to be towed past Marshall. The mommy mobile passed, a couple of little kids gawking from the back.

Marshall pivoted, turned the corner at La Paz Street, and headed back to the campus. He felt flushed. Finn had a point. Marshall was broad-shouldered and five foot eight and would seem like a bully if he beat on Finn.

Across the street, James walked by with his friend Scotty. The two should be okay, playing video games at Scotty's house like they usually did. James shot Marshall a worried look but kept going, his fingers rubbing the back of his neck.

On Beverly Lane, the cat at the yellow house across the street froze and stared at him. Marshall must have walked by that cat lazing around in the flowers a billion times, but this time it inspected him like he was a dog. Then it arched up like a Halloween cat and *fuffed* at him. *What the hell?*

Marshall passed the driveway that led back to Vision Charter, tucked behind the elementary school. He kept straight on Beverly Lane to *his spot*, a picnic table on a splotch of grass. He splayed himself like a starfish on top of the table. The afternoon stretched before him.

His school was a bunch of portables surrounded by chain-link prison fences. Marshall preferred Oak Tree with its lawns and the big field he'd cut across where little kids played T-ball in the spring.

When he'd gone to Oak Tree, a lot of the kids rode their bikes or walked to school like him and James did. They'd fit in.

On the occasions when the charter school called to bug his dad about his volunteer hours, Marshall seized the opportunity. "I'd be happy to go to Pacific." Pacific was a real middle school. At Vision Charter he was stuck with kids all the way down to kindergarten.

His father scratched at specks of paint on his arms. "Vision is a better school."

"Pacific has a music program."

"Academics first. Guitar second."

On the picnic table, Marshall scooched down to let his legs drape off the end, his orange Converses dangling. Clouds drifted. Every few moments, the sun would pop free, warming his face and glinting on the sun-bleached strands of his honey-colored hair.

Maybe he could persuade his dad by telling him about Finn. *What a little punk.* He should have smacked the freckles off his face. Then he and James could both go to a regular middle school.

He never argued hard against his dad, though. Because his dad's face sagged, and Marshall knew he'd rather be surfing, out where the waves could wash away his sadness. Instead, his dad spent his time cooking mac and cheese and hauling his kids to Target to buy new underwear. His dad had campaigned for two years to get Marshall into Vision Charter. Once Marshall was there, it had been easier to get James in. It wasn't really about academics; his dad wanted him and James together in a small school, surrounded by a fence, where he thought they might be safe.

Rolling thunks of skateboard wheels traveled toward him. Marshall sat up. His one friend, Rocky, was grinding on the curb of the parking lot, which he wasn't supposed to do, which was why Marshall liked him.

Rocky landed a flip trick, then jumped off his board, caught it by the tip, and lifted his chin at Marshall in greeting.

Marshall patted the pocket of his shirt and put his thumb and forefinger to his lips.

Rocky loped toward him, carrying his board. A new black skull decal shone on the dark side of the skateboard deck.

"That's tight."

Rocky tucked long blond hair behind an ear. "My mom bought it for me." He laughed.

Marshall laughed too, but not without a hollow thump in his chest.

Marshall's mom had brought him here—right here—holding his hand for his first day of kinder. He'd been a big baby, sinking down to the concrete and screaming to go home. Rocky was lucky to have a mom even if she was so young kids went around saying she was a MILF, like they'd ever had sex with anyone besides Rosie Palm.

By silent mutual consent, the two boys headed to the gate that blocked the street. They slipped around it on the pedestrian passageway and crossed Beverly Lane. They passed Big Al's Iron Works and automotive shops before turning onto a road that bisected an empty field. It used to be a place that sold rocks. For some reason, as a kid, Marshall had been fascinated by the piles of pebbles and stacks of bricks. Now there was nothing but grit and bits of gravel.

At the end of the short road, Marshall led the way along a fence. Usually, no one and nothing was around. That was why they came here. But today, a huge green dumpster hulked on the asphalt. The dumpster looked like one you'd get for a demolition. Maybe the one-room office for the rock business was going to be torn down.

Behind the dumpster, Marshall sparked up a joint, took a hit, and passed it to Rocky.

Rocky barely inhaled before he handed it back. He threw down his skateboard and tried to knock open one of the dumpster's lids. It banged back shut, loud as a gunshot.

"What the fuck?" Marshall pinched the end of the joint and stuck it in his pocket. They'd come back here because it was quiet, but Rocky never seemed to think about stuff like that.

"Why is this dumpster here?"

Marshall shrugged. Rocky acted like he had ADD. "You know what, dude? You should have your mom get you medical marijuana. Calm you down." Although the hit Rocky had taken hadn't done any good.

Rocky didn't answer. He picked up his skateboard and used it to wedge open the heavy lid.

"What're you doing?"

Rocky grabbed the edge of the dumpster. "Make sure the lid doesn't fall on me."

Marshall couldn't reach the high end of the lid, so he held the skateboard steady to keep the lid propped open. Rocky hopped and levered himself over the rim. The top half of his body folded into the container, his hair flipping forward off his back. "Dude, this is weird." His voice echoed. Rocky slid out to the pavement, trawling a backpack and jacket. White powder, like sheetrock dust, covered the bottom of the pack. But the rest of the dark blue fabric was shiny new.

"Hey!"

Marshall whipped around, pulling loose the skateboard. The lid slammed. On the road through the old rock yard, a skinny girl in a skirt straddled a pink cruiser bike. Older than them, like maybe a senior. She rocked a short tee shirt that stopped below her tits and revealed ink of a snake.

"Whatdaya have?" The girl put her UGG boots on the pedals and coasted forward. Marshall dumped the skateboard on the ground. She eyed the pack in Rocky's hand. Rocky acted totally uncool, dropping the jacket to the ground and sticking the pack behind his back like a little kid.

Marshall stepped toward her. "None of your business."

She stopped and propped skinny arms on the handlebars. Thick make-up ringed her eyes. They narrowed at him. Her bike tire turned toward Rocky.

"Give me the pack."

"No!" Rocky said. "We found it."

Rocky scooped up his board and ran with it under his arm until he was past the treacherous pebbles. The girl stomped the pedal of her bike and raced after him. Marshall chased the girl. Lunging, he caught the metal rack over the back fender. He lurched forward. Then he yanked back, skidding on the gravel. The bike juddered to a stop.

The girl tipped sideways. She put a toe down, her UGGs sliding on loose rocks. She didn't fall over, but her skirt flipped up and black lace peeked out. Marshall gawked.

"You little fucker!"

Up close, her blue eyes were red-rimmed, but she was still beautiful. A spicy perfume rose from her body.

When she drew herself upright, he quit staring and sprinted toward the elementary school to catch up with Rocky.

"That's not yours! You and your stupid friend are going to pay for taking it!"

The bike tires whirred behind him. He couldn't figure out why Rocky was running from a girl or why she was bothering to chase him, but he cut sideways before she could ram his leg. When she cranked back toward him, he headed over the curb toward the grassy area of the school. She looked too weak to jump a curb with a cruiser, but then she was a crazy hopped-up psycho chick trying to run him over with a bike.

"Run!" Rocky screamed at him from the playground. The idiot stood on the other side of the jungle gym, grinning and swinging the pack above his head as though it were a weapon he intended to hurl.

As soon as Marshall caught up, Rocky whooped and ran. His hair streamed and shimmered behind him. Something bumped around inside the backpack like a noisemaker for a football game. Rocky headed toward the fields, a good idea. On grass, they'd be able to move faster than the bike.

Marshall's head throbbed. At this point, both schools were closed for vacation. The gate out from the field would be locked.

He glanced back. The girl had thrown her bike down on home plate and was yanking something from the waistband of her skirt. She put it up to her face, and he knew it was a cell phone.

His armpits were wet, but his mouth was dry. He and Rocky could climb the chain-link, easy enough. But it was threaded with brown plastic privacy strips, and right now the sun angled into blinding glitter through the cracks.

The girl acted as if they'd stolen her stuff, but it was a man's pack. Who was the girl calling and what would be waiting for them over the fence on Del Amo Street?

31

Chapter Six: Dwelling

Vivi paced her left-behind feeling around the kitchen. As the baby of her family and the only girl, she'd been adored and protected by her brothers, but also considered a pain in the butt to be ditched at every opportunity. Not that Ben had ditched her.

She sighed and wondered if Ben would be able to identify the person the police had in custody.

A skateboard *ka-thunked* down the street, a grating noise. Now that she wasn't jacked up with adrenaline, now that she was alone in the house, uneasiness settled around her. The intruder had had a gun. She locked the back door. *Forget the fingerprints.* She'd smeared them already anyway.

She found herself holding a ladle and didn't know why. She set it down. Standing in *tadasana*, she tried a simple *pranayama*, observing the breath without changing it. On the third breath, she shook her hands in irritation. In class, when Winn offered this exercise, she wanted to shout, "You cannot observe something without changing it." Even a houseplant responded to attention.

She picked up a sponge, relapsing to her ingrained way to restore order—swiping at the counters she'd already cleaned. The tracked-in mud and mess in the bedroom had to stay. The police would want to photograph, wouldn't they?

If they'd detained someone, it must be the burglar. There weren't many young black men in Playa Maria.

Over the years, she'd worked with at-risk students, kids teetering on the brink of disaster. What life—what stupid decisions—had led this one to point a gun at Ben?

But anyone could make stupid decisions. That was for sure. Bubble-wrapped in teenaged ignorance, she'd gone into nude modeling to earn college tuition money. Everything had been fine—for a year.

Vivi opened the refrigerator and blinked at the contents with the vague notion she should eat something. They'd had no lunch.

Maybe it was time to tell Ben, and yet, right now, when he'd almost been shot, seemed like the worst time possible.

She backed into the kitchen, nibbling a piece of cheese.

Once, she'd tried to unburden herself of her secret—to an English major she'd crushed on for a semester of *The Bible as Literature*. The first time they had sex, in a long, post-coital talk, she'd told him.

His eyes had glistened but he unlatched his hand from hers and said they should get some sleep.

In the morning, he told her it wasn't a good idea to dump something that heavy early in a relationship. That moment, over a bowl of Cheerios, she stopped adoring him. Just as well. He never called.

Her story had taken on the quality of Double Dutch—don't rush in too early—but if she waited too long, the opportunity twirled away. And it was easy to put off the telling because under her anger rested a bedrock of shame. Why share it? It wasn't like she'd murdered someone, or anything like that.

Revived by sharp cheddar, Vivi considered how Ben might react. By the time she'd known nothing would scare him away, she also knew he wasn't someone who would let the matter lie, even if it had happened more than thirty years ago. He would want justice.

To give attention to her secret, to expose it to air, would change it, as certain as paying attention to one's breath expanded it. She preferred the experience remain in a little box, under her control, neat and tidy.

The thief had turned things upside down, but now was not the time to tell Ben what had happened in Hollywood.

Chapter Seven: County

WEDNESDAY - late afternoon

The officer escorted Dwayne toward the wing he'd been in six months ago, the jail's wings dividing people according to their crimes. Alleged crimes, Dwayne prepped himself. Everyone in lock-up was innocent, unless they shot off their mouths. Sucking in his lower lip, Dwayne clamped his mouth shut.

Linoleum stretched in front of his load of two sheets, two blankets, one cup, and a spoon. No pillow—that was lame. If you wanted to smother someone, a folded-up blanket would do the job.

The guard stopped in front of the familiar pod. Down the hall, they had a special place for pervs. They better keep those fuckers locked up tight. If one of them touched his baby girl, he'd put chrome to the dome and pull the trigger for sure.

As the officer assessed the guys watching television, Dwayne steeled his face. The day area was crammed with triple-decker bunks, which meant he wasn't getting a cell. Last time they'd paired him with another black guy who must've been fifty—in for a hit and run while driving on a suspended license. The drunk snored like someone had shoved corks up his nose. But that would be better than the current situation.

Fuck it. He didn't expect to stay. Long as the police didn't find the gun. He shifted his weight.

The guard buzzed the control room to unlock the door. Before entering,

Dwayne stole a glance at the bedroom-sized exercise room connected to the day area. On the concrete floor was the person he wanted to see—Buster. Still there. At Dwayne's last stint, Buster had already served a year in County. He was bench-pressing a stack of plastic chairs balanced on each hand.

The guard nodded to a bunk. "Your ride. Top tier."

The other guys checked him out—the new arrival. With hooded eyes, Dwayne met their stares. They went back to the television program. A white guy named Troy, leaning against the wall, dipped his chin at him. He was barely older than Dwayne. A year ago, he'd looked like some chick's Instagram fuck boy. Now his skin had that oil-slick sheen from life on the streets. Once they'd done a smash-and-grab together. Troy didn't have any heart, though. He'd rather beg for cash downtown. *Pathetic.*

Dwayne sauntered to the bunk and plopped his stuff on top. Reclining on the bottom mattress and chewing a twist of paper, a wiry guy gave him side-eye. He had gray hair, leathery skin, and the twitchy fingers of a smoker coping with the county's smoke-free environment.

"Gonna climb aboard my Cadillac."

The wiry guy glared, the whites of his eyes yellowish. "Don't put your stinkin' feet on my bed."

Dwayne turned away like he didn't give a shit. He should talk to Buster now—deal with the gun. He crossed the room to an empty chair. Troy scooted along the wall until he was next to him. They'd gotten high after unloading a stolen GPS. Dwayne wasn't sure if they ever settled up.

"Hey," Troy said.

Dwayne tipped his head at his bunkmate. "What's up with that guy?"

"Has a germ phobia thing." Troy scratched at his arms like he had the itchy blood. "Doesn't even like the guard to touch his food tray."

The crazy looked over.

Troy put a hand on Dwayne's shoulder. "Nah, man. Chill."

Dwayne shrugged away. He strolled to his tier of bunks and stepped a sandal onto the bottom cot.

His bunkmate sprang up, flinging his paper wad to the floor, his body tensed. "Get your filthy shoe offa my bed."

Dwayne ground his second sandal onto the mattress and hoisted himself. The guy grabbed at his legs. Dwayne kicked, one sandal flying off.

The crazy latched on to an orange pant leg and pulled, howling like an animal. The waist of Dwayne's pants caught on his boxers and both were dragging down his ass. He lurched back, letting the guy yank on empty pant leg, and then pistoned the other foot into the crazy's chin, the other sandal flying across the room. The guy's head snapped back, followed by his off-balance body, his full weight yanking Dwayne's pants further down his legs, exposing his cock.

The circled inmates were laughing now, Buster towering behind them. When the sinewy germ-phobic crazy staggered back, Buster caught hold of him. Guards with Tasers poured into the room and ordered everyone to face the wall.

Dwayne's pants dangled from his toes. He reversed them up his legs and drew his legs up onto the cot. The bed was in the middle of the room, so there was no wall for him to face. "I need a cell, man," he said to the nearest guard. "That motherfucker is racist. Thinks I have germs."

Buster let go of the wiry guy so they could comply with the order, but the crazy didn't turn to the wall. He panted and pointed at Dwayne. A guard approached him and asked if he was injured.

"Don't touch me!" the man shrieked. His body convulsed and he stabbed a finger toward Dwayne. "That guy rubbed his dirty shoes on my sheets. I need new sheets."

Beside the crazy guy, Buster pressed 'I surrender' arms to the cinderblock. The guard by Dwayne's cot barked, "Get down!"

He hopped to the floor.

"Let's go."

Perfect. Maybe he'd end up with a cell. If he got lucky, maybe they'd put him with Troy. If only they could take care of this fast. He needed to talk to Buster.

Behind him the crazy howled that his bed was contaminated. The guard allowed Dwayne to toe on his sandals. They slapped along the wide, dim hallway. A blank distance stretched to the office where a correctional officer named Steverson processed arrivals. The escort guard's mouth was set in a way that didn't open to chat, so Dwayne was pushed back into his thoughts.

He needed his shortie Espie to get the gun. If the cops found it, he was screwed. He should be negotiating with Buster right now, but what could you do? If you backed down from a fight, you might as well tattoo yourself 'Lil' Bitch.'

If anyone had a set-up phone account with credit, it would be Buster. He'd hacked up his main squeeze and disposed of her in the Playa Maria River. But with only a piece of one hand, the DA wasn't rushing to trial, and the public defender favored the community's loss of memory, so Buster had been moldering in jail, building an empire.

Yeah, Dwayne thought, he should've tapped Buster first. Got word to Espie. Had her retrieve the pack. Take the gun to his fence for cash. Put the money in his commissary account. Boom, gun off the street, and bargaining power.

The guard deposited him in the dumpy little office. Steverson lifted his face from his computer and turned to Dwayne.

Guys who did this kind of work all had *the look*—soft faces, bad haircuts, and clothes from Target. Dressed like civilians to make inmates believe the intake meetings were casual.

"Back so soon." With a foot, Steverson pushed out a chair for Dwayne. The guard cuffed him to the table and left.

Dwayne slumped and stretched his legs. Jail wasn't so bad—just boring being locked up with a bunch of guys, watching television, arguing about sports, and talking about their bum beefs. How they were going to get out. But most of them didn't make any plan. Not like his bro. Wesley had taken a jackrabbit parole from a roadwork crew. Maybe he could do something that epic—get the gun himself. His mind started clicking.

He'd get out and go back and wipe the judgmental look off the face of that shrimpy old motherfucker who'd put him here.

Chapter Eight: The Great Escape

WEDNESDAY - late afternoon

Rocky pitched his skateboard over the chain-link fence and twirled the pack to hurl it.

"Don't throw the pack!" Marshall hollered. For the girl to be chasing them, there must be something valuable inside.

Rocky spun around, his hair flying like he was in a metal band. "Why not? It'll be easier to climb the fence."

Marshall glanced over his shoulder. The girl mounted her bike on the street.

Without waiting for an explanation, Rocky slipped one strap of the pack over his shoulder and launched himself at the fence. The wire rattled, and the threaded plastic boards whirred like a weird instrument.

Marshall scrabbled up after him. His friend dropped to the other side, landing gracefully with knees bent. By the time Marshall plopped to the earth, Rocky had already swooped up his skateboard. They crossed a strip of bare soil to the sidewalk.

Marshall looked up and down Del Amo—not far from where he'd confronted Finn, James' bully. The school traffic gone, it was a quiet street. Big new houses lined the other side where there used to be a chicken hatchery. His ears perked at the sound of a car.

It turned off La Paz Street onto Del Amo. Marshall was about to tell Rocky to run when he recognized the forest green and decal of a sheriff's cruiser. The vehicle traveled toward them. Marshall angled toward Rocky but kept an eye on the car. As the vehicle approached, the deputy studied them. Marshall tried to walk casually, but his legs felt like the knees didn't bend. The doobie rolled in his pocket.

"You look like you're going to piss your pants," Rocky said.

"You look like you're going to shit yours."

Rocky doubled over and laughed.

The cruiser rolled up, slowed, and pulled over. They kept walking.

The deputy climbed out. Marshall peeked back. The deputy was taller than Marshall's dad and buff, with muscles pushing at his uniform. His dark hair was cut like a Marine's. "Gentlemen, I need to talk to you for a minute."

Marshall stopped and turned. No one said *gentlemen* unless you were in trouble. He stayed at a distance, so the cop would be less likely to sniff the marijuana. At first, Marshall didn't think Rocky was going to comply, but his friend did a slow pivot.

"Yeah?" Rocky said.

The deputy used both hands to hitch up his belt, heavy with a gun, baton, spray, Taser, and a device that whipped out like a pointer. Must be like going around wearing scuba weights, Marshall thought, getting dragged down all day.

"Have you been hanging out in this area today?" the deputy asked.

They glanced at each other, trying to gauge the importance of the question. "Since after school," Marshall said.

"School?" The officer raised one eyebrow.

"We go to the charter," Marshall said.

"Have you seen any unusual activity?"

Rocky tapped the tip of his skateboard against the sidewalk. "Like what?"

Marshall looked away. The chink, chink, chink of the board against concrete was driving him crazy.

The deputy nodded at the backpack, hanging loose and book-free over Rocky's shoulder. "Doesn't look like you plan to do much studying."

"Nope," Rocky said. "Just gonna eat a lot of turkey and mashed potatoes at my grandma's house."

Marshall's throat clenched. Rocky's words had a sassy tone. He'd seen Rocky smart-mouth teachers, but he couldn't believe he was lipping off to a deputy.

But a smile quirked up on the deputy's face. "Don't forget to eat your vegetables."

He strode back to his cruiser, folded himself inside, and pulled away from the curb. Marshall heaved a sigh of relief. But the rumble of another car engine whipped his head the other way.

A lowered tan Impala—a gangbanger car—turned from La Paz. The girl on the pink bike rounded with it, hanging on to the driver's open window. She pointed at them and released her hold.

Marshall's heart jumped. "Run!" He sprinted toward the stop sign. Rocky zoomed past him on his board.

"Rocky!" Marshall raced across the street. Rocky executed a ninety-degree turn and jumped the curb, following him. Marshall ran down the side street. Rocky rocketed past him. The driver gunned his engine. The lowered car couldn't go fast, but it would be a hell of a lot faster than they were.

The car, though, was limited to the street. Marshall darted up the next walkway, bounded onto the porch, and hammered on the red door. Panting, Rocky stood beside him. Marshall pushed the doorbell, over and over. Inside the dog yipped. A little Yorkie named Joey. Marshall walked by this house on his way to Rocky's. One time he'd told the old man who lived here, "Nice roses." And the stooped, bald man had snipped a bouquet of every color. "Take 'em home for your mom."

Marshall had taken them home. He'd rinsed dust off one of his mom's vases and placed the roses in the center of the table. His dad and James were both out. He'd put his head down on his arms and cried, surrounded by his mom's favorite fragrance.

But now there were no footsteps inside the house, no one peeking out, even though the Yorkie was home.

Sweat beaded on Marshall's forehead. Where the hell was everyone? Gone for the holiday? Why wasn't anyone coming to this street for Thanksgiving?

The Impala idled noisily at the end of the walkway, waiting for their retreat from the door. The girl on the cruiser pedaled up and talked through the window to the guy in the car. She whined "Rico" like she was trying to persuade the driver of something.

He and Rocky were trapped on the porch of an old man Marshall didn't really know.

"Come on!" Rocky pulled himself onto the porch railing. Even with a pack over his shoulder and a skateboard under his arm, he balanced as gracefully as a gymnast. Marshall clambered up behind him.

The banger in the Impala kept glancing back toward them, but he didn't get out of the car.

At the end of the porch, Rocky stepped into a juniper tree.

"Why don't you just throw the pack to them?" Marshall asked. "That's what they want."

"No way this pack belongs to that girl." Rocky climbed up the tree.

Marshall thrust himself into the spiky needles. Cobwebs glommed onto his hair. A scent, powerful as Vicks VapoRub, invaded his nose, but at least the tree had close-together twisty branches for climbing.

At this angle, he could see why the two had stopped at the curb. Down the street, a young couple was loading up a little red car, the woman strapping a child in the back and the guy hefting suitcases into the other side. For a second, the sight of the red car—like his mother's—stopped Marshall's breath. They shot wondering glances at the out-of-place vehicle, but apparently couldn't see him and Rocky in the tree. Rocky chucked his skateboard over the rooftop and it clattered down the back side into the homeowner's yard. Then he pressed out of the tree, grabbed the drainpipe, and snaked onto the roof.

"Keep down," Marshall hissed.

But it was too late. Rocky had already popped up and was pounding over the guy's roof, up to the chimney and down the back side, the young couple staring with what-the-fuck expressions on their faces.

On the other side of the roof, there was no convenient tree. "So now what?" Marshall said.

Rocky peered over the edge. "It's not that far down." He tested the gutter with a sneaker. Before Marshall could protest, his friend backed off the roof, dangled from the gutter, and dropped to the grass. "Piece of cake." He crossed the yard to retrieve his skateboard.

Shaking, Marshall followed Rocky's lead. He eased his legs into the air, gripping the metal. The gutter screeched. His body lowered an inch as the metal wrenched loose from the roofline.

Marshall released before the whole gutter ripped off. His skating instincts kicked in. He fought the urge to break his fall with his hands and instead bent his knees, tipped sideways, and landed on his butt. He glanced up at the hanging gutter, feeling bad that he'd damaged the property of the old man. Rocky raced by him. "Dude, come on!"

They scrambled over the side fence and encountered a little boy pedaling around in a toy car. His mother flew out a sliding glass door and screamed at them. Marshall wasn't even sure what she said. He was already climbing over the next fence into a yard where two Chihuahuas leaped against the boards and bared their teeth.

The two yapping Chihuahuas chased them. A person could punt them, but Marshall didn't have the heart to kick a dog. Teeth latched onto the bottom of his pants. He shook the chihuahua loose. It landed on its tail with an angry yelp.

They huffed across the next yard—a calm patch of grass, the house of the young couple packing their car.

At the end of the block, they paused at the last fence. Rocky peeped through the cracks. "He's at the corner."

Marshall peered through an empty knothole. The Impala had driven down the street and turned the corner. It idled at the curb. Marshall didn't see the girl. He wiped the sweat dripping from his forehead. "What now?"

"We just have to get across the street," Rocky said. "On the count of three, we'll go over together."

On three, Marshall climbed over. They leaped down together and sprinted toward the apartment building where Rocky lived.

The car roared to life, raced thirty feet, and screeched to a halt. The man jumped out. He wasn't very tall and was a little on the skinny side, but he had neck tattoos. And a knife.

Rocky started yelling, "Mom! Mom! Mom!"

They cleared the street, the guy chasing after them.

Rocky kept screaming, "Mom! Mom! Mom!"

Marshall and Rocky took the shaking steps of the apartment building two at a time. The man hesitated. Then he turned around and hustled back to his car.

Chapter Nine: The System

WEDNESDAY - later afternoon

Steverson's "office" was nothing more than a cut-out in the hallway. Steverson leaned way back in his desk chair and laced his hands behind his head.

"So what brings you back?" Steverson asked.

"The guy in my bunk is racist. I need a cell. To be safe." *Safe* was the word to play. The jail was getting bad press lately over two inmate deaths.

"Uh-huh." Steverson tipped his chair upright and swigged at a paper cup of coffee. "What makes you say that?"

"The guy didn't want my black feet touching his mattress."

"Let me guess. Your bunkmate is Adams. Adams isn't racist unless a person can be racist against germs."

"Why does he think my black feet are germy if he's not racist?"

"He's completely nondiscriminatory about germs. He thinks everyone's feet are germy. Their hands and faces, too."

"Then he's not safe because he's crazy." Dwayne's foot bounced as seconds ticked by, each one an opportunity for the cops to find the gun.

"Everybody has issues," Steverson said. "Ever notice that? Some people are afraid of heights. Me, I have a phobia of spiders. With some people, it's a fear of not being able to game the system."

"That's messed up."

"What is?" Steverson asked, all innocent-like. "Seriously, a spider gets on

44

me, and I'm like a little girl."

"No, what you said about me. That's messed up."

"You?" Steverson raised his eyebrows. "You mean that part about gaming the system?"

Anger bubbled in Dwayne. He narrowed his eyes. Steverson thought he was so smart. He'd like to run into him in a dark alley, see how smart he thought he was. Dwayne's focus slid around the room, searching for a photo, a sign of something personal. "You have daughters?"

Steverson shook his head.

"Hey, man, you ashamed of your kids?"

Steverson exhaled loudly. "I guess we're done here."

"What about my safety?"

"A guy who can leap over fences shouldn't have any trouble getting into a top bunk without agitating Adams."

"Allegedly hops fences," Dwayne muttered.

"I said 'a guy'—not you. Hypothetical."

"How 'bout a hypothetical cell?"

Steverson shook his head. "Ain't gonna happen. Anything else I can do for you today?"

Dwayne leaned toward him, but the guy didn't flinch. "What programs you got?" He was antsy to go, but as his brother Wes said when they trolled parking lots, jerking on car door handles and found one unlocked: "Seize the day." Dwayne was here now.

Steverson's chair squeaked. "Programs?" He tapped his fingers on his desktop. "Better to discuss those after your arraignment. They'll probably send you back to River House."

"Isn't that your job to set us up with programs? Rehabilitate us?"

"Just what kind of *program* do you have in mind, Dwayne?"

"Christian."

"You mean back with Lavonne?"

"Yeah." Lavonne was perfect—a sweet, angel-faced woman who would've been beautiful if she didn't have a double chin and weigh two hundred pounds. Truly dedicated to converting sinners and making the world a better place.

Steverson cleared his throat. "Yeah, well, Lavonne. When you passed through last time, she wrote something like 'introduced to the gospels by his maternal grandma, but was ...'" He rubbed his head with his knuckles as though to scrub up the memory. "Let's see—she used some interesting adjective. *Tepid.* That's it. 'He was *tepid* in his participation.' Do you know what that means, Dwayne?"

"Fuck you."

"*Fuck you?* That doesn't sound very Christian."

* * *

When Dwayne returned to the pod, Buster wrapped a massive arm around his neck and gave him head noogies. "Look who's back," he razzed, like Dwayne was his prison bitch.

Dwayne struggled against the chokehold. The other guys gawked with stupid smiles on their faces. When Buster chose to release him, Dwayne backed away, shaking it off.

Buster chortled. "Like I'd want a piece of your black ass."

Dwayne's body zapped with fury. So much for establishing his manhood up front. It was accepted as fact that Buster had chopped up his girlfriend, while he, Dwayne, had been a pussy at crunch time, not able to squeeze one off. He wondered how long he had before that got around.

He needed to man up, now. Dwayne eyed Buster's size, a 'roided-out freak show. "I have something to discuss with you."

The hulk laughed like an evil Santa Claus. "You came to the right man for *bidness.*" A mammoth paw motioned Dwayne into the exercise area. Two stories up, it opened to the air, the edges circled with razor wire. "What can I do for you, sonny?"

"Phone call?"

"I'm the man. Mr. Verizon."

Dwayne didn't know if he was joking. "You have a phone?" Guys like Buster had associates that came and went through County. They could hoop in a phone like they did drugs, especially now that some lawsuit had stopped cavity searches.

"A phone?" Buster laughed harder. "Ain't you a sweet pea? Sure I do, but there's no reception in here." Buster flashed ultra-white teeth like he had Crest strips brought in to him. "They have a blocker for the whole jail."

Eyes slitted, Dwayne leaned back on the wall. "Why you have a phone then?"

Buster rolled his head as if to loosen up muscles. "Now, son, check the attitude. In transport, I can sneak out a text. So could you, for a nominal fee."

No one was going to the courthouse, or anywhere else, on the day before Thanksgiving. Or on Thanksgiving, or Friday, or the weekend. Not unless an inmate got stabbed or something. Dwayne ground his teeth as his options slipped away.

"But, hey, I'll call for you, kid. Ten bucks. It'll be recorded, but by now, they sure as shit are sick of monitoring my calls."

Seriously, Dwayne thought, for a guy like Buster, facing a life sentence, what did an inappropriate call matter, anyway? What would they do? Restrict his phone use?

It was just annoying that Buster had to be the man.

"I don't have money yet."

Buster pursed his lips and rubbed his thumb and two fingers together. "But the call will generate some?"

"Yeah."

"This is the way it works. In twenty-four hours, the money is in my commissary account, or the fee increases."

"Increases to what?"

"Way I see it, Sweet Pea, you ain't in a position to negotiate."

Dwayne squatted behind the chairs, his back to any passing guard. He wished he had a different person for Buster to call, but he didn't know if his brother Wesley was out, and Rico had been pissed at him since their last job together. He wasn't tight enough with Jessika. That left Espie, and Espie was totally unreliable.

He told Buster Espie's number. Buster repeated it to him.

"What do I tell her?"

"Tell her I'm in County."

Buster picked at an ultra-white tooth. "Don't she know that by now?"

With Espie, maybe not. "Tell her I've left a present for her, and she needs to get it. Now."

Buster listened to the directions. "A dumpster fifty yards in front of a new peace sign on your third-grade school?"

"Right."

"If they listen to the recording of this call, they'll sure as shit know something's up. Will your squeeze understand this top-secret shit?"

From under hooded eyes, he studied Buster. All brawn, no brains. The ape thought he was stupid. The message was supposed to be *secret.* Coded. If it wasn't, Buster would send one of his own associates to the spot.

Dwayne stood up. "You might have to repeat it to Espie a few times."

"Is she retarded?"

If he had his gun, he'd blast those sparkling teeth out into orbit—no doubt.

Chapter Ten: The Press

THURSDAY, THANKSGIVING

B en liked the peace of early morning, that time before any bad news descended. Luna greeted him, bopping his hand for pets and food. He put on the coffee for Vivi—darkly brewed French roast. Splash of half and half. He knew the exact color it should be.

He made tea for himself. When he heard Vivi stirring, he delivered the mugs to the bedroom and then padded outside in his bare feet to pick up the newspaper. He took a long draw of crisp autumn air, stopped on the porch, and flipped to the Police Blotter section.

There it was. He spread open the sheets of the *Playa Maria Reporter* without folding them. They trembled in the breeze:

Resident Pursues Armed Burglar

An 18-year-old Playa Maria man was arrested Wednesday after he allegedly burglarized a house and was pursued by the resident. The burglar threatened the resident with a gun, police said.

The resident and his wife returned to their home on Beverly Lane near Scenic Drive about 1:30 p.m. and found suspected burglar Dwayne Williams in their home, said sheriff's department spokesperson Lt. Samuel Rose.

While being chased, Williams dropped stolen items and fled along the creek near Bay High School, closed for Thanksgiving.

Sheriff's deputies and Playa Maria police spotted Williams in a residential neighborhood near an area of freeway construction. After a brief chase, Williams was apprehended on the 400 block of Dewey Street about 2 p.m. Authorities searched for the gun but had not found it by 4 p.m. Wednesday.

Williams was arrested on suspicion of assault with a deadly weapon, burglary, and resisting arrest, deputies said.

Williams is being held in County Jail in lieu of $250,000 bail, according to jail records.

Ben folded the paper, went inside, and deposited the article in Vivi's lap. Propped in bed, she plucked up her reading glasses, resting on a stack of mysteries. Without a word, she snatched up the newspaper. Her brow furrowed with laser focus. There was no use saying anything to her now. If a plane fell out of the sky while Vivi was reading, she wouldn't look up.

After a minute, she peeked at him. "Our local hero." She smiled. "I'm going to buy you a cape for your birthday."

"I hope he rots in jail." He settled into bed in his gym shorts and torn Phillies tee shirt.

"Were you able to sleep?"

"Not much. How about you?"

The dark frames of her glasses didn't hide the puffiness around her eyes, but he liked the Smarty Pants look. Even first thing in the morning with her short silver hair sticking up in rooster tails, she was beautiful.

"I kept hearing every little creak."

Ben read the article again. "Does this mean he could be out on bail, maybe right now?"

"It's a huge bail—$250,000. I don't think he's going anywhere soon."

"How about a bail bondsman?" he asked. Vivi absorbed a ton of crime factoids from her consumption of mysteries.

"The family would have to put up ten percent that they may never see again. Twenty-five thousand is a lot."

His legs and arms felt heavier than after a session with weights at the gym.

"Do you think he's into drugs?"

"He looked too healthy to be a serious addict."

"Yeah, but young bodies can take a lot of abuse."

"Only eighteen." Vivi *tsked*. "When I was teaching, we had a seminar on the brain." She adjusted into a more upright position on her pillows. "At that age, his frontal lobe, his impulse control, hasn't even fully developed." She snagged her lower lip with a tooth. "I thought he was older, more like twenty-five."

"I'm glad he's spending Thanksgiving in jail." He leaned forward to meet her eyes. "He threatened me with a gun. Remember?"

Luna pounced onto the bed, turned a circle, and nestled next to Vivi's thigh. "I wonder why the bail is so high." She stroked the cat's tortoise-shell-patterned fur.

"Probably the gun." Skimming the article again, he sipped his tea and searched for a clue he might have missed.

"Maybe priors." Vivi removed her glasses and rubbed at an eyebrow.

"Could be because he wasted all that manpower for a whole afternoon." His face tightened. "And they still didn't find the gun."

"But Big Al's apprentice saw it, right?"

He thumped down his mug of tea. Hashimoto's statement about *catch and release* ricocheted in his head. The whole idea someone could break into their house, steal their stuff, threaten to kill him, and be released to walk around and do it all over again made him grind his teeth.

He sat up and tugged on his athletic shoes.

"Where are you going?"

"Down to Big Al's."

"It's Thanksgiving."

"Maybe someone will be there." As an artist, Big Al was unchained from conventional business hours.

Vivi eyed him skeptically.

He yanked his laces tight. "A guy could be getting back on the streets with a gun and a grudge and our address."

Chapter Eleven: The Gun

THANKSGIVING - a moment later

After the door clicked shut, Vivi marched down the hall to lock it, but Ben had already thrown the deadbolt to safeguard her.

The cool solidity of the doorknob penetrated her jangle of thoughts. Were they being paranoid? Understandable, but not rational. Rational thinking said their burglar was behind bars. Rational thinking said no one was coming to burglarize them while they were home. Rational thinking said they'd lived together in this house for fourteen years, and nothing like this had ever happened before.

She released her grip and walked down the hall. The burglary was over. Done. Gone. At this moment, she was safe in her house, the wooden floor beneath her bare feet.

She crawled back under the covers, thinking about when she was six years old, and her friend Nina persuaded her to go into the town's grocery store to steal candy. The good stuff—gum and candy bars—were displayed behind the checkout stand, manned by Mrs. Rafferty.

The woman watched them pass, but Nina led Vivi confidently down an aisle full of cake mixes to a shelf lined with little plastic canisters full of cake decorations. Nina grabbed a container of chocolate sprinkles and stuck it in her pocket. Vivi took decorations meant for a wedding cake that looked like silver bb's. They'd been about as tasty—hard little pellets of guilt.

She'd never stolen anything after that. Well, not until she was nineteen.

But that had been different. *Justified.*

The burglary was thrusting forward memories as though Dwayne Williams had stripped away a shield, leaving her bare and vulnerable. Restless, Vivi hopped back out of bed and went to the hallway bathroom to brush her teeth. She paused with her mouth full of toothpaste. A noise. Scraping on the window pane. No tree grew near the frosted glass.

Her heart thudded as she crossed the room. What if, as the girl on the bike had suggested, the burglar had an accomplice?

No shadowy form moved beyond the glass. The toothpaste stung her mouth. Saliva gathered behind it. With sudden resolve, she slid open the window.

Birds fluttered from the feeder. A gray squirrel made a brilliant flight from a tree across the yard to the fence top. Her eyes scanned the narrow yard. Empty. It must have been the squirrel.

She completed her morning ritual and fixed another cup of coffee. What was taking Ben so long? Was his reaction normal or was he a little unhinged by the trauma?

Marching down to Big Al's was in character. Ben didn't sit and let things happen. After all, he'd continued chasing the burglar after having a gun pointed at him. But was there more to it than his desire to protect their house? To protect her. Did the thief remind him of Art?

According to Ben, his first wife, Leanne, had been his way of punching back at his parents. She'd been a groupie, dancing in front of the stage. When she got pregnant at nineteen, Ben dealt a satisfying blow to his father, who said there were two kinds of blacks, the hard-working ones and "the other kind." Yet, three years later, when the marriage fell apart, Ben's parents hired a high-powered attorney who showed Leanne could not properly care for Arthur. Ben ended up with full custody, putting a damper on his drumming ambitions.

Now he occasionally subbed for local bands.

She felt sad for his lost dream, but the saddest part was how unprepared and seemingly—from what she could glean—uninterested in parenthood both Ben and Leanne had been.

She rinsed the turkey, extracting the neck bone and giblets. After returning the turkey to the refrigerator, she went to the front window, but the trees at the side of their yard prevented a view down the sidewalk. Outside, brisk air cut through her flannel pajamas. With no school in session, the street was deserted. Her flip-flops smacked the walkway. On the sidewalk, she could see past the three houses to the gate, Big Al's, three tall palms in the far distance, and mountains beyond.

Ben hurried toward her.

"Any luck?"

"No Big Al. But look." He held up a ridged metal item the size of a pea.

"What's that?"

"The twist-on cap to my drum tuner."

"Where did you find it?"

"By the school dumpster."

"So you were searching for evidence?" With her arms wrapped around her torso, she hurried toward the house. "Maybe it flipped out when he pulled the gun."

Ben caught up to her and stopped abruptly on the porch. Even though the morning air cut through her pajamas, she stopped with him.

"The gun is a big deal, Vivi."

"I know it is. I'm just cold and want to get inside."

He followed her through the door.

"I don't want this guy to get away with robbing us and threatening to kill me." His eyes widened. "I don't care if he's eighteen. What about next time he burglarizes a house?"

"He's in jail. And twenty-five thousand is not an amount most people have kicking around." She started toward their bedroom. "I'm going to get your tea and warm it up. You only drank about two sips."

He trailed her. "I don't want it to come down to his word against mine."

"So what if it does?" She spun around in the hallway. "Do you think a jury would believe you or someone 'familiar' to the police?"

"I wonder how hard they searched for that gun."

"The newspaper indicates they were still searching at four."

"It's a big area. They picked him up two miles from here."

She didn't know what to say. His body stood rigid, his dark eyes blazing. "The gun is crucial."

She continued into the bedroom and seized his mug, sloshing tea onto the wood floor. "Why do you keep acting like I don't think it is?"

"I don't want you to go all soft because he's eighteen." His voice was gentler but still adamant. "If this goes to trial, only one person," he held up a finger for emphasis, "just one—has to doubt the existence of the gun, and he could walk."

"Only on the gun charge," she said. "They'll get him for the burglary and resisting arrest and God knows what else."

Ben took a napkin from the bedside drawer and wiped up the dribble of tea. His face flushed.

"The punk was in there, Vivi." He gestured at the open drawer. The heat of embarrassment crawled up her neck. A stranger had pawed through these personal items—Ben's reading glasses, his tooth guard, lubricant. In the other corner of the drawer Ben stored a packet of valentines she had made for him, one for each of their seventeen years together.

Dwayne had come into their house, cracked open this space, and raked his hands through their most private things. It was like being groped. Another hot surge of memory and drops of sweat gathered at her temples.

Ben focused on her forehead, noticing. "The deputy told me that without the weapon, this could be a catch and release."

"Look," she said. "It's Thanksgiving. Instead of our usual hike, let's go follow this guy's trail. See if we can find that gun."

Chapter Twelve: Big Al

THANKSGIVING - late morning

Al scrubbed at his fingernails with a brush. That was one thing he hated about ironwork—the rust and grease in the creases of his palms and under his nails, the way his hands took a beating and were rough against Angie's skin. He wished he could make them a little more presentable for the Thanksgiving meal.

Other than that, he was pretty happy with his business, in spite of the chaos yesterday. Normally, he thought Beverly Lane was an okay location—fairly safe with a school there. He was a lucky man, doing what he loved: making sculptures. The bigger, the better. Ideally, he would create something a few stories high, a sculpture that erupted into the sky.

Not that he could climb up to work on a piece like that. He wasn't tall and had legs like tree trunks. He weighed a lot. *Too much.*

After drying his hands on the towel, he hung it up straight the way Angie liked. He inspected his shaving job in the mirror. Dropping his head, he checked his scalp. He'd been shaving his head since he was thirty, when his hair started falling out.

The meal would be just Angie, him, their daughter Stella, and her husband, but Angie had been preparing the Thanksgiving meal since yesterday, baking apple pies from scratch. So it was a big deal. Al rinsed out the sink. Angie hated when he left a ring.

He went out to the kitchen. The smell of roasting turkey filled the room.

Pressed against the sink, Angie was peeling potatoes, her face rosy from the heat. She turned a little and smiled. "Hi, Sleepyhead."

He kissed the top of her thick honey-colored hair. Her fragrance and the roasting turkey were so much more pleasant than his everyday smells of propane for the forge and microwaved shop food.

"Stella, why don't you help your mom with these potatoes?"

Stella's and Chris's heads showed over the back of the cream-colored leather couch. In front of them, images of the Macy's Thanksgiving Day Parade flitted across the flat-screen television.

"I've got it," Angie said.

But irritation welled in him. Stella and Chris were kicking back while Angie was sweating in the kitchen. They weren't exactly guests. Their daughter had moved back in with them, husband in tow.

Al plopped heavily into his La-Z-Boy. Residual tiredness hit him so hard on holidays that sometimes he thought it would be better to keep rolling through the week. Yesterday had been especially grueling, trying to make a table for a woman who didn't actually know what she wanted. Then his former customer Ben came screaming down the street, pursuing a thief. His young worker had scrambled off like a hound, chasing after adventure, and later, the cops came by to ask questions. They never did get back into the groove of their projects. His apprentice was so jacked up he kept making stupid mistakes. Al may as well have closed the shop.

Angie had put a dish of salted peanuts on the coffee table. Stretching forward, he scooped up a handful. "What is that balloon supposed to be?" He pointed at the screen.

"Sonic the Hedgehog." Stella and Chris answered in unison. They huddled against one another and both gave him an incredulous look.

"The Sonic Hedgehog, huh?" His words had a bite to them.

"Al," Angie warned from the kitchen.

He couldn't help it. The whole situation irritated him, going back to Stella majoring in music. How did she expect to find a job with a degree in music? If you wanted to do art, you needed to start with a practical skill like he had. He'd learned to weld and had done that for years, pursuing his art on the side.

And then there was her husband—Chris—he was nice enough, but he played bass in a band that gigged mainly in San Jose and San Francisco. He claimed that he couldn't fit in a job with a regular schedule between gigs. So, when Stella and Chris had received a rent hike, they'd moved in with him and Angie until "they got on their feet." Two months already.

He reached for another handful of peanuts.

"Don't fill up on those," Angie sang from the kitchen. "We're going to have turkey, mashed potatoes, gravy, sweet potatoes, Brussels sprouts, and homemade apple pie with ice cream."

Al crunched the peanuts. The grinding soothed him. It was tough for young people now, vying for jobs with older laid-off workers and retirees whose 401Ks had been obliterated by the stock market crash. He'd lost a bundle himself, but at least he'd had the good sense to leave his money invested. Buy low; sell high. Most people didn't have the balls for it and got out at the wrong time.

He regarded the young couple staring at the television. The housing bubble burst had driven up rents. The situation wasn't all Stella and Chris's fault. Kids moving back home was so common they had a name for it—Boomerang Kids.

The longer he gazed at his daughter, the more she dissolved into his baby, the five-pound preemie, whose difficult birth meant she'd be their only child. They'd both treated her like a little dewdrop that might evaporate. But Stella had been oblivious to the miracle of her life, dancing around the house and singing with the voice of an angel. They'd spoiled her.

Blushing, his daughter glanced over at him as though she could read his thoughts. With her perfect skin and blue eyes, she looked like Angie about the time they got married.

Chris turned his way, too. "Angie told us what happened at the shop."

"Yeah?"

"Maybe this will persuade you to come out to Baker's and shoot a few rounds with me."

Big Al's gaze fell critically on his son-in-law, the long dark hair gathered into a curly pouf. Metal discs stretched out the kid's ear piercings like he was some kind of a wanna-be tribal native.

"I prefer golf." People never guessed he was a golfer. He was built like a football tackle, disliked wearing shorts, and wouldn't be caught dead in a peach-colored golf shirt. Ironwork and golf didn't, on the surface, seem to have any connection. But when he clamped a red-hot rod of steel into a vice, gripped the rod with a crescent wrench, and bent it into a graceful arc, he imagined explaining: "Here's the connection, buddy. It's all about how you get something to move through space from one place to another." Al had a talent for that—assessing distances, calculating the tricks of perspective—a spatial intelligence.

It made him a good shot with a gun, too, although he didn't care about guns—one way or the other. He owned a Smith and Wesson, but hypocritical as it may be, he didn't like the idea of Stella with a guy who kept a firearm. When they'd moved in, he had insisted Chris store his gun in the garage.

"I wasn't thinking about the sport of it," Chris said. "I was thinking that burglar could have broken into your place."

"The shop's alarmed." And he kept his revolver there.

"Okay," Chris said, "but a guy with a gun was like twenty feet away from your shop. When it was open."

"I don't have time," Al snapped. "When you own your own business," he added pointedly, "you work pretty much twenty-four seven."

"Alan, would you come here, honey," his wife called from the kitchen.

Uh-oh. He tilted the La-Z-Boy forward and circled around the partial wall to the kitchen. Steam rose from a pot on top of the gas stove. Angie banged a frying pan next to it, probably for the gravy. The aroma of turkey filled the house, but it hung most heavily here in the steam. His mouth salivated. He felt bad. He wanted Angie to have a good Thanksgiving.

"He's trying to reach out to you," Angie hissed at him.

"So you think I should waste my time with target practice?"

She smiled tightly at him. "Not target practicing. Bonding."

If he stripped away the bullshit, she was right. He was stubborn. He'd been to the shooting range before and enjoyed it. And seriously, if he meant to deter some punk from robbing his shop, he needed to keep up his skills.

Angie opened the oven and checked the turkey. "Take a four-day weekend like other people do."

"I have workers, Angie, who expect some hours tomorrow."

She rested against the counter, her blue eyes bright in her flushed face. "I know they need the money, but you, Mr. Boss Man, can leave whenever you want."

Angie smiled at him, and his resistance melted. He'd never been able to say no to her. He didn't want to say no to her. "You're right. I'll see if Chris is up for Baker's tomorrow."

Chapter Thirteen: The Money

THANKSGIVING - late morning

Brenden's fingernails were ragged from his tiling job with Frank. His mom had pushed him to take the work, but she wasn't going to like these hands at her Thanksgiving table. *Oh well.*

He didn't think Frank would tell his parents about the burglary and the run-in with their customers—Ben and what's her name, the wife. He was supposed to be the one sealing their grout, but that wouldn't be happening.

Jessika leaned over his dresser to insert her nose ring, red spandex gripping her small buns. The smell of her perfume swirled around her. Exotic, like her. His eyes lifted to her reflection in the mirror.

She wiggled her butt at him, but he didn't smile. Scrolling to his parents' number, he pressed call.

"Where are you?"

"Sorry, Mom." He didn't like his mom coming at him that way, but he still felt guilty. "We should be there in a half hour."

"I'll tell your father to get the grill ready by himself."

"See ya soon." He wanted to be there. The family tradition was for his father and him to clean the Weber and put on the turkey. One of his sisters baked the pies; the other prepared the salad. They spent the morning cooking together in their farm-style kitchen.

He didn't have to tell his mom they were late because of Jess. His mom assumed any problem was because of her, and she was usually right.

Jess turned, her blue-black bangs falling across her eyes. She hitched herself onto the dresser and wrapped her legs around his waist. "What's wrong?"

"Are you going to wear this?" He snapped a red stretchy strap.

She thrust him away and sprang up.

"We're going to my parents' house." He sounded whiny, even to himself.

"Well, der. I know where we're going." She turned away. "What kind of family starts Thanksgiving in the morning?"

Not yours, he thought. Eileen, Jessika's twice-divorced mom, had produced a far-flung dysfunction of half- and step-brothers. He grabbed Jessika's arm on the fangs of her snake tattoo.

"Keep your hands off me."

"I'm trying to have a conversation with you."

She twirled, hair flying. "That's what you call it?"

He backed up. She was capable of launching at him with fists, and no one would hear his story. He was a big guy; she was a small woman.

He fought for control. "Yeah. That's what I call it."

"I call it Fascism."

He'd been attracted to her firecracker personality when they were rooting for the Niners or were in bed, but lately....

"You know how my parents are."

"Yeth. I do."

This time he heard it. She did have a lisp, her speech impaired by her tongue stud, like his mom said. His eyes ran over the pearly face and down to the calligraphy VIP on her chest, the rest of the word, the ER, hidden by red spandex. "You're not helping the situation."

Her face flushed. "Why am I supposed to adjust to them? Why not they adjust to me? I'm your girlfriend."

"A *girlfriend* might do me a solid here."

She crossed her arms over her chest. "How's that? By dressing in a sack to please your parents?"

He sighed. "It's more than that."

"Yeah? What else?"

"The tile job with Frank."

Jessika looked over his shoulder. "We don't have much time, especially if I *must* change my clothes."

"Jess."

"What? I'm changing already. How about jeans and my sweater from Macy's—the one with sparkles?"

"Jessika."

She pulled the tight dress over her head. He candidly assessed her body, the jutting ribs, the perfect little breasts with rosebud nipples.

In that moment of opportunity, when he couldn't see her face and the spandex confined her arms, he asked, "Did you tell someone about the money?"

Her face popped free, and the fabric lifted her hair into spikes. The thick, mascaraed lashes blinked.

"You told your friends about the money, didn't you?"

She hurled the balled-up dress onto the floor. "Fuck you, Brenden."

"So which lowlife did you tell?"

"I'm not putting up with this shit." She turned away, pawed in the dresser drawer, and pulled out jeans and a sweatshirt. She bobbed around him and tugged on the tight pants.

"Frank took me off that job," he said.

She shrugged.

Brenden spoke to her back. "You told Espie, didn't you?"

The sweatshirt glided down Jessika's slender back and dropped over the mole at the curve of her hip. She whirled around. "Why do you blame me for everything? I didn't steal the goddamn money." She slid one bare foot into her worn UGG boots parked by the door.

"No one stole any money."

She froze with the other boot hoisted in the air.

"You heard me right. Espie's boyfriend, or whoever the fuck broke in, didn't get any money."

Jessika's body thawed back into motion. She stuck the other foot into her UGG, hobbling while she yanked it on.

Brenden's stomach turned. If she left, she didn't have anywhere to go. He might be ready to call it quits, but he didn't want her to end up on the streets. Not on Thanksgiving. "Wait, Jess."

She grabbed her jeans jacket from a wall peg. "Go see your mommy and daddy by yourself." She slammed out the door.

* * *

Jessika glanced back at the stucco granny unit, but Brenden wasn't at the window. And he didn't come running after her.

A lump blocked her throat. Brenden's place was so cute, tucked deep in a paradise-like backyard. His boss, Frank, knew the owners in the front house and had vouched for him. No wonder Brenden was angry. The granny unit was a score in Playa Maria. He didn't want to piss off his boss and lose it.

Stepping along the stone path, she snagged her pink cruiser from its spot against the wood fence. She weighed her options. She'd been hooked up with Brenden for the last couple of months. What would she do now? It wasn't like her mom would be happy to see her. The last time Jessika had tried to sneak into the house, the locks had been changed.

All cuz of Dwayne.

She rolled the bike out to Del Amo. The new locks weren't about Dwayne; they were about her—keeping her out. Dwayne never would've been there if not for her. Then he'd had the balls to bitch the gun wasn't loaded, that he had to *procure* ammo. Compared to his brother Wesley, Dwayne was a whiny little bitch.

Her arms felt itchy with the need for a little bump, but yesterday had yielded a big fat zippo, zilch, nada. After chasing those kids through the neighborhood, all she and Rico had was the location of the pack. And from what Brenden said, it didn't even have money in it.

It must contain something good, though, the way that little skater punk held on to it. If she could get it, she might be set for a while. Those kids were an easy target.

She pedaled up La Paz and turned the corner at Beverly Lane, as though muscle memory dictated her course. There was the yellow house, silent and empty, except for the cat balanced on the porch rail.

Some idea was percolating down in her gut, but she didn't even know what it was. She dipped into a pocket of her Levi's jacket. The twenty-dollar bill she'd lifted from Brenden's wallet comforted her.

She rode to a Starbucks on Scenic. The girl at the cash register acted like she didn't recognize Jessika from back in high school. Jessika let it slide. Her mom had always harped, "If you want extra money, get a job." *She'd die before being a cuntista at Starbucks.*

Sitting in a corner, Jessika nursed a latte, letting the espresso loosen twisted-tight nerves. She texted Brenden, but he didn't respond.

A call to Rico netted voicemail. She didn't leave a message. *Fuck it.* The customers who'd kept the girl and the teenage male barista busy at the counter took their drinks to go—off to be with their families. The counter girl shot a look at her but turned away as soon as Jessika stared back.

"Hey, Francine," Jessika trilled, knowing the girl would hate hearing her full name.

The girl tucked her head and whispered to the barista. Jessika heard her whole name: Jessika Fitzgerald. The guy peeked at her.

Jessika rubbed her forehead with her middle finger. Then she texted her mom: Happy Thanksgiving, Eileen!!!!!! Followed by a pile of poo emoji. Electronics couldn't completely erase sarcasm.

What kind of mom cut you loose for taking a little cash? Eileen wasn't hurting for money. She just had a stick up her ass. *My way or the highway.* Jessika scratched at her arms. Ninety percent of the time, she'd choose the highway.

The cold emptiness of the coffee shop drafted around her. Francine laughed. Jessika jerked her head up, but the two workers had their backs to her, going on about their jobs.

At least the caffeine had kicked an idea into Jessika's head. The boys had taken the pack, but tossed Dwayne's jacket on the ground. She hadn't checked it. Maybe there was something in the pockets. And that old lady from the yellow house said Dwayne stuffed the pack. When the kids took it, it looked almost empty. So where was the loot?

Leaving the dirty cup and a shredded napkin on the table, Jessika biked toward the abandoned rock yard.

Chapter Fourteen: Mr. Verizon

THANKSGIVING - very early

On Thanksgiving morning, Dwayne woke up too early. The deep breathing of sleep surrounded him, an in-and-out shush like the ocean. The eerie quiet reminded him of the first time Wesley took him along.

He had been eleven and squirmed through a doggy door, landing in a foreign silence like this. A dim light above a stovetop had revealed a kitchen.

All he had to do was throw the deadbolt.

The next day, Wesley had patted a twenty into the chest pocket of his shirt. "Just remember, crime don't pay." He'd laughed.

Dwayne felt displaced with no Espie spooned against him, the baby squeezed between them, Espie's little sisters in the bunk against the other wall. Her aunt didn't like him around, but he had a right to see his kid. *Tanisha.* How come his baby popped out so dark? *Black eyes and all that?* Espie had almost blonde hair and smokin' green eyes. And his Mama and Grammy Rice and him were all light. Espie claimed her grandpa lived in the *Costa* region of Oaxaca. "People there look like that."

Espie liked to hold on to him, even when it made his back sweat. She had abandonment issues—her dad in prison, her mom deported, and her aunt not happy about having four kids, plus Espie's baby, dumped on her.

Life's a bitch, and then you die. With his hands behind his head, Dwayne lay flat. If he rolled wrong, he could fall off.

Even if it was the middle of the night, he wouldn't be staring at the ceiling for too long. They served breakfast at five-thirty, and you had to be there for headcount.

His body searched for a way to stretch. He drummed the mattress with his heels. The whole three-tier structure shook.

For the whole of Wednesday evening, the 'roid freak Buster wouldn't say whether he'd made the call to Espie. Buster had bumped past him in the common room. "Line a mile long," he'd said and winked at him.

Now who was being *top-secret*? Buster wouldn't wait for his turn to use the phone. Dwayne had picked the guy for a lot of reasons. That was one of them.

Buster was fuckin' with him. Because that was the kind of guy he was.

If she got the message, Espie would pick up his backpack. She would borrow her aunt's car, or just take it, or ride the bus. She would do anything he asked. That wasn't the problem. The problem was that Espie screwed up everything. She was unreliable. She'd go up to a cop and ask for directions when she was high. She had no sense.

The inmate under him flipped over, making the upper deck wiggle. He farted loudly.

A putrid stench exploded like a stink bomb. Dwayne leaned over. "What the fuck, man?"

But the guy breathed like he was asleep.

Dwayne nibbled a cuticle. Right now, the most serious charge against him was the possible assault with a deadly weapon. He doubted they had the gun. Without the gun, they didn't have much. He'd learned that in second grade when he'd stolen some Pokémon cards. Pointing his finger, the sissy student ratted him out.

The teacher had narrowed her eyes but hesitated. Dwayne had been her only black student. The school had learned from his older brother Wesley that his mom would be there in a hot minute. He and Wesley could be "guilty as sin," as his mom put it, but they were her boys. Especially Dwayne. His problems were his dad's fault, The System's fault, and, after that, Wesley's fault.

The teacher had walked down the aisle and stood, towering over his desk. "Is it true?" she asked. "Did you take his Pokémon cards?"

"I don't have them." He had jumped out of his seat and turned his pockets inside out while all the kids watched the drama.

"He took them." His accuser had curly gold hair and actual tears in his eyes.

Turning toward the kid, the teacher clasped her hands tightly together, and her forehead wrinkled.

Dwayne glared at the kid. "Did you see me take them?" All the Mexicans in the class would be on Dwayne's side, even though at least one of them had seen him snake into the kid's pack.

The wuss shook his head.

And while he had this advantage, Dwayne added: "He's racist."

The teacher's head swiveled back and forth between them, weighing the situation. "We'll continue this conversation during lunch."

Earlier at recess, Dwayne had tossed the cards on the roof. Even back then, he'd known that lack of evidence made a weak case.

If all the cops had now was another burglary and violation of probation, they might weigh the fact he was eighteen and let him walk. Or do a few months at River House.

He propped himself on his elbows, but with the bunk in the middle of the room, he couldn't even sit against a wall. He switched from biting his cuticle to worrying his hair. If Espie didn't pick up the gun and the police found it, everything changed. Use of a firearm. Robbery, not burglary. Assault with a deadly weapon. Hard time.

He could sense the day getting lighter, the dawn sifting down into the open exercise area and sneaking in under the door. Today was Thanksgiving. They'd serve turkey slices for lunch.

When he was little, they went to his Grammy Rice's house. She made sweet potatoes with baby marshmallows on top, baked to gold perfection. His mouth watered.

Grammy Rice liked to clasp his cheeks between her two palms and say, "You are a good boy." By the time he was eight, he was shrugging away in embarrassment. But she kept doing it—still did the part of clasping his face between her two palms—as if she wouldn't let go of the baby he'd been, peering into his eyes like she could divine some golden glow deep down inside. Nowadays she said, "You have to change this path you're on. There isn't anyone can do it for you. There's so much life and future ahead of you. So much possibility."

Dwayne flopped back flat on his back.

"Stop shaking the bunks," Adams growled up at him. "I don't want your lice sprinkling down here."

"Shut up, Looney Tunes."

At least the interruption chased away thoughts of Grammy Rice. This Thanksgiving he'd miss getting high with Espie and lifting Tanisha up and down in his arms, making the baby smile and drool.

That time, with the Pokémon cards, he'd asked Wesley to help him onto the roof.

When Wesley saw the cards, he'd slapped him upside the head. "You stupid little bitch."

The impact had made his eyelids tap wildly like thumbs texting a message. "You take stuff!"

"You stole Pokémon cards?" his brother hissed. "We climbed up here for Pokémon cards!" His hand slipped into Dwayne's pocket. It came out empty. "Didn't the kid have money? No candy?"

As Dwayne stretched on his jail bunk, he smiled to himself. What a stupid runt he'd been. Pokémon cards. He didn't even know how to play with them.

* * *

After breakfast, he edged up to Buster. The giant's round head sat between massive shoulders like a boulder in a valley. The boulder rolled slightly to indicate the exercise area.

"Try lifting these." Buster shoved two chairs across the concrete.

"I didn't come out here to lift weights."

"I know, Sweet Pea," Buster said, "but you better be doing something besides standing here jawing with me. Feel me?"

Dwayne lifted one chair up over his head. "Satisfied?"

"No!"

He banged it down.

"That looks like you're getting ready to throw it. Try this." Buster squatted, grabbed a metal chair leg in each fist, and rose, extending each arm at shoulder level. He lowered the chairs to his thighs and winged them out again.

"I ain't doing that."

"Why? 'Cuz you can't?"

Dwayne sucked his teeth. "Just tell me about the phone call."

"You tellin' me what to do?" Buster kept lifting the chairs. His expression didn't change.

"No."

"Then pick up some chairs and act like you're doing something besides having a little heart-to-heart with me."

Dwayne separated two chairs from the stacked pile. He dipped down and fisted a leg in each hand. When he tried to stand, the chair leg in his right hand pitched sideways, wrenching the muscle around his shoulder. Both chairs crashed to the floor.

Buster snorted. "Need to work on your technique." He placed his two chairs on the concrete and squatted. "Grab both legs in the same place, in the middle. Make sure you're balanced before you stand."

Dwayne rubbed at his shoulder, but crouched.

"Okay," Buster said, "I talked to that piece of yours."

When Dwayne tried to stand, both chairs wobbled. "What did she say?" His arms shook. He pulled his elbows inward and lowered his body back toward the floor.

"Not so easy, is it?"

Dwayne tried to stand again with the chairs in his hands. "Not hard."

"That's it—work on that manhood." Buster resumed his workout, grunting on his upswing. "She said 'Uh-oh.'"

"*Uh-oh*, because I'm in jail, or *uh-oh*, about the stash?"

"*Uh-oh*, like how the hell do I know?" Grunt. Exhale.

"What did it sound like?" Dwayne dropped the chairs onto the concrete.

"You want me to interpret your ho's *uh-oh*?"

Dwayne viciously twisted a piece of hair.

Grunt. Exhale. "She said *uh-oh* like my hard cock was coming at her."

Because your shriveled 'roid nuts scared her. Survival instinct kept Dwayne's mouth shut and his body locked in place.

"Let's see you do some reps." Buster's chairs rose and fell in smooth arcs. "She sounded like she already knew something was wrong."

"But she was going to go pick it up?"

"Said she'd get it." Buster let the chairs bang to the floor. "You just make sure that squeeze of yours deposits the cash. I need that Jack Mack and chocolate to keep my strength up. Wanna have us a nice Thanksgiving." Buster wiped his forehead and left the exercise yard.

Watching the hulk lumber into the communal area, Dwayne shook his arms to stop his muscles from shaking. If he didn't get money for Buster's commissary account by that evening, the price would go up to some unknown amount. And if he didn't get the money at all, he was in for a world of hurt. Even if they transferred him to River House, Buster would get his payment. It might be in blood, but he'd get it.

Chapter Fifteen: Wedding Ring

THANKSGIVING - late morning

Before they left to search for the gun, Vivi tried to compose an email account of what happened to send to friends, but her eyes kept straying out the window. Luna perched on the ledge of the gate, oblivious to the drama, the morning sun highlighting the gold in her fur.

Finally, she put together a short message saying she was relieved Ben had not been shot, grateful neighbors had rallied to help, and thankful the police had arrested the thief. She linked to the newspaper article.

In the "TO," she typed the names of four brothers and stopped. She wouldn't be adding her mom's name. Another gap in the family. Her dad and middle brother—her favorite—were long gone. Her brother had been killed when he was thirty-two by an overeager, novice deer hunter. After all these years, the thought of it remained almost unbearable. Vivi blinked back tears.

She added more names: Ben's son Art and his wife. She wondered if they'd bother to respond. Or if Ben would write a separate message to wish them a Happy Thanksgiving. Either would be good; neither seemed likely. Ben's attempted conversations with Art were painful even to listen to—tired, with awkward pauses, as if they were both trudging through the mire of the past.

After some thought, Vivi included Anne and Bob, friends she and Ben shared.

She signed off as Vivi and the Local Super Hero. But launching the message into cyberspace created a backblast of loneliness—no children of her own, no close siblings (her brothers were rabid Republicans except the youngest who lived in France with his wife)—her colleague friends caught up in busy lives.

Thank God for Ben. What if she'd come home alone to find a man in the house with a gun?

She shivered.

Ben may have been crazy for chasing the burglar, but he was brave. Like her father, who'd run through machine gun fire to rescue a fellow soldier. That was crazy, too, but no one questioned the valor. In a foxhole, you wanted a man like Ben, not someone like Winn, advising you to meditate on *shanti*. If anyone had suggested a yoga peace meditation after the burglary, she would have wrung his *vishuddha* chakra, she thought with a wry smile.

She crossed the room to the closet, dug through a dusty box, and pulled out a map of Playa Maria. Leaning in the bedroom doorway, she studied the ragged paper as Ben swapped his shorts for Levi's jeans.

Between Ben's account of his chase and the newspaper article, she was able to trace the burglar's general route. Excitement stirred in her. The idea of hunting for clues, of searching for a gun, appealed to her. Like the heroine of a mystery.

"In all the chaos yesterday," Ben said, "I forgot to put on my wedding ring." He reached for the small gold box where he stored the ring so it wouldn't get scratched on the gym weights.

When he opened the box, she knew before he spoke.

"Another thing that shithead took."

They stood silently. They'd chosen the design, enthralled by the jeweler's idea of including meteorite, of Ben wearing something fallen from space, a reminder of how humans evolved from stardust.

Ben dropped the empty container to the dresser. "I'll have to make an amended report."

The burglar must have been in their bedroom for a while, combing through their things—taking the drum tuner out of its case, opening the gold box to see what was in it. He'd flung aside items like the photo album of Art but as if to clear space for his search. Overall, he'd been systematic.

Had he stood there viewing the photos tucked into the maple frame of the dresser mirror? The one of her in Mexico, laughing and dripping wet in her bathing suit, flopped like a fish into a boat, her snorkel fins up in the air? The picture of her and Ben, much younger, sitting at a café table in Baños, Ecuador?

"We can look for the ring where he dumped the other stuff." She said it for herself as much as for Ben.

Ben picked up Deputy Hashimoto's card from the dresser, punched in the number, and after speaking to someone, waited, tapping his foot. Then he explained the situation—the burglary the day before, the report, opening the ring box....

Vivi walked down the hall and tipped their matching blue jackets from closet hangers. She envisioned the ring resting in the parking lot, waiting for them. Anxious to go, she twirled the jackets on her fingertips like nunchucks.

"About a thousand dollars," Ben was saying to the person on the phone. After a silence punctuated by a series of okays, he hung up.

"What did they say?"

"Call any pawnshops in the county, asap. The burglar might have stashed it for an accomplice. Or if it fell on the street, someone might find it and try to sell it."

"An accomplice?" There was that idea again. She told Ben about the girl on the pink bike. "She said there was a guy ducking down in a car around the corner on La Paz Street."

Ben frowned. "I don't buy it. If Dwayne had a partner, the guy would have picked him up."

"How about the girl on the bike?"

"What?" He screwed up his face. "She'd ride off with him on the handlebars?"

The idea was a stretch. The girl had been in the vicinity; that didn't mean she and Dwayne were connected. "Let me Google pawnshops. See if any are open."

She slid into the office and perched before the computer. The old pawnshop in Playa Maria was closed for the holiday, and the one at the other end of the county looked to be out of business. Who needed a pawnshop in the age of eBay?

"We may as well continue with Plan A. Go on the hike to look for the gun." *And the ring.*

"Better pick up our pumpkin pie first." Frowning, Ben twisted the watch face toward her. "Look at this."

Scratches, from being thrown on the ground, marred the surface. She shook her head, wondering what they'd discover next. "I'll go with you," she said, not wanting to be alone.

They pulled from the driveway, abandoning their home. With school out, the street was deserted. On La Paz, their CRV was the only moving car. "It's like the rapture happened, and we got left behind."

"At least I got left with good company."

They turned onto Del Amo, a broader street where small houses on large lots were giving way to whole developments. Even here, a mile back from the beach, Playa Maria property was being snapped up. A girl rolled her bike from the back yard of one of the old houses, her UGG boots stomping, black hair sticking out from her head.

Vivi rapped on the window. "That's her."

"The bike girl?"

Vivi cranked around to watch the girl climb on the pink cruiser and ride off in the opposite direction. Did she live there? Where was she headed like that on Thanksgiving Day?

* * *

After the crush of people in the bakery, Vivi was relieved to have dropped off the pie and to be outside in the crisp air. A couple of crows strutted down their street, pecking at walnuts they'd cracked open by bombing them onto the asphalt. The birds didn't seem at all concerned about two approaching people. *Cocky creatures. No wonder Poe chose a raven to haunt his narrator.*

She and Ben hurried toward the metal gate that split Beverly Lane, turning it into two cul-de-sacs.

"Where did he first point the gun at you?"

Ben posed in front of the gate. "Right here."

Vivi stooped down. "Stuff was already falling from his pack so when he pulled the gun, the ring could have flipped out. Did he draw the gun from the pack?"

"I'm not sure."

In a crouch, she circled the dumpster, her gaze sweeping back and forth. Even though small, the gold ring should glint in the sunlight.

"My main concern, right now," Ben said, "is the gun."

Not the ring? Annoyance sparked in her heart. The search had been her idea. Now Ben was commandeering it—too much like her brothers. If she'd ever managed to mention an idea they embraced, like climbing trees, it remained her idea for about five seconds before they were making rope swings and playing Tarzan, relegating her to Jane.

Past the gate, Ben crossed the street and entered a narrow parking lot that ran beside Big Al's Ironworks from Beverly Lane through to Scenic.

Vivi scanned the asphalt.

"He still had the gun here," Ben said. "He pulled it again at the far end."

"I'm keeping an eye out for the ring."

"We can look for that on the way back." Ben paced forward like a dog on the scent tugging a leash. "Here." He pointed at the final parking spot before the driveway out to Scenic. "This is where he pulled the gun the second time and started dumping stuff."

A long tan sedan occupied the space.

"Three cars in the whole lot," Ben said, "and one has to be right here."

She squatted to inspect under the old-model car. It had an expired registration tag. "I bet this car's been dumped."

Scenic Drive was a major thoroughfare off the freeway. It was a common location for abandoned vehicles, and Thanksgiving offered the perfect time to dump them.

Normally, she and Ben would have committed the license plate to memory—each taking a part—to report to the Vehicle Abatement Program.

77

Today Ben shoved forward to an adjacent lot for an auto parts store. "Dwayne didn't dump the gun there," he said over his shoulder.

She dropped to hands and knees, anyway, lowering her chest as though in yoga's melting heart pose, scanning the blacktop under the car, unable to relinquish her hope of finding the ring, of saving the day, because she'd always wanted to be swinging on the rope as Tarzan, not sitting in the tree fort as Jane.

"You're not going to find anything," Ben said. "I searched that spot yesterday. So did the police." He poked around in the juniper bushes that divided the two parking lots.

"Yes, but you didn't know the ring was missing then." She straightened up, her knees cracking. "There's a test where you study a wall and note everything red for ten seconds. When you turn around and you're asked to list red stuff, you can say all kinds of things." She brushed dirt from her jeans. "But asked to name green stuff, chances are you won't be able to say a single thing. We notice what we're looking for."

"Okay, Nancy Drew. But I didn't know what the shithead had taken. I wasn't focused on one thing like the color red. We were looking for anything."

"My point is more that you weren't looking specifically for your ring."

He didn't reply.

"Is this where the tow truck driver showed up?"

"Yeah."

"And the sheriff who had your watch?" she asked.

"Yeah."

She felt like she was back in the classroom, trying to lead a reluctant student, squelching her own frustration, fighting for an encouraging tone. "A mechanic gave it to him?"

Ben nodded curtly.

"So where did the mechanic find the watch?" she asked. "Dwayne must have continued on this business side of Scenic until he lost it. Not everything fell out of the bag when he dumped it." As she cut a diagonal across the lot of the auto parts store, her gaze swept the asphalt, on alert for a gleam of metal. "Didn't you lose sight of him about here?"

"Yeah. I turned to the tow truck driver. When I looked back, he was gone." Ben swung his body one way and then the other, as though mentally reenacting the scene. "When they picked him up, he didn't have his jacket, his pack, or the gun. My guess is he ditched it all at once. He didn't have time to do that here. I would have seen him."

Vivi continued past the auto parts store. Another narrow driveway turned off Scenic and fronted a couple of workbays and the office of an auto repair shop. The wooden fence at the end of the drive snagged her attention. "Maybe Dwayne cut back there." She pointed. "He's pretty good at hopping fences."

"Doubled back?" Ben scratched under his Phillies cap. "Seems risky."

"He doesn't strike me as a risk-averse person." She hurried down the driveway. "This could be where he dropped the watch." She peered over the fence. A green dumpster bulked on an empty lot. "Let's check that out."

She toed her shoe atop the crosspiece and hefted her flat stomach onto the top ledge. Pulling one leg up and over, she awkwardly straddled the fence before scooting off the other side. "If I can do it, so can you."

Ben hoisted himself up and glided down beside her. He reached up to lift the lid of the dumpster. "How are we going to see inside?"

Stretching, she grasped the grubby lip of the metal lid. "I'll hold this, and you can pull yourself up."

Ben smiled grimly. "You really do think I'm Mighty Mouse." He grasped the top of the container and did a pull-up. He dropped back down beside her. "Nothing in there but a bunch of sheetrock."

Inspecting the ground, she circled the dumpster.

"Let's concentrate on the gun, Vivi."

"Don't you care about the ring?"

He stopped. "Of course I do."

"But?"

"Finding it will not make any difference."

"To the case," she said.

"Yeah, to the case," he said.

Back at the fence, he squatted, offering laced fingers as a stirrup. When he boosted her, a curve of pink metal flashed in her eyes.

Chapter Sixteen: Jessika & Espie

THANKSGIVING - midday

"Wait!" Vivi tumbled out of Ben's cupped hands and landed on all fours.

"You okay?" He helped her up.

She wiped her stinging palms. "I grew up with five brothers, remember?" Across the barren rock yard, a clump of overgrown weeds twined through the cyclone fence.

"That bike is over there. The one that girl was riding." It had been flung on the asphalt of Beverly Lane. She imagined the girl hit by a car, lying helpless.

Ben tore off in the direction of her point. She raced to get in front of him. He caught her arm. "Vivi, stop. That sounds like a fight."

Grunts and scuffling ricocheted toward them, caught in a weird acoustical echo bouncing from the peace sign painted on the school building across the street.

She sprinted toward the noise. On the ground, two girls were locked together. The Shakespearean phrase *beast with two backs* flitted through her mind, though this conjoined tumbling was far from having sex. The girl from the bike cocked a puny fist and punched at the face of another girl, who clutched a hank of the bike girl's black hair and screamed *cabrona, puta,* and a stream of other Spanish swear words. The Latina released the hair and bared long claws that ripped at the bike girl's cheek, leaving a dotted line of blood.

"Stop!" Vivi mustered her authoritative teacher voice. But these weren't her students. She had no sway over them. Still, she'd physically broken up student fights in her day.

Stepping behind the bike girl, Vivi scooped an arm under each of her biceps and locked her hands behind the girl's neck. She yanked up. Freed of her attacker, the girl on the ground leaped up, flushed with anger. As she lunged toward her now helpless enemy, Ben latched onto her shoulders.

The girl released a stream of Spanish cussing and elbowed his stomach. "*Omph.*"

That was sure to piss Ben off.

"Stop!" he growled. "It's over." He released her.

She spun around, a thick braid of hair twirling. "And who the fuck are you?"

"Nobody you care about."

"*Esa es la verdad,*" she muttered. That's the truth.

The bike girl quieted in Vivi's hold, but her muscles were tensed, ready to spring. "Let me go."

The other girl pivoted. She was packed into a pair of jeans and glowered from under eyebrows plucked to a thin line. But the baby skin of her face betrayed her youth. *A freshman, sophomore tops.*

"Are you going to stop fighting?" she asked the bike girl, but in a voice loud enough for the other girl to hear.

Bike Girl nodded.

The fighters glared at each other. The Latina's bottom lip was split and puffy, contrasting with swooping eyeliner as though she'd set out to a party. She had her hair braided, though. When Vivi had been teaching, if a girl who wore her hair down came to school with it plaited tight, that was a tip-off of an impending fight.

"Walk away," Ben said to her.

"*Puta!*" The girl charged toward her target. Vivi swung, turning Bike Girl with her like a matador's cape.

The other girl flew by them. She slid, turned, and lowered her head like she would charge again. "I know you took it, Jessika." She aimed a finger at the thin girl. "You're fucking dead, bitch." She wheeled around, grabbed up a dirty jacket from the ground, and stomped off down Beverly Lane.

Vivi relaxed her hold on the girl—Jessika—but didn't release her. "Took what?"

Jessika struggled without any real effort, just enough to stir her spicy fragrance.

"What was that all about?" Vivi tried again.

"Nothing."

"What were you up to over here?" Ben asked.

Silence.

When the Latina had put about fifty yards between them, Vivi let Jessika go. Without a word, she wiped off a thread of blood on her cheek, mounted her bike, and rode off in the other direction toward the passageway around the gate. She clearly knew the neighborhood.

"Do you think that's it? Or do you think she'll pedal around the block, and they'll start up again?"

Ben shook his head. "What was going on there?"

"Who knows? Boyfriend, maybe."

"No, I mean with you. You could've gotten hurt."

She brushed strands of hair from her jacket. "But I didn't."

"That was stupid."

"And chasing a guy with a gun wasn't?"

"I didn't know he had a gun."

"You did by the time he reached the dumpster."

"Yeah, and our mission now is to find said gun. Not to stand here having a ridiculous argument."

"You started it." *Oh my God.* She sounded like she was ten years old. But she couldn't help herself. "I guess the only one in this family who gets to play hero is you."

Ben stalked across the lot back toward the dumpster. But at the wooden fence, he made a finger stirrup for her again. Vivi had seen a horoscope chart once that linked signs to grudges. Ben's Libra sign held a grudge for .02 seconds. Her sign, Taurus, could hold one for a lifetime. She frowned at his hands.

"Oh, come on, Vivi."

With his assist, going over was easy. As Ben clambered over, she scouted along the roll-down doors in front of the automotive repair bays. In a further peace offering, Ben bent down and said, "I wonder if the gaps are big enough for a ring to slide under." He walked over to the office door. "They're open tomorrow. I'll come back and ask if anybody found a ring."

When they reached the sidewalk, Vivi stopped and shaded her eyes with a hand. "He must have crossed Scenic near here. And over there is a fire road."

They jogged across the four lanes. Scenic Drive curved and wound like the country road it used to be connecting small, distinct communities. Now the towns had grown together, and Scenic was a main artery through Playa Maria County. But on this side, away from the ocean, vestiges of open countryside remained—ramshackle, spaced-apart buildings with the fire road leading down into overgrown brush. She backed up to get an angle to see the roofs of the buildings. A school custodian had once told her that students threw contraband onto the rooftops. Behind her, Ben opened the business's dumpster.

"Anything?" she asked.

"Nothing. Their garbage was probably collected Tuesday, like ours."

Along the dirt fire road, she picked up a Manzanita branch for a walking stick. On this north-facing slope, the temperature fell ten degrees, the earth damp from the rain days earlier.

A cluster of run-down houses ran along a lot behind the businesses. Ben opened their garbage and recycling cans.

Vivi whacked into brambles with her stick. "A backpack!"

Chapter Seventeen: Fire Road

THANKSGIVING - early afternoon

Ben watched Vivi trudge into the brush toward a rotting blanket, a litter of plastic bottles and tin cans, a school desk whose laminate top had been shredded. The backpack on the ground was smashed and slick with pooled raindrops.

"Don't touch it! That's not it."

But she didn't listen. She stubbornly inched past a faded Burger King wrapper and stepped over a white sock patterned with daisies.

"Watch out for needles."

"We should have worn gloves." She pinched up the pack and unzipped it even though mold grew on its strap. She dropped it back on the trash heap.

It was empty, as he'd expected, but a gentle warmth filled him at her determination to find the gun.

They returned to the fire road. "How do you suppose Dwayne got that gun?" she asked, her voice flattened with disappointment.

"Previous robbery."

"Probably."

Thoughts snaked through Ben's mind. Had Dwayne used the gun before? Did he pull the trigger then?

One squeeze and his head could have been blown off. The thought infuriated him. Separated from death by a finger. And the shithead could go free.

Beside the fire road, the brush tangled into an impenetrable mass—brush woven together with wild berry vines. Vivi was walloping it with her walking-stick branch. "If he went charging into there," she said, "he'd get scratched up and poison oak to boot."

"He could have shoved everything into the pack and hurled it." Frustrated, Ben sped ahead. But Vivi had a point. He scouted for paths into the foliage, a spot for Dwayne to hide stuff.

"Dwayne steals to get money for something," she called after him. "Maybe drugs, but it could be something noble like baby formula for all we know."

"Nothing about Dwayne struck me as noble," he muttered back at her. "He intended to kill me." He was here, scuffing at this road, because of dumb luck. Why didn't Vivi get that?

She caught up and took his hand. They walked for a moment in silence. Then she said in that pondering way she had, "A gun seems like a valuable score. But he didn't sell it."

"Exactly." He released her hand. "He kept it to threaten people—like me."

To him, the idea they might find the gun was growing more ridiculous by the minute. He focused on the side of the fire road that sloped away gently, allowing access into the brush.

Down the road, a beaten footpath entered overgrown weeds. He veered onto the trail. Then he halted and lifted his arms to maintain his balance and stretched them to block Vivi's path. "Don't take another step." Ahead of him, the brush moved.

Chapter Eighteen: What Up?

THANKSGIVING – mid-morning

On Thanksgiving morning, Marshall sprawled on top of his twin bed, flipping the cover of his phone open and closed. He stopped, worried that the *click, click, click* would wake up James, even though his little brother slept scrunched down, his head crushed sideways into his pillow and covers pulled over his ears. It usually took Marshall or his dad throwing off the blankets and tugging James' toes to wake him up.

Marshall hesitated to call. His dad was strict about the phone, even if it was like the cheapest one possible. Marshall was too embarrassed to take it out on campus, even though he kind of agreed with his dad how ridiculous it was that some of his classmates had new iPhones costing hundreds of dollars.

On his flip phone, Marshall got exactly sixty minutes per month. "For emergencies," his dad said. He probably wouldn't have any phone if it weren't for what happened to his mom. Not that a phone would have done her any good. She'd been driving along minding her own business one minute, and the next, she was smashed flat. He fought against the image of her red compact car flattened liked a can for recycling. Her body, too destroyed for an open casket. His throat swelled, and he was filled with an unbearable urge like he needed to explode; he couldn't contain the amount of feeling. He shook his head violently and willed away the memory before it overwhelmed him like a rogue wave. He pushed his thoughts back to the day before because, as crazy as it had been, it was better than thinking about the accident.

He and Rocky had been lucky to escape that guy Rico in his Impala. When they'd reached the top of the stairs, Rocky's apartment had been empty, all of Rocky's shouting to his mom a ploy, the smartest thing Rocky had done all day.

The two of them had watched out the window. Rico seemed more like a teenager than a man, and he wasn't very big, but he looked tough, like a gangbanger, and the knife glinted in his hand. Rico and the girl didn't hang around long. The Impala rolled away with the girl on her bike, holding onto the open window for a free tow. He and Rocky had waited until they were completely out of sight, then Rocky had slipped the backpack off his shoulder and unzipped it.

Rocky's hand flew from the pack, his fist wrapped around the butt of a gun. "Holy crap!"

Fear flashed through Marshall. "Dude, don't point it at me."

Rocky aimed the barrel at the carpet, and Marshall reached toward the weapon, wanting to feel it, confirm its realness. Rocky jerked away, bumping into the coffee table.

"Don't even think about it," Rocky said. "I found it." His mom's clown statue rocked on the table.

"Okay. Chill." Marshall threw his hands in the air. "I'm not gonna take it."

Rocky sat on the arm of the couch, turned the gun over, and inspected it. "How do you get the cartridge thingy to pop out?"

"I don't know. You could check YouTube." Sweat trickled down Marshall's face. From running, he told himself. "That could be loaded."

"You think?" Rocky said sarcastically. "That's what I'm trying to find out." Rocky tugged at the barrel. It snapped back. A bullet flew onto the floor. "Holy crap!"

Marshall's heart hammered. "You know now."

"Cool." Rocky picked up the bullet.

"What you gonna do with it?"

Rocky laughed. "I can think of a few people I'd like to shoot. How 'bout that punk Finn that's always messing with James?"

"Be serious, dude."

"I don't know." Rocky pocketed the bullet and sank into a couch cushion.

It always struck Marshall as weird to see his friend in this apartment, his high skater socks and shredded shorts against the flower print of the couch. The scuffed Vans on peachy-colored carpet. The skull decals on his board and the butterfly decals on the window. The girly décor seemed doubly weird, with Rocky staring at a gun in his lap.

"You could tell your mom," Marshall said.

With a nervous giggle, Rocky flopped onto his back. "If my mom knew I had a gun, she'd ground me for the rest of my life." He aimed the gun up at the pebbly ceiling.

Wiping his forehead, Marshall backed to the door. "I better get home."

Rocky rolled his head toward him. "You look like you're shitting bricks." He sat up and pointed the gun at the glass clown. "Pow!"

"Jesus, Rocky." Marshall opened the door. On his way out, he pointed back at his friend. "That's not a toy."

Did Rocky even understand that? As Marshall lay on his bed snapping the phone open and closed, he thought the situation qualified as an emergency. He needed to talk to Rocky, in a way so Rocky would pay attention. He scrolled and found the number.

With each ring, his heartbeat quickened. What if Rocky had already done something stupid? Marshall didn't want to leave a message. His head bobbed to a frenetic drumbeat in his mind.

Rocky finally answered, sounding groggy. "Dude, it's not even nine."

"Yeah, well, I need to talk to you," Marshall whispered, watching James. But James remained conked out with drool making a wet spot on his pillow.

"Hey," Rocky snapped awake, like he went from zero to sixty in a second, "do you have any more ice cream?" Their code word for dope.

"Nah." Marshall looked around the room as though his dad could appear through the walls.

"So, what up, dog?"

"You know." How could Rocky be asking that? "What happened yesterday?"

"So? We got away."

"That guy and crazy chick know where you live."

"You need to chill. What are they gonna do?"

Marshall's heart rose to his throat with possibilities. Why didn't Rocky ever worry? "They could come back." When he and Rocky had crashed through the unlocked door, the apartment had been quiet enough to hear the people next door talking. Rocky's mom worked and went out on dates. Rocky was there by himself—a lot. "We should tell somebody."

"Dude," Rocky laughed, "you are such a girl."

On the other twin bed, James groaned and rolled onto his stomach. Without opening his eyes, James snaked his arm toward their shared bedside drawers. On his neck, a remaining ink line poked into his shaggy brown hair. Marshall fought an urge to scrub at it with a licked finger.

"Look, meet me today, same time, same place," he said to Rocky. Marshall leaned closer to his brother. At the spot where the ink line went under James' p.j. collar, his brother had a purple blotch on his skin like a hickey. Had Finn been doing more than writing on him? Pinching him?

"I can't," Rocky said. "We're going to my grandma's for Thanksgiving."

"Tomorrow then?"

"Nah. We won't be back 'til Sunday."

"Sunday, then. Three o'clock?"

"Can you get some more ice cream?" Rocky asked.

"Yeah."

"Okay," Rocky said. "Laters."

Luring Rocky with dope meant he had to go back into his dad's stash to sneak another pinch. His stomach swirled. Last time he'd found a photograph in the drawer—a hot girl stretched out on the sand, her oiled body glistening in the sun. Just a blue bikini bottom and no top. Propped on her elbows, one knee lifted, she smiled at the camera, her face half-hidden by ginormous white sunglasses. He had picked up the photo, excited, and embarrassed that his dad was a perv. Then the curve of the full lips, the long neck, the little mole by her ear jolted him, an electric zap of recognition. He dropped the picture of his mom. He felt like he'd eaten old baloney.

Marshall watched James' soft fingers wiggling around on the dresser like blindworms. He wondered what Rocky would do if he showed up with no weed and what would happen to James if he didn't learn to defend himself. And what was gonna happen with that friggin' gun.

Chapter Nineteen: Do Words Matter?

THANKSGIVING - early afternoon

A burly man crashed out of the brush, staring belligerently at Vivi and Ben. "Hey!" He gripped something in a massive hand.

Vivi startled and backpedaled. Ben reversed, mud making sucking sounds under his boots. He kept his body in front of hers, arms wide to shield her.

Through the brush came a woman's voice. "Do you know where Sarah's binkie is?"

"I've got it!" the man shouted over his shoulder. He turned back to them. "You continue down this path, and you'll be up to your ankles in water."

"Thanks, man."

The man plunged back into his hidey-hole, the army-green canvas of an ancient tent about twenty feet up from the muck in a sunny spot.

"All the years I've lived in this area, I never knew there was a swamp down here," she said. "Did you?"

"Nope. Never knew homeless were living here either."

"Unsheltered," Vivi said.

"Homeless. Unsheltered. What does it matter? The guy has a home; he has a shelter. It's just that it's a fucking tent. Saying *unsheltered* is like repainting the stripes on a chewed-up highway."

They stepped back onto the solid ground of the fire road, the sadness of the situation deflating them.

"The paper did refer to a 'creek bed,'" Ben said. "The gun's probably out there. In the water."

"Maybe. If Dwayne's number-one goal was to get rid of evidence."

"What else would he be trying to do?"

They continued along the road, but their pace was slow. "Well," she jabbed at the dirt with her branch, "he wanted to get the jacket off because he was hot from running, and he wanted to look different."

"He was a black guy in our neighborhood. Pretty hard not to stand out."

"He was encumbered by that pack," she insisted. "That's why he started throwing stuff out. Or, maybe he did that to stop you. Anyway, what I'm saying is he valued that gun, and rather than throwing it into the water, maybe he stashed it to pick up later."

"Yeah, that's possible, but he's in jail now."

"He didn't know he'd get caught."

"Oh, he knew," Ben said. "There must have been seven cop cars just on the street where they arrested him."

"Hope springs eternal. He was trying to evade them until the last minute. You said yourself—the gun is a big deal."

"Exactly why he might have tossed it." He fell silent. His shoulders drooped.

Hope might spring eternal, but Ben was losing his. He sounded defeated, so unlike him.

Her stubbornness kicked in, the strong yellow blaze of her *manipura chakra*. "At first this seems like a great place to get away from the police," she said, "but it's pretty stupid. The freeway curves around the area, blocking off escape unless a person wades into the muck and goes through a culvert. That would have been the smart thing for Dwayne to do."

"We're not dealing with a mastermind. He's not pulling off a final heist and retiring to Hawaii to sip mai tais."

She took his hand to snap him out of his funk. "Still, it's possible that he kept the gun and the wedding ring until he knew he was going to get caught and then stashed them for someone to pick up."

"Let's go home. We have a turkey to cook."

His enthusiasm had drained into that swamp.

"Look," she said, shaking his hand to command his attention. "You searched the place where he dumped our stuff. Your wedding ring wasn't there. Why didn't it dump with the rest of the stuff?"

"I don't know. Maybe he stuffed it in a pocket. Maybe it snagged in his pack. Or maybe we just didn't see it." His voice was clipped.

"Or maybe he kept it because it was small and the most valuable thing he took. If he threw it and the gun away, he would have nothing to show for his trouble."

"He has nothing to show for it anyway." Ben took off down the road, his hiking boots spitting up wads of mud.

Chapter Twenty: A Good Man with a Gun

FRIDAY AFTER THANKSGIVING

Big Al expected the ten-mile ride to Baker's Gun Shop with his son-in-law to be strained, maybe even tense, but Chris climbed into Al's truck cab, sucked in a deep breath, and said, "Ahhh, that new car smell."

"First off-the-lot vehicle I've ever owned." Big Al's hand proudly traced the arc of the steering wheel. The remark was pointed, and he knew it, rubbing in again how hard and long he'd worked for things.

Chris didn't seem to notice. "How you liking it?"

"*Motor Trends* named it Truck of the Year, both 2015 and 2016." He found himself eager to share all the great features of the Chevy Colorado. He gunned the engine to show Chris the truck's power.

"And the mileage ain't bad. About twenty-two miles per gallon around town." They rolled smoothly along an open expanse of freeway. In the distance, sunshine glinted on the ocean. Life felt good. "And you'll appreciate this," he said to Chris, "it comes with a thirty-day free trial of Sirius XM."

"What kind of music do you listen to?"

Big Al used the steering wheel controls to turn on the Outlaw Country station.

"Oh, yeah," Chris said. "I like Outlaw Country. Wide range of stuff. Allman

Brothers right along with Johnny Cash."

Big Al bopped his head to Willie Nelson's "On the Road Again." Something about traveling along, listening to this music, made him feel young. He had to admit, he was enjoying himself. "In the shop, I mostly listen to metal."

"Metal for metal," Chris said with an impish grin. In spite of the ear discs, he was a good-looking guy. Big Al had to give Stella that.

"Metallica, Tool," Al said. "Stuff like that."

"Did you know Lars Ulrich originally went to Los Angeles to train to be a professional tennis player?"

Big Al shot Chris a look. "That right?"

They discussed bands and music until Big Al found himself at the south end of the county on a short industrial street, not even sure how they'd gotten there. The drive had been quick and effortless.

As Big Al drove past Baker's Guns, Chris craned his neck.

"The lot in the back has room."

"It might not stay that way. And those spaces are narrow. I don't want someone banging his door against my truck."

"Copy that," Chris said. "This is a dicey neighborhood, though. They have security cameras in the lot."

Big Al climbed from the cab. "I'm not worried about that." Chris joined him outside on the street, where a person could hear the muffled gunfire from the shooting gallery. It was a beautiful fall day, the air crisp, the street quiet—some of the industrial shops still closed for the holiday. "And in a minute, we'll be armed."

He circled to the truck bed, where he'd locked their guns in one of his toolboxes. Chris was beside him. Big Al had the key in the lock. Chris's head jerked up.

Two men slid from the side of a building. They headed right toward them.

Chapter Twenty-One: Rocking the Chakras

FRIDAY - morning earlier

On Friday morning, at five minutes to eight, Ben was headed down the street to Big Al's. Ten minutes later, he slammed back into the house. Vivi knew the visit hadn't gone well. She leaned against the kitchen counter, finishing her coffee. "What's the matter?"

"The apprentice won't testify."

"He just came right out and said that?"

"No, I started out by thanking him for chasing the thief, and the little shit was really unfriendly, wouldn't even look up."

"Big Al wasn't there?" she asked.

"No."

"Where was he?"

"How would I know?"

"Don't take out your frustration on me." She opened the dishwasher, rattled the mug into place, and shut the door more loudly than necessary.

"That gun is important. The deputy said so, too."

"Do you want to go look for it again?"

"It's hopeless."

But in spite of his words, his head had lifted.

Luna was peering in the door, leaving nose smudges on the glass. He let the cat into the kitchen and sprinkled kibble into her bowl.

"We can go as soon as I get home from yoga," she offered.

"Yoga with the hot teacher?" he teased.

She smiled, glad he was regaining some of his sense of humor.

He scrubbed his face with his palms. "Do you remember if the pawnshop was going to open today? Next thing would be to call them. Put them on the lookout for the ring."

"And the gun," she said.

Listening to Ben make the call brought the burglary right back, a rush like her life had sailed without her on board. When Ben went out to the garage to practice his drums, the uneasiness spread even though he was right there. She reminded herself that it had only been a day and a half.

She had another hour before yoga. In the comfy desk chair in the office, she tried to fill the time by writing comments on students' papers. Volunteering in a high school writing program was not proving to be a satisfying retirement activity. The students weren't hers, and half the time she thought the teacher wasn't doing an adequate job.

With their sound-proofed garage, she couldn't hear Ben's playing, but the vibrations traveled through the vents and along the floor, connecting her bare foot to Ben's body fifty feet away, his haunches lifted, his weight over his kit. "A muscular drummer," he'd said when the band took a break, and he came over to talk to her. She'd been waiting for a colleague friend and leaning back against the bar admiring the thick black curls tossing around as he played.

"How did you start drumming?" she'd asked.

"My Grandma Russo gave me a drum set because she hated my mom. She wasn't Italian. Worse yet, not Catholic."

Vivi stirred from the memory to find herself staring at the photo of her mom over the desk. Ninety years old, but she sported a red hat, pluming with red feathers.

Talons squeezed Vivi's heart. She leaned back and closed her eyes, then blinked them damply open. She avoided the photograph by looking out the window to the garden gate. The one Dwayne had crawled over.

This was not going well. Everywhere she looked blew up another emotion.

The doorbell chimed. Her hand jerked, sending the computer mouse crashing off the desk. She picked it up, hoping it wasn't broken, and checked out the window before heading to the door. A sheriff's vehicle sat at the curb.

Holding a paper in his hand, Deputy Hashimoto stood on the steps. "Good morning, ma'am. How are you doing?"

"I'm pretty jumpy."

He nodded. "I came by to see if you would take a look at a six-pack of mug shots. See if you can identify Dwayne Williams."

She invited him into the entrance hallway. "Would that do any good?"

"Why do you ask that?" Cops were supposed to keep a neutral demeanor, but Hashimoto was particularly hard to read.

"I saw his photo in the newspaper yesterday. That seems prejudicial."

"I would say give it a try anyway. It could be one of these men or none of them." He showed her the sheet.

She bent close. Studied the first row, then the second. She turned on the hallway light and repeated the process. None of the black-and-white photos resembled the one in the newspaper. "All these guys have bushier hair than the burglar."

"Just do your best."

"I know how unreliable eyewitnesses can be," she said.

"Maybe. But eyewitness accounts are one of only two kinds of evidence not considered circumstantial."

Surprised, she flicked a look at him. "What's the other?"

"Video."

His words weighed on her as though her choice could affect the outcome. She reached for the six-pack, and the deputy relinquished it. She held it close, considering each face. She'd encountered the idea of the cross-race effect in her teacher training; most people were unable to distinguish well the physical differences in another race, but she'd never experienced it in such an acute way.

"I don't know. Maybe this one." She pointed to the young man with the fairest skin, the feature she remembered the most.

Hashimoto didn't flinch or tic, but she sensed that she'd chosen the wrong one. "That's not him, is it?"

"I can't say."

* * *

When she entered the gym, Vivi couldn't wait to start yoga, to find some calm. Picking a face from the six-pack agitated her, made her worry that she'd undermined Ben. She unrolled her mat, but kept a corner tucked, the way Winn had students signal they were okay with adjustments. She bowed to a couple of yoga buddies, then bent her legs into full lotus.

Winn was out of the room. *The Mantra for Healing* played on the sound system. She shifted on her sitz bones to get centered.

Winn breezed into the room and turned off the music. She didn't know much about him except he didn't depend on yoga for a living. He'd let it slip one time that he trained EMTs.

She waited hopefully for the process of following her breath, listening to Winn, and escaping a barrage of thoughts about Dwayne Williams and the gun. She should be thankful Ben hadn't been murdered, but it was pretty frickin' hard to reach a state of gratitude just yet.

Winn unfurled his mat without hurry, as though his every action taught yoga. She smiled at the memory of Ben suggesting Winn had checked her out, a silly yet flattering idea. But then there had been that weird electricity when he'd touched her arm. What was that about?

The teacher's unlined face suggested someone younger than her fifty-seven, but maybe that was the effect of regular meditation. Besides, if chemistry existed, did the years matter?

Sitting in *virasana*, Winn reminded the class of the upcoming retreat in Mexico. "Two spaces still available." He looked right at her, and her heart lurched. "Tropical beach. Yoga under a palapa."

The peaceful image tugged at her. She'd absolutely love to be there, to escape the tension from the burglary. But that was why she couldn't go; she needed to support Ben.

Breathing together, the class quieted. She rolled her shoulders.

Winn talked almost non-stop, but his voice was melodic and the patter informative.

"Right now..." Winn said.

Perfect words.

She set her intention for class: be present. *Not so easy.* They had a gun to find, and she'd possibly fingered the wrong person to the sheriff's deputy. Plus, whenever she became still, her mother's absence visited. And had she made the right choice to retire?

She counted her breathing, eight beats inhaled, pulling in air from the back of her throat, eight beats out, the sound like air soughing through wheat, a sound from her childhood.

"As we close our eyes, we close off the outer world," Winn said. "Of the eight branches of yoga, many classes focus on only one, the *asanas*, the postures. But in the Tibetan style I offer today, we concentrate on the inner world. Closing our eyes eliminates sight, which informs us that I am here and you are there, that we are separate and things are solid and fixed.

"In reality, we are moving electrons—energy—and we can change and move that energy, that prana, that chi. We can change the stories we tell ourselves, and when we do, we can free ourselves from the prison of our minds. We can change the way we operate in the world, and then we start to change the world."

Be the change. Cliché. She adjusted her right hip down toward her turquoise mat, her lower vertebrae clicking into place. She peeked at Winn, the toned biceps outside the sleeveless tee. A fantasy embrace snuck in. *Oh my God.* She rolled her eyes. "Focus."

"We sit here in the same class, listening to the same words, feeling the same breeze through the window," he continued in his liquid honey voice, "but some of us will be thinking, 'When will we get out of this posture?' and others might think, 'When will he stop talking?' and others may say, 'This is so relaxing,' so what is the truth of this moment? What narrative do we tell ourselves?"

He had his eyes closed. She was a naughty spy. She closed her eyes and tuned back into his words.

"We have control over the story, and that creates our reality. Why not create a reality in which everyone can be happy and free?" He directed them to cup their hands into gentle fists, to breathe in, and to stir the energy up from the first chakra. "As we breathe out, we'll offer that energy to the world with the thought, 'Wouldn't it be wonderful if we could all be happy and free?'"

Not Dwayne Williams. She didn't want him to be happy and free. Was she practicing yoga if she hoped he was miserable and locked up?

On the inhale, she lifted her spread fingers. *Maybe?* He was only eighteen and needed to hit some kind of bottom to rise up. Like Ben's son Art.

Her exhale shrouded her in sadness. Dwayne Williams was a kid. During her career, she'd encountered too many students for whom it was a heroic feat to make it to school—kids from shelters and migrant camps. People all had choices, but not all had the same choices.

Inhaling. *Dwayne has time.* Like her, he was energy in flux. But she could only visualize him running from her home. Living the life of a thug. Using a gun.

Winn started their *asana* practice. As she pushed into her first downward dog, his footsteps padded across the floor. He placed a hand on each of her hipbones and gave her pelvis a tug back toward his body. Blood rushed to her face. He gently ironed her spine with one warm palm. "Beautiful," he whispered.

* * *

Vivi and Ben returned to the fire road off Scenic, the place where Dwayne had almost certainly fled after the burglary. They passed the footpath that led to the homeless family. The swampy water shouldn't have been a surprise. Playa Maria County was a watershed. Each community had a river from the mountains as well as numerous little creeks running down through it.

As the fire road rose away from the dip, sunlight dappled the dirt.

A certain slant of light. The phrase popped into her head even though Emily Dickinson had been writing about oppressive pale wintery light, not the soft light of autumn.

Ahead of them, a couple with a yellow Labrador retriever veered off the fire road through a copse of eucalyptus.

"Remember how the newspaper article about Dwayne mentioned construction?" she asked Ben.

"Yeah."

"It's right up there." She pointed after the couple. "And Dwayne had to get off this fire road. Cruisers can drive down it."

He stopped with her to study the possibilities. Here the slope of the road faced south, and the trees grew taller and farther apart with less underbrush.

"Let's follow them," she said. "They look like they walk here all the time and know the way through the trees. The path Dwayne might have taken."

"Okay. Let's do this like in the movies. You go over there." Ben indicated a spot beyond where the dog walkers had turned. "I'll start here."

Vivi stepped into the soft earth, scattered with rotted leaves. Neck bent, she combed the ground with her gaze. Slick spears of bay laurel and fingered maple leaves on a sprinkle of rusty pine needles. Then she saw it. Stopping abruptly, she kneeled. "Look at this!"

Ben hurried over. He studied the ground. "What?" His face crumpled in disappointment, as though he'd expected to see the gun.

"See this gouge in the dirt?"

"So?"

"About four feet up is another one."

He leaned closer.

"Look how they're curved. Those are heel indents. Wednesday the ground was damp. Dwayne would have been running, hitting the ground hard."

He smiled. "Nancy Drew. How did you get so smart, anyway?"

She puffed with pride even though the discovery didn't mean much. At least not by itself. Unless the imprints led to the gun.

They followed the trajectory of the prints up a bank of dried grass and came out onto a neighborhood street. It dead-ended at a fenced-off, wide swath along the freeway. On the other side of a chain-link fence, a backhoe, grater, and dump truck rested near blocks of concrete and piles of mangled rebar. "Maybe he threw the gun there."

"If your theory is correct, and Dwayne held on to the gun until the end, more likely he ditched it as he started cutting through back yards."

"But that would be hard to retrieve." *And the family or some little kid might find it.*

Ben turned away from the chain-link and crossed to the nearest house. He peeked through the cracks of a wooden side fence that butted up to the freeway fence. He studied the height of the planks.

Vivi grabbed his arm. "We can't go into people's yards." Ben's decisiveness had saved them many times, jumping them off a bus with bad brakes in Costa Rica, commanding her to run from two men in Venezuela before she even saw the glint of their knives. Still, his quickness to act never failed to make her anxious.

"I know."

"When you made the field I.D., did the sheriff bring you down this street?"

"No. I'll show you."

They walked down a block of small homes, quiet except for the pervasive freeway hum. A white minivan rolled by with a dog—a boxer—panting a bright pink tongue out the passenger window.

At the end of the block, Ben said, "One more block, that's where the arrest was made."

"He cut through a lot of back yards."

"One of the homeowners called 9-1-1. That's how they nabbed him."

On the return home, they altered their route, checking the garbage cans of the continuation school next to Bay High School. It served students at risk of not graduating from normal high schools. The cans were empty except for small candy wrappers and bits of paper stuck to the gunk in the bottom.

They cut back to the fire road near where they'd seen the heel prints. She found another backpack, but it was smashed and covered with mold. "Who knew backpacks were such common trash?"

"We're near schools." He sounded discouraged. "And homeless camps."

When they reached Scenic Drive, they crossed to search the area beyond the automotive shops, in case Dwayne had run along the boulevard longer than they thought. She moved ahead of Ben, who shuffled along behind like he'd given up. But the thought of the gun had taken up residence in her head: Dwayne didn't have it, and neither they nor the police had found it. Where was it?

Chapter Twenty-Two: Break In

FRIDAY - later

Now that she was paying attention to the apartment building, Jessika decided it couldn't be uglier. The afternoon sun revealed all the smudges on the two-story, half-block of beige stucco. Scruffy grass ran along the front of it.

She and Rico circled to the back to look for what he called "ports of entry." A wooden fence and a string of carports separated the apartments from an alley. Rico moved a recycle bin over and clambered on top of one of the low-slung carports to get a better look.

She didn't need to climb up. It was hopeless. The back of the building presented a sheer wall unbroken by any convenient trees.

Rico bounded down. "So you know, I hate second-story jobs."

"There must have been something good in that pack or Dwayne wouldn't have sent Espie to get it." Jessika's UGG boots crunched over broken glass. "She thought I took it. She was really pissed." A tinge of sadness tweaked through her. Espie was like a little sister.

Rico followed her toward the mouth of the alley. "You still with Brenden?" He tried to sound casual, but Jessika knew he was in this alley because of her. The score alone wasn't enough incentive.

"Guess not. I sort of walked out on him on Thanksgiving. He hasn't texted."

He caught up and walked beside her. "Where you been hanging?"

"Home."

They turned along the side of the apartment building. "Didn't your mom kick you out?"

"She didn't know I was there."

Her mom, in fact, had changed the locks and installed an alarm system, but she had tried the old code to the garage door and presto. And not alarmed.

Rico snorted. "You're sneaky."

So far they hadn't spotted any alarm signs on this property. At least that was good. They got back to where they'd started, on the sidewalk in front of where the boys had run up the steps.

Carrying a fat pug, a middle-aged woman emerged from the door next to the one they were watching. At the bottom of the steps, she sat him on the grass. The dog waddled behind her down the walkway.

"Cute dog," Rico said.

The woman stopped and smiled.

"What's his name?"

"Buddy."

Rico squatted and extended his fingers for the dog to sniff. "There's a good boy." The woman beamed.

Rico patted the wrinkled head. "Is it okay to give him a treat?"

The woman stiffened a little. "Where's your dog?"

"At the vet," Rico said. "Getting de-wormed." He sighed up at the woman and rolled his eyes.

He deserved an Oscar.

"I know how that is," the woman said, giving a nod of approval for the treat.

When she and the dog were out of earshot, Jessika whispered, "Do you always walk around with dog treats?"

"Tool of the trade."

Burglary, Jessika thought, was more interesting than any subject she'd taken in high school.

They strolled along the sidewalk, keeping an eye out for the neighbor on the other side of the kid's apartment, although there'd been no car in the corresponding carport, and the curtains were drawn.

"Probably gone for Thanksgiving," Jessika said.

"I'm going up."

He loped up the stairs. Jessika's heart banged. She followed. The thrill, the rush, was almost as good as crystal.

"Knock on the neighbor's door," Rico said.

"Are you two looking for somebody?" The woman with the pug was calling up to them from the grass. She sounded less friendly.

That was the shortest dog walk ever. At least no one had responded to her knock.

"Rocky's mom asked us to check on the place while they're gone." Rico was stone-cold smooth. All that time the two boys had been yelling to each other, she'd hardly paid attention to their names, much less which name belonged to the apartment.

Down on the grass, the woman waved a dismissive hand beside her ear. "*Pawh*, she'd be a hell of a lot safer if she didn't leave the key under the mat, just inviting in some burglar."

* * *

Jessika stood shivering on the sidewalk, the street quiet and the night black around her. Streetlights and landscaping lights cast dim beams, diffused by a cold mist off the ocean.

"I prefer mid-day," Rico muttered. "Fewer people home."

He spied up the free-standing concrete steps. "Second-floor is for shit. No way out the back."

Jessika rubbed her goosebumps. Didn't bother to call him a pussy. He'd said all this before. A few times. And he was still here.

His black clothes disappeared up the walkway steps.

He was stealthy; she could barely hear his sneakers. He reappeared in the weak light beside the apartment door, then became a shadowy figure as he slid to the other side of the door away from the light.

She reminded herself to watch the sidewalk and road instead of Rico.

Chapter Twenty-Three: Rise and Shine

SATURDAY - morning

P ropped in bed with a couple of pillows, Vivi opened the local paper to the police blotter. Since their burglary, she went right to it, appalled by the commonness of break-ins and meth busts. The headline *Man Shot at Gun Store* grabbed her attention.

Ben leaned over to see what she was reading, his shoulder warm against hers, his dark-framed reading glasses accentuating the quick intelligence in his eyes. "What's on the menu today?"

"Two guys went to Baker's for target practice. While they were unlocking their guns, two hoodlums accosted them and demanded their weapons."

"What happened?" Ben tugged at the paper.

"Hey." She yanked the paper back. "I'm telling you."

"The paper used the word *hoodlums?*"

In her clear teacher voice, she read: "The two Playa Maria men refused to hand over their firearms and tried to tackle their assailants."

"Don't read it. Tell me what happened."

"I thought you didn't want to hear words like *hoodlums.*" Turning away, she lifted her mug of coffee. "One of the good guys got shot."

"Dead?"

"No. Wounded. The other guy dived under their vehicle."

She handed him the paper.

He scanned the article and rested the paper in his lap. "Should we get an alarm system?"

Across from them, a black-and-white framed poster advertised Sam Shepard's play *Fool for Love*. "It's not something I ever thought about." She never tired of the poster, how the woman's long pale arms twined around the man's neck, and her face disappeared into his shoulder. "But maybe we should look into it."

"Are we losing our perspective by reading this Police Blotter?"

"Probably. Or maybe we were naïve before. Living in our bubble."

"I'll get some bids."

* * *

When Ben left to go to the gym, Vivi settled at her desk to read student essays. Out the window, the back gate loomed. Dwayne Williams had scaled it and landed in their lives. She swiveled back and forth in her chair. Now that she was alone, disquiet was creeping into her body.

A hummingbird lit on the stem of a lavender pelargonium blossom. His spot. She'd be typing away, lift her head, and there he would be, still and quiet after fluttering his wings eighty times per second. A gift to her, day after day, glinting scarlet and teal. As the bird calmed his madly beating heart, he calmed her. A perfect yogi coming to his mat.

Vivi gave up on the idea of critiquing essays and clicked on her email folder. Messages responding to her notice about the burglary flooded their inbox. Seventeen today. Most of them were way-to-go messages. Her second-oldest brother greeted her as Vivianne. The old-fashioned sound of her full name normally rankled her, but from her brothers, it confirmed her identity in a tribe. *Glad you are both okay*, he wrote. *Stay safe, little sister. I couldn't take another loss.*

The message stabbed her heart, their mother's death still fresh. As much as she missed her mom, this brother had been the one back home, visiting her every day.

The next e-mail rained exclamations.

Hey, we're waiting for the lowdown! Ben, man, you rock! Brave, brave, brave!

Don't you guys own a gun? If not, this should convince you to buy one. (Or two!)

I hope things are back to a cautious normal.

Love,

Anne (and Bob)

From Anne, the gun question wasn't a surprise, but it made her itch. Vivi pushed her sweater above her elbows to make sure she hadn't contracted poison oak. No red dots. Plain irritation.

Anne and Bob owned a dozen guns—collectibles, but also, according to them, ones for protection. Usually Vivi tucked this fact to the side and enjoyed their monthly get-togethers for dinner and pinochle.

Now her shoulders tightened. What a stupid idea that a gun would have done them any good, like they would have strapped it on to go to the grocery store. And for what? To shoot some guy for breaking into their house? And if the gun had been in their house, wouldn't Dwayne have stolen it? Most likely the way he got the gun he pointed at Ben.

And how about the guys that got shot at Baker's Guns? They had guns. What good had that done? If they hadn't been carrying firearms, they wouldn't have been targets. Their assailants wanted weapons, not money. That's why they'd staked out a gun store instead of a 7-Eleven.

And then there was her brother. An accident. But so much destruction—to his wife and two children, to her mom and dad and herself. To her brothers. To the hunter, a fourteen-year-old boy. Lives altered forever. None of it could have happened without a firearm.

Her fingers tapped the keys without typing. She couldn't respond now. It would be a rant.

She breathed in, counting the inhalation. She breathed out, matching the length. What would Winn advise? How did one apply yoga here?

Cautious normal. A normal that now included no mother and a friend who thought she should buy a gun. The hummingbird had flitted away, and she was left to stare at the gate.

* * *

111

Anne's e-mail bugged her throughout yoga class. Instead of following her breath, she composed replies to Anne in her head. She barely heard Winn's words. The idea of an alarm nagged at her, too. Robert Frost's poem *Mending Wall* crowded into the mix: *Something there is that doesn't love a wall/That wants it down.* In that poem, the mending of a stone wall ironically brought two neighbors together. Nothing magical like that was going to happen with a virtual wall, although it would hopefully keep the likes of Dwayne out of their house.

At the end of class, she squatted and rolled her mat as others left the room. She packed slowly. Today she was dead last. Standing, she rubbed her hips.

Winn slid his mat bag over his shoulder and padded toward her. "Hard class?"

"My hips are like concrete."

"Seat of emotion," he said. "That's where prana gathers when a person holds anger. Has unresolved issues."

"Sounds about right."

"Are you headed next door?"

Vivi nodded. "I'm going to get a juice drink."

"I could go for a cup of coffee."

"You drink coffee?"

Deep dimples etched into his square chin. "I'm a yoga teacher. Not a saint."

* * *

In the café, Vivi joined Winn at his table.

Dark eyes smiled at her over his mug. "Vivi," he murmured, "is that short for anything?"

"I was named after my mom, Vivian. I'm Vivianne." Her response sounded worn, like an old record played too many times.

Winn took an unhurried sip. "Is she alive?"

Vivi's eyes brimmed with tears. She was used to little things—like the sight of a red hat—punching her, but not this standard question. She flushed with embarrassment. Winn waited, receptive.

"She passed away in September." It came out pretty good, only a tiny quaver.

"I'm so sorry." His hand moved toward her, but she kept a grip on her cup, her other hand stashed in her lap.

"She lived to be ninety and had a full life."

Winn folded his arms across his chest. "That doesn't stop her death from hurting."

Nodding, she sucked on her straw. Why had she even said that? She hated when people tried to comfort her by pointing out how long her mother had lived, as though that eased the pain. If anything, having shared life with her for so long made the loss harder.

Winn's gaze traveled her face, eyes warm, waiting. Patient.

She chewed on the end of the straw. In his silence, Vivi realized his hypnotic voice was one of his most alluring qualities, and his face became handsome when he smiled, which meant he lived a life where people wanted to hear him speak and to make him smile. *A charmed life.*

Heat bounced between them. She didn't wear her wedding ring to class because it spun on her finger, and the diamond bit into the neighboring digits. Although she'd never given him reason to believe otherwise, Winn might not know she was married. Her thoughts deviated, and the heat of a blush crawled up her neck.

When she didn't add any more about her mother, Winn said, "You have a committed yoga practice."

"I have the luxury of being retired."

He gave her his full dimples. "You must have retired *really* early."

A smile played on her lips. He was flirting. "This year. I wasn't planning on it, but the school district offered a golden handshake too good to pass up."

"Wow." He lifted the white ceramic coffee mug in tribute. "Retirement, then the death of your mother. Two of the top ten stressors." He paused. "A transformative time."

Transformative. She hadn't even told him about the burglary.

Right now she should mention Ben, and that the early retirement was possible because she was *married.* She could slip in how she needed to get home to help her husband locate a gun. But she didn't. Instead, she asked Winn how he got into yoga.

"Death of my wife." Sadness shadowed his eyes. "It hurled me into an abyss."

She bent across the small mosaic table, wanting to touch his arm, but now Winn was the one leaning back into his grief, pulling away.

"When was that?"

"Ten years ago. Breast cancer. Age forty-six." He stopped talking.

The café's blender whirred, crunching ice.

When the roar subsided, he added, "Yoga helped me climb out of a deep, dark hole."

His vortex pulled at her. Vivi wanted to edge close and peer inside.

Chapter Twenty-Four: Secret

SUNDAY - midday

At the elementary school, Marshall perched on top of "his" picnic table, his orange Converse sneakers tapping the bench. Rocky was later than usual. He could have forgotten. Rocky was the kind of kid who only sometimes did his homework, or at least copied it. Marshall doubted Rocky would graduate from eighth grade. Rocky didn't seem to care since he'd go on to high school, anyway. He'd just have to take remedial classes.

Rocky was not responsible. Which was why Rocky should not have the gun. Marshall lay back on the warm wood and clasped his hands over his wavy hair. *How to convince Rocky to give him the gun.* "I found it," Rocky kept insisting. Even after they'd been chased by the guy in the Impala, and he and that crazy bike chick knew where Rocky lived.

Marshall lurched up. Glanced around again for Rocky. Bounced his foot. He watched a leaf fall from a tree, floating side-to-side, taking like *forever* to reach the ground.

He didn't have any weed to bribe Rocky since he couldn't bring himself to raid his dad's stash again—to see that photo again.

At the sound of footsteps, he whirled. Rocky strolled up with the pack slung over his shoulder like there was nothing to hide. *What an idiot.* But at least that meant no one was pursuing him. Not yet. Marshall let out the breath he'd been holding.

Rocky slid the backpack onto the wood surface. "You're right, dude. We should stash this at your house."

Marshall tensed. "What changed your mind?"

"When we were at my grandma's, that banger and bike girl broke into our apartment."

"How do you know it was them?"

"Who else?" He punched Marshall's shoulder. "I thought you were the smart one."

Marshall's heart thudded. He eyed the pack. "Why didn't they take that?"

"I had it with me."

Marshall didn't know if that was lucky or not. It might be better if the two had taken it, or if he and Rocky got rid of it. It wasn't easy to figure out what to do with a gun.

"But," Rocky twisted his mouth to the side, and Marshall's stomach turned, "my mom asked if I knew what they were searching for. She probably thought I had some weed. Now she's gonna be all on high alert. You know how moms are."

Rocky stiffened. "Oh. Sorry, dude."

"Don't worry about it."

The pack reminded Marshall of a story in English class. *The Monkey's Paw*. A treasure that's cursed. If he remembered right, someone ended up dead. "Did your mom call the police?"

"Nah."

"Why not?"

Rocky shrugged. "She says that's the good part of being poor—nothing to take."

"They didn't take anything?"

"They took the money from my swear jar."

Marshall had seen the glass pickle jar where Rocky's mom made him deposit a dollar when he swore—the reason for Rocky saying "crap" instead of "shit."

"Some old Vicodin," Rocky continued. "Mom says she wore or packed all her good jewelry. And she had her phone and purse. She has another little stash of money, but they didn't find it." Rocky smirked. "She keeps it in a tampon box."

Marshall wrinkled his nose.

"Exactly." Rocky swiped hair behind his ear. "Mom says most thieves are guys, and they react like that." He pointed at Marshall's face.

Marshall batted away Rocky's hand. "Doesn't she want the police to catch who did it?"

"Right. Like they ever catch anyone. She thinks it was kids looking for drugs, and reporting it would be more hassle than it's worth."

Rocky nudged the pack toward Marshall. "You need to take this."

This whole thing was becoming too complicated for Marshall to ever explain—to the police, to his dad. Especially to his dad. He'd worry and be angry and drop everything to deal with it. He'd feel like he couldn't depend on Marshall to take care of things.

"Okay. Let's take it to my house," Marshall said. "Watch for that psycho chick."

* * *

Marshall's dad always told him to count himself lucky they owned their house. Real estate was crazy expensive in Playa Maria. But when Marshall walked up the sidewalk, the weedy grass embarrassed him. It was his chore to mow it; it was also his job to unload the dishwasher, to fold his own clothes, and to vacuum.

He opened the dented screen door, unlocked the front door, and they entered the empty house.

"I wish I lived here, dude," Rocky said. "It's like a man cave."

"Your place is better."

"No way."

"Way." The pink bathroom at Rocky's smelled like soft-powdery things, and the refrigerator was plastered with photos of Rocky and his mom with their extended family and friends. Not that Marshall was gonna say any of that.

Rocky didn't care about the cramped quarters of Marshall and James' bedroom or the childish Avengers comforter his mom had bought for him or the dinosaurs on James' comforter, as though they were still eight and five. Rocky didn't even seem to notice. That was what Marshall liked about him.

Throwing the backpack on the twin bed, Rocky plucked up Marshall's guitar. He slung the leather strap around his neck and slammed the strings like an arena rocker hitting power chords. Marshall's unmade bed swayed as Rocky clambered on top and pogoed over the mattress, singing, "I'm a king supreme/I'm a human being/I'm making a scene…." He paused for inspiration. "I'm CeeLo Green…."

"You don't sound like CeeLo."

Rocky's long hair flew up and down. "I'm great at peeing." The pack bounced with him.

"Knock it off, Rocky." Marshall rescued the pack and sat it on the floor. He nudged it under the bedframe and flailed an arm toward his prancing friend. "That's not a toy."

Rocky handed over the guitar. "That's a pretty good song, though, don't you think?"

By the time Marshall planted the instrument in its stand, Rocky was kneeling on the carpet. "Under the bed? Seriously? Kind of obvious, don't you think?"

"There's no room anywhere else." Marshall got down on all fours and shoved the pack farther until it hit against the wall. As he backed out, the comforter pulled away from his head. Footsteps came down the hall. The door popped open.

Marshall jerked up and tugged the comforter off the side of the mattress. He sat on the edge of his bed. "I thought you went with Dad."

James balanced along the invisible line that ran down the middle of the room, arms out as though he walked a tightrope. He hadn't gotten his growth spurt, and a little-kid vibe clung to his pudgy body. Greasy brown hair swept across his forehead. "What was that?" James asked.

"What was what?" Marshall angled toward the end wall of the room and

118

examined the four-foot-high Jimi Hendrix poster that his dad had given him.

Rocky climbed back onto Marshall's bed and held a hand out to the poster. "Greatest guitarist of all time." Strutting across the mattress, Rocky played air guitar. Then he switched hands. "Do you wish you were left-handed like Hendrix?" he asked Marshall. "Ever tried to play with your teeth?"

"Shut up, Rocky." Out of the corner of his eye, Marshall watched his little brother.

Elbows on his knees, propping his head, James didn't glance at the poster or Rocky. He gazed right down to where Marshall had been on the floor. "You hid something under the bed." With the heels of his checkered canvas shoes, James kicked away a pair of his underwear.

"I'm not hiding anything."

James' torso stretched forward, crossing into Marshall's space, his hand out to grasp the draping comforter on Marshall's bed. "Then what was it?"

Marshall dropped to his knees. "No big deal." He hauled out the pack.

"What the fudge?" Rocky shrieked.

"Where'd you get that?" James asked at the same time Rocky swore and said they should have left it at his place.

"Found it," Marshall said.

"So why were you hiding it?"

Marshall narrowed his eyes. "I wasn't hiding it."

"It looked like you were hiding it."

"Just shut up!" Marshall snapped.

Rocky hopped off the bed, close to James. "You better not tell anyone."

Marshall popped up, spun, and shoved Rocky. "Don't you threaten my brother."

Rocky backed up, dramatically throwing his hands in the air. "Geez, get real. I'm not threatening him."

Eyes cast down, James plucked at the bottom sheet of his bed.

"It's nothing," Marshall said in an even voice, "just a pack we found."

"Did you steal it?"

"I just told you we found it."

119

"Why's it a secret then?"

Marshall flew across the small space, pushed his brother back on his bed, sat on his chest, and pinned his arms. "Listen," he hissed. "Don't even think of touching that pack. Or telling Dad."

"Don't threaten him, huh?" Rocky said.

James didn't struggle. Instead, he smirked up at Marshall. "No big deal, huh?"

Chapter Twenty-Five: Visiting Hours

SUNDAY - afternoon

"Dwayne Williams." The intercom voice summoned. Dwayne twisted his hair and edged to the door—glad for the escape, not knowing when Buster would leave the exercise room and feel the craving for a Snickers. And not knowing whether Espie had added money to Buster's account to pay for it. The tension kept mounting, the giant not indicating anything one way or the other, like he enjoyed dicking with him.

The other inmates backed away from the door. At the electronic click, Dwayne stepped free from the pod.

A correctional officer loomed before him, a beefy guy he didn't recognize. "You have a guest."

Dwayne had filled out Visitor Clearance Forms for only his mother and Espie, and his mother wasn't coming.

The guard turned a wrist up, indicating Dwayne should ready himself for bracelets.

"Does she have plenty of junk in the trunk?" Dwayne shaped large parenthesis with his hands. "Round Nicki Minaj ass?" Excitement bubbled inside him. He hadn't been able to put down what they called a Government ID number for Espie. She drove, but when he'd finally made his collect call to her, she'd whined, "I'm fifteen. You know I don't have a driver's license."

Keeping a serious face, the guard spun his hand, signaling Dwayne to turn around. Probably didn't know who Nicki Minaj was. Dwayne tucked his hands behind him in compliance. The guard clicked on the cuffs and waved him forward. Dwayne wanted to see Espie and ask her about stuff they couldn't discuss on the jail phone. Had she picked up the pack? Got some money? If Buster hadn't been paid…Dwayne cut off that thought.

"I'm a minor," Espie had complained on the phone. "They're not gonna let me visit."

"Get your aunt to bring you."

He swore he could feel her huff through the phone. But she must have managed it somehow.

Dwayne hustled toward the room, the correctional officer beside him. When they came around the corner, the guard moved ahead, opening the door to where inmates met attorneys. He swept an arm as though Dwayne was a king entering a palace.

Near the table, a sheriff's deputy stood.

Dwayne balked, stepped back, but the officer nudged his shoulder.

"Where's my visitor?"

"This is your visitor," the guard said. "Have a seat."

"I don't have to receive visitors."

"In this case you do." The meaty correctional officer shoved him hard. "Have a seat."

"Did you see that?" Dwayne asked.

The deputy's expression didn't change. Dwayne plopped down into the plastic chair. The correctional officer cuffed his ankle to the leg of the bolted-down table and positioned himself by the door.

Dwayne lowered his eyelids and gave the deputy a veiled once over. "Come to visit me, huh?" He made his voice flirty.

The deputy's hairy eyebrows drew together. He started the Miranda warning from memory.

"What the fuck? I'm already here."

The deputy tugged a pad from his pressed uniform shirt. He flipped a page and stared at it a while. Finally, he said, "I'm here to place you under arrest."

Dwayne heaved forward, the tether to the table wrenching his back. "This is insane. I'm already arrested."

"Sit!" the correctional officer barked, whipping out his baton.

Dwayne dropped into the seat.

The deputy remained standing on the other side of the table. "Let's get down to business."

Dwayne scooted forward, scraping the legs of the chair up to the table. He dogged the sheriff's deputy. The tag over his pocket said Zepeda.

"Dwayne Williams, you are under arrest for two additional counts of felony burglary."

"Say what?"

The deputy consulted his notes. "A burglary committed October 15th at 1111 Scenic Drive. And a burglary November 7th, a residence located at 2513 Scenic Drive."

"I want a lawyer."

"You'll get one. In the meantime, sounds like you have a regular route along Scenic."

"Fuck you."

Zepeda arched his caterpillar eyebrows and puckered his lips like someone's disapproving mama. "If you want to be that way." He had a deep, sports announcer's voice. "But maybe you'd like to discuss this other person. Your partner. Hispanic male. Small build."

Zepeda came around the table and sat on a chair near Dwayne. He waited in silence, giving Dwayne time to sift through the information. Dwayne's mind fired into overdrive, trying to connect the addresses to jobs. Scenic was his route. Sometimes Rico had been with him.

The deputy glanced down, reading from notes. "Hispanic male jumped out the window at the 2513 address."

"I'm not a snitch."

"I admire that, Dwayne," Zepeda said. "Loyalty to friends."

Dwayne narrowed his eyes. "What are you? The bad cop and good cop rolled into one burrito?"

"That's right." Zepeda wiggled his furry eyebrows. "Plenty of salsa. Spicy."

Dwayne slouched in his seat. The deputy was playing him. He ran his tongue along his teeth, waiting, letting his sullenness fill the room. This Zepeda could get on with his little show.

"We matched your prints to a nice perfect thumbprint on a jewelry box at the 1111 Scenic Drive incident."

The glossy black box, varnished wood.

"The woman there doesn't care about the burglary, Dwayne," Zepeda said. "She just wants her grandma's cross back."

Zepeda's beady eyes studied him like he was supposed to break down and cry. *Boo hoo. Someone lost a cross. The world's gonna end. As if returning the cross would get him out of trouble.*

Still, he saw his Grammy Rice slowly lowering her eyelids and shaking her head.

Zepeda cupped his chin and worked a finger up and down his cheek like he was some great philosopher. "From where I'm sitting, I've always found things go better for those who cooperate."

"Not where I'm sitting." Dwayne folded his arms. In here, if you couldn't keep your trap shut, you lost face. Or worse. He squirmed a little, though. Rico wasn't in here. And wouldn't be if he could help it.

Zepeda scooted his chair closer. His face hardened. "Three felony burglaries. Priors. Probation violation. You know what all that adds up to?" After a tiny pause, he leaned back and remembered to add the personal touch, "Dwayne?"

He could do the math, all right. *Three strikes. Twenty-five to life.* Dwayne kept his focus on the scratched tabletop, but his jaw muscle was vice-tight.

"Maybe we should review other burglaries near the Scenic Drive bus route." Zepeda glanced down at his pad. "Like the one in August. Theft of a handgun. From one Eileen Fitzgerald."

Dwayne raised his head. That threat was plain stupid. If he was going to have three strikes already, what difference would it make if they connected him to another burglary? "Step off my dick."

"Want to help yourself out and tell me about your accomplice?"

"Go fuck yourself."

Zepeda's face remained blank, not even the little phony disapproval.

Finally, Zepeda looked at the correctional officer. "Guess we're done here." He stood. "Goodbye. Dwayne."

* * *

Back in the pod, Dwayne slumped in a chair, the football game on the television not penetrating his skull. His whole life right now could be boiled down to Rico. Or to the gun.

He stretched his legs and crossed his ankles. His life had pretty much sucked since he could remember—his dead dad and the family on that side that didn't want anyone his mom's color in the house even though they were a bunch of crackers themselves, and before that, Grammy Rice, raising two teenaged daughters by herself. "I waited a loooong time for the perfect man," Grammy said, "but maybe that weren't such a good idea since he up and died on me." She tapped her cane. Grammy Rice wasn't too old, but diabetes had crippled her feet.

Dwayne rubbed a fist between his ribs with a sudden ache for his grandmother, the way she clasped his cheeks and her eyes drilled down to this spot, like she could see a golden heart there. She knew he was a thug but refused to believe that was the end of his story.

Grammy Rice could remember her Great Great Grandma, who lived to be 102 and had been born into slavery. "They had her training in the plantation house when she was knee-high to a grasshopper," Grammy Rice said.

Before a smile at his grandma's way of talking could slip across his lips, Dwayne slapped on his game face. He rolled his head to inspect the room. Everyone stared at the blaring football game.

An inmate across from him leapt out of his seat. "Interference! Interference!"

A guy next to the inmate drawled, "The only interference is you."

The riled football fan threw his arms wide and looked down at the speaker. "You blind?"

"Right now, with you standing there, I can't see shit." The speaker remained seated. Relaxed. Typical jailhouse banter.

How was it, Dwayne wondered, that his Grammy Rice never got riled? Dwayne couldn't wrap his head around that. How could a person not be bitter when history stretched like that football receiver, the ball in his fingertips, only to slam down on the turf?

Chapter Twenty-Six: Alarmed

MONDAY - morning

Ben walked into the rolled-up garage opening of Big Al's. Noise reverberated inside the dim interior of concrete walls. Covered in a gray jumpsuit, Big Al hammered at a bar of iron glowing red from a small propane forge. Goggles hid his eyes, and a tattered cap, brim backward, covered his bald head.

Big Al continued to bang at the metal. "Hey, where's your worker?" Ben shouted to be heard. Big Al didn't respond.

Finally, Big Al stopped, rested the ball peen hammer on a long wooden table, and pushed up his goggles. His cap fell to the floor. He didn't smile, speak, or pick up the cap.

"Is your apprentice here?" Ben asked.

"Nope."

"When do you expect him?"

Big Al brushed thick hands down the legs of his jumpsuit. "Why?" He swabbed his damp forehead with a gray sleeve.

"Did the police question him?" Ben asked.

"They questioned both of us."

"If the case goes to trial, will he testify?"

Al picked up the ball peen and tapped his palm with it. "I wouldn't know, Ben. He quit."

"He quit?"

"This morning."

Big Al was angry. About what, Ben had no clue. It had to be about more than the kid quitting his job. All Ben knew was that the whole friggin' case against Dwayne Williams seemed to be falling apart. "Where can I find him?"

"I don't know. He said he was leaving town."

"You must have some address on his job application."

"I don't go around sharing that kind of information."

"What's wrong?" Ben asked.

"Did you read the paper yesterday?" Big Al turned and pounded the wooden table with the tool. A row of crescent-moon dents indicated this wasn't the first time Big Al had vented this way.

"I read the paper every day," Ben said, irritated.

Al spun toward him. "Did you see the article about the shooting out at Baker's?"

"Yes." He froze. "That was you?"

"Me and my son-in-law."

Ben's heart sank. "He got shot."

"That's right." Big Al bit off the words. "Serious injury." He walloped the table again. "He's in the hospital. Won't be out for a while." His face flushed redder than it had been from the furnace heat. Even his bald dome was pink.

"I'm sorry to hear that." Ben backed away.

"We wouldn't have been at Baker's," Al muttered, "if it weren't for you." He pointed the hammer at Ben, "Chasing that burglar like some nut job."

* * *

Vivi scrubbed at the pot she'd used to cook oatmeal. When Ben banged through the door, she jumped. He came into the kitchen, eyes stretched wide and unblinking. "Remember that article about the shooting at Baker's? That was Big Al and his son-in-law!"

She leaned back against the counter. Ben remained in the middle of the room, spilling his news.

"Big Al blames me. You believe that?"

She wiped her hands on a towel even though they were dry. "That doesn't make sense."

"I just talked to him," Ben said. "He was barely civil. Apparently he went to Baker's because of our burglary."

"He's been through a trauma." Their own experience was like someone had hurled a rock through their windshield, the craze cracking out from the point of impact. And that was without Ben being shot. In Big Al's case, someone had been shot. "He's looking for a place to direct his anger."

"You're taking his side?"

"I'm not taking a side." Anger erupted like primordial lava. Winn would tell her she could choose her feelings, but how could you control a force of nature? "I'm trying to make sense of Big Al's reaction." She struggled to keep her voice even. "I understand how you feel, too."

"Oh, you do? You understand how it feels to have a gun pointed at you and to think you're going to die?"

"No." She clamped her lips, but then spoke. "But I know what it is to lose someone you love to a weapon." The doorbell rang. Luna streaked down the hall.

When Vivi opened the door, the representative from the alarm company bore a serious expression. If a client needed an alarm, it was no smiling matter, she supposed, or maybe he'd heard them arguing. In his charcoal slacks and blue windbreaker, he looked like a retired cop. He skimmed a big hand over crew-cut gray hair and introduced himself as Henry Bilstead.

"Come on in."

She waved Henry toward the kitchen, wondering if he could sense the tension in the air. For the most part, it had dissipated. That was the weird magic of relationships—you could be irritated with each other and still snap together as a unit within seconds.

Ben shook Henry's hand and spoke about installing alarms *after* burglaries.

"That's the way it usually works," Henry said dryly. "I installed an alarm system a couple of months ago for a woman after she'd had her firearm stolen. But that doesn't mean this is frivolous. You'd be surprised how often people are hit a second time. A thief robs you, waits a month for you to replace everything nice and new, and then returns."

"Our guy is in jail," she blurted.

"Sometimes they have buddies."

A fat lot of good Dwayne's incarceration did then.

The three of them pulled stools around the butcher-block table. Henry accepted a glass of water, opened a glossy blue folder, and continued his pitch—smooth and practiced. A pro, Vivi thought.

By the time he reached his grand finale, Henry had moved to home invasions. "You may have heard about that case in Los Gatos—a couple came home from a dinner and were accosted in their driveway by two thugs with guns. One of the robbers was a friend of their son."

Henry's gray eyebrows quirked in inquiry—did they have anything like that to worry about? She glanced at Ben. His son Art had left his cocaine-fueled indiscretions in the past. He'd met a nurse in rehab, married, and had worked his way up to manage a top restaurant in Santa Barbara. For all the strain between him and Ben, Art would never have anything to do with something like that now. Would he?

"How does the alarm work with a home invasion?" Ben asked.

"If they force you inside—those kids up in Los Gatos had a sawed-off shotgun—and coerce you to turn off the alarm, you enter a second, special code instead of the usual one. That will alert us, and we can deploy our personnel."

"What if on a normal day, we confuse the two codes and punch in the wrong one?" Vivi asked.

"When you use your special code, we call to see if you used it on purpose. You won't be able to say much if you have a gun to your head, but what we do is agree upon a password."

"Like the name of our cat," Ben offered. "Luna."

"That would work. You insert that word into the conversation. Like, 'Everything is okay. *Luna* jumped and triggered the motion sensor.'"

They wrapped up and Ben stopped on the porch with Henry to review all the information—make sure he had it right. She left them to it and returned to flip open the blue folder and then slap it shut, tired of everything

· it represented—the invasion of their home, the fracturing of their lives, this business that capitalized on crime. Each day plunged them into more fallout, and she couldn't, now that the burglary had stirred up memories of Hollywood, find a good time to confide in Ben. She put the water glass in the dishwasher.

When Ben came back to the kitchen, she plucked up the folder and dropped it back to the table. "We've been slimed. Was that meant to scare us or what?"

"That's how to sell alarms."

"Just what we don't need."

"You've changed your mind about getting one?"

"No, I mean we don't need an extra dose of fear about thugs waiting for us with a sawed-off shotgun."

He stood at the table, head bent, thumbing through the contents of the folder. "Expensive, too."

"Didn't those kids in Los Gatos kill that couple? Would a *deployed* rent-a-cop have stopped them?"

"In that situation, the company would contact the police."

"Even so, the couple would have been dead."

"Yeah. You're right." He closed the folder.

Now that the salesman had gone, Luna ventured back into the kitchen and raised her head for a reassuring pet. After obliging, Ben glanced up. "The rep was trying to upsell us."

"We don't need all those bells and whistles."

He stood, knees cracking. "Some people just put up an alarm company sign."

"Maybe more than that. An actual alarm might have scared Dwayne Williams away."

"You're right," he said again.

"Wow, a record." She smiled. "Right two times in one minute."

He started down the hall to get his gym bag, and she followed, making her case. "All we need is an alarm to go off. The burglar won't know what services are attached to it."

He added a fresh towel to his duffel bag. "At least this meeting clarified

131

what we want. I'll make an appointment with another rep." He grabbed his Phillies cap from the closet and put it on.

The bedroom phone shrilled behind them. Luna raced under the bed again. After the talk about people being shot in their homes, she felt like joining the cat. Vivi snatched up the receiver. Outside the bedroom window, the pelargonium bush swayed in a stiff breeze.

"This is Assistant District Attorney Cheryl Smith."

She mouthed the words although Ben was pressed close and had probably heard the booming, confident voice. The call surprised her. Their friend, a public defender, had cautioned them that the justice system was overburdened. "Don't expect to hear from the DA's office for a week," he'd said.

This Cheryl Smith must be on the ball.

Ben pulled the phone away from her, so like her competitive brothers. Or maybe like the entitled only child he'd been. She hovered to hear the conversation.

"The arraignment for Dwayne Williams has been set for tomorrow," the attorney said.

"The two-hundred-and-fifty-thousand-dollar bail should hold him until then." Ben's statement lilted up at the end like a question.

"Two hundred and fifty thousand?" the ADA said. "Where did you get that number?"

"The paper."

Cheryl Smith chortled. "You can't believe everything you read."

"What is it then?" Ben asked.

"The typical twenty-five thousand."

"So he would only need twenty-five hundred to be out?"

"Believe me," the lawyer said, "you don't have to worry." The voice was clipped now, signaling that she did not plan to elaborate.

"I want to go to the arraignment," Ben said.

"That's not necessary. It'll be over in five minutes. It's just a time for Dwayne Williams to formally hear the charges and for the court to decide the bail."

"Didn't you just say it was twenty-five thousand?"

"That's a schedule amount." Before they could ask what that meant, she said, "Because of the gun, we'll be pressing for robbery."

"What's the difference between burglary and robbery?" Vivi asked.

Ben repeated the question into the mouthpiece.

"Robbery involves physical force or the threat of physical force. Longer sentence, typically."

"Good," Ben said.

"I want to prepare you, though," the assistant district attorney continued. "After the arraignment, given Dwayne's age, and the overcrowding in the jail, and the fact he didn't shoot you, and we can't prove the gun—yet—they may move him to River House in South County."

"But he'll be locked up." Ben's voice insisted at the same time the timbre again pitched upward in question.

"Yes. But River House is for non-violent offenders. They offer various release programs."

"What does that mean?" Ben choked on the question like he had food stuck in his throat.

"It means with good behavior inmates are allowed outside the facility to do things."

"Things? Like what?"

"Clean up along the freeway, that kind of thing. Under supervision, of course. The facility also has a strong relationship with a local church."

From behind, Vivi circled Ben with her arms. She didn't blame him for being nervous. The alarm rep, Harvey Bilstead, who looked like a former police officer, had spent the last half hour in their kitchen spinning worst-case scenarios of home invaders with shotguns.

"They can go to church?" His voice tightened.

"Don't worry. It would be extremely unusual for the defendant to come for you," Cheryl Smith said. "Actually, they'll probably hold him in the jail until after the prelim. Make it easier for the court and the defense attorney. River House is twenty miles from here." The lawyer's voice emitted crisply from the handset. "I do want to advise you, though, that sometimes relatives or friends show up at hearings."

"Is that a danger?" Vivi asked, loud enough to be heard through the receiver. This ADA was about as reassuring as the alarm rep.

"Dwayne's brother Wesley is locked up." The ADA paused. "Although his release could be about now." She stopped again. "I'll have to check on that. But when we get to the prelim, if you go—"

"Oh, we're going!" Ben said.

"Be mindful," Cheryl Smith said. "I'm sorry that I have to cut this short. In the meantime, be careful whom you talk to. If someone comes out and identifies himself as 'with the DA,' be on the alert. That is the oldest trick in the book. He's not exactly lying, but he means DA as in defense attorney."

"That's sneaky," Vivi inserted over Ben's shoulder.

"It's part of the game." Cheryl Smith's voice contained a smile, as if the ADA relished the contest before her. That kind of energy might be beneficial for their case, Vivi thought, but she didn't like it. Nothing about this seemed like a game.

Chapter Twenty-Seven: Blues

MONDAY - after school

Marshall rested on his twin bed, the blue pack underneath sending radiation up through the mattress. The pack had to go somewhere else before James got too curious. If he found the gun, he might do something stupid, or tell their dad, who would go ballistic. Or worse, sit Marshall down for one of those serious, disappointed conversations. Marshall stared at his Hendrix poster, waiting on inspiration.

He and his brother shared the superstar's real name—James Marshall, although at birth Hendrix had been called Johnny Allen. The name was changed a few years later, part of Hendrix's messed-up childhood. But the fact he and James split the legendary musician's name was cool, even if his brother had the first name.

Marshall's dad had actually named Marshall after Eminem, thinking what kid wouldn't love that, but his mom put her foot down on the naming of the next baby. Their dad had been named James after his father, who had died in Vietnam before their dad was even born. Their dad carried the name in their grandpa's honor, and their mom insisted James carry it forward. It was like a tribute to a ghost, or maybe to their biology.

Lifting his guitar off its stand, Marshall cradled the maple against his body. He strummed a G chord, then a C and a D, then he mixed it up and added a blues riff. How had they decided to make blue the color of sadness? He knew only why blue sang sadness to him.

Playing the easy, opening lick to the Rolling Stones' *Satisfaction*, a song he knew by motor memory, left him free to worry about James. Their mother had always taken his little brother's side. James even had the creamy skin and wide apart, big eyes of their mother. And like their mom, James cried easily, which was a big problem.

Marshall was the spitting image of his dad. They just clicked—maybe it was that first-born son thing. *Whatever.* Their parents' preferences had been obvious, but maybe they thought it didn't matter, that it balanced out. Marshall was his father's son. James was his mother's. In photos, his brother snuggled up against their mom while he stood by his dad, his father's hand on his shoulder. His dad taught him to surf while James built sandcastles near their mom, reading a book in a striped beach chair.

He slammed a power chord, trying to drive away the gathering image of himself, a kid, sprinting over cobalt-blue creatures, each smaller than his palm, littering the sand. He bent down, such a pretty, pretty blue.

"Are these jellyfish, Daddy?" A fin stuck up from each blob of bright blue, his favorite color. The fin looked like the glass of a jelly jar.

"No, son. People think that's a Portuguese-man-of-war, but that's a Velella velella."

Marshall rolled the words around in his head, the la la sounds like something to sing. "Do they sting?"

"Nah."

His father lifted one by its transparent wing. "Actually, this isn't one thing at all. Each Velella is a colony." And then because Marshall didn't know the word colony, "A family."

"Why are they here today and not other days?"

"The wind has to be just right. Some people even call them 'by-the-wind sailors.'"

Marshall ran a couple of yards up the sand to avoid an incoming wave, but his dad remained still, letting the freezing water splash around his bare ankles. The ocean whooshed back out, little bubbles popping where crabs ducked for cover.

Marshall followed the sandpipers that chased the surf, drilling their long beaks down after the tasty treats.

Back at his father's side, he asked, "So the Velella velellas sailed here?"

"Yes."

"Why?"

His father dropped the creature to the sand, but it didn't sail magically. It fell straight down. He faced the water and scanned the horizon before squatting down to look into Marshall's face. "They've come here to die."

Plucking up a Velella velella, Marshall tore off along the edge of the surf, his feet spraying wet sand behind him. A little dog lunged at his flying leg. The lady on the other end of the leash said something.

"Mom!" Marshall dashed up the soft beach. "Mom!"

She raised her head from a book and smiled at his excitement. James stopped digging with his yellow plastic shovel and stared at him. His mom sat down her book to receive his prize.

"The Velella velellas sailed here to die!"

His dad trudged up behind him, his bare chest tanned and his hair sparkly with gold. His mom's face lifted toward him. She lowered her sunglasses and frowned, pinching up the blue creature.

"He asked," his father said, "so I told him."

"I'm eight years old," he'd said to his mom's look. "I know all about things dying."

But he hadn't known anything about dying. But then, did a person ever get old enough to grasp his mom dying? That day at the beach was the last clear memory he had of her. Even now he couldn't shake the sense of cause and effect, that he'd handed her that blue bit of death and cursed her.

Yup, they'd picked the right color for sadness. He swiped away a tear and practiced some barre chords.

"If the Velella velella is a family, did they all die?" He'd squinted into the sunlight circling his dad's head.

His mom scooped a hole in the sand with James' shovel and buried his gift.

Marshall didn't remember what his father said, but he'd learned the answer. Now that his mom was dead, the organism of their family was dead, no longer able to scud over the ocean. He and James and his dad had been reincarnated as something else. As sad as that was for Marshall, it had to suck worse for James, who had been so connected to their mother. No matter how he and his dad tried, James seemed alone.

The responsibility to try to fill the gap left by his mom pulled Marshall down like an undertow. It was tricky. Just that morning he'd been trying to explain it to his dad.

"Sure I stick up for him at school. But that's not necessarily a good thing."

His father had spun all the way around in his computer chair. "How's that?" His eyes inspected Marshall from head to toe the way he did when Marshall tried to weasel out of a chore. Marshall glanced away at the invoice up on the screen.

"Conflict resolution and all that stuff is good in theory," Marshall croaked.

His father leaned back in the black office chair. His arms crossed over his tee shirt, pulling the ratty white cotton against the definition of his chest. "That right?"

A dot of blue paint beside his father's eye tugged at Marshall's fingers and heart. "Look, Dad, I don't care what they say in those programs. If some kid comes after James, *James* has to stand up to him—or he might as well slap a target on his back."

His dad's forehead wrinkled. "Is some kid harassing James?"

"I'm just saying, Dad."

His dad stayed quiet, but his foot jiggled on the floor. "If anyone is bullying James, I want you to tell me."

"Okay," he mumbled. His dad didn't get it, and he didn't know how to get him to understand.

Marshall had already gotten in the face of that little shit, Finn—smaller than James, but sneaky and mean. It didn't help James' rep to need a big brother to protect him. Especially when Marshall would be off to high school next year.

As Marshall nestled the guitar into his body, the perfect place to hide the backpack came to him, but it didn't change his blue mood. It made him sadder. Putting down the instrument, he got up, dragged the pack from under the bed, and stuck it inside his guitar case. It was like sticking the worst thing in his life inside the best thing.

But at least James shouldn't look there. Marshall's music stuff was strictly off-limits.

Chapter Twenty-Eight: Fall Out

TUESDAY

In the courtroom, Dwayne's crazy bunkmate sat in the chair beside him in the jury box. The guy's mouth chewed even though there was nothing in it, his teeth clicking. Then his jaw jutted forward like he wanted to bite. The weirdo's name was Harrison Adams, a name that sounded like the court secretary got it backward. He was first up on the docket.

Dwayne listened to the charges against Harrison Adams: drug possession, resisting arrest, failure to appear. *Boring stuff.* He shifted around. The seats weren't that comfortable. Three inmates in sweats from River House filed in to join them. Dwayne bent forward, but he didn't recognize any of them. In front of the divider, three young women in red jail threads sat on chairs. He stared at their long hair. None of them turned around. They weren't fine like Espie, anyway.

With the last name Williams, he'd be at the end of the docket. The judge called up people from the gallery, offenders out on bail, dressed in civvies. A couple of them made an effort with bad-fitting suits straight out of Goodwill, but one defendant showed up in a NorCal shirt. The guy was either clueless or had huge balls. On certain people, NorCal screamed gang affiliation. The judge would be looking at that shirt while making his decision.

There was no one familiar among the spectators either. An elderly man glared at the jury box as if someone seated there might have killed his grandson. Dwayne turned his eyes away to the dark wood and flags and official seals. In front of the judge, a woman hunched over her recording machine and a skinny redheaded woman across from her sorted through files, reading glasses slipping down her nose.

When they reached the R's, his defense attorney finally appeared. She cruised over to whisper to him. She introduced herself: Criminal Defense Attorney Shawna Morrison, all decked out in a suit and tie like she was going to a lesbian wedding. Shiny shoes and a fresh haircut. One of those high-class lawyers the county sometimes used when short on public defenders. He'd won the jackpot.

On the other side of the divider, Morrison flipped through his file as if this was the first time she'd seen it. If she'd looked like a public defender—like she slept in her shirt—it wouldn't surprise him if she'd been too busy to read his file. But if she was a contracted lawyer, the county was getting screwed.

Disappointment knotted in his chest. For a second, he'd thought he was catching a break. *What a fool.* At least a public defender wasn't in it just for the money.

"You'll plead not guilty, of course." Her dark eyes barely turned up to his face.

"Yeah."

She tapped the divider a couple of times with all her fingers together. Blunt nails. Buffed, no polish. No rings. "We'll talk later."

As she crossed to the defense table, he inspected her shapeless back. She whispered to another attorney, not even glancing at him.

When his name was called, Dwayne stood, head bowed. The judge's reading included the new charges. But not robbery. *No gun.* His insides relaxed a fraction. The gun would be worse than the three strikes. Even if Rico talked, the three strikes were a maybe.

"Do you understand?" the judge asked.

"Yes. Your honor."

"How do you plead?"

"Not guilty."

He was the last customer. A guard opened the side door and the seven

141

of them returning to County filed out a back passage to the underground garage. In the van, he rocked with the turns, glad that they'd be back for lunch. He was starving. Adams swayed toward him. Dwayne jerked away so their shoulders wouldn't touch.

Adams jutted out his jaw. "Whatcha staring at, dickwad?"

Dwayne ignored him. Did the crazy want to start something in the van?

"You and me will be going to River House together." Adams' teeth chattered like he was freezing. "You and your smelly feet."

As they swung around a corner to the jail, the other inmates watched the mini-drama. Instead of turning toward Adams, Dwayne steeled his gaze on a squat Mexican across from him, tattoos masking his face. "You think this is some fucking episode of *The Wire?*"

Reddish eyes narrowed. Dwayne knew the guy didn't understand him. He'd needed an interpreter in the courtroom.

Adams didn't say anything more, just clicked his teeth.

When they reached the jail, the prisoners shuffled into the portal for transporting inmates, Adams backing into a corner, away from the other bodies. The officer shooed others forward to another guard, then escorted Dwayne and Adams back to their pod, careful not to touch Adams even when removing his cuffs. Needing air, Dwayne bee-lined to the exercise area.

From the other side of the doorway, a hammy arm lowered, like a parking lot gate, blocking his path.

"How'd it go?" Buster's eyes tightened to piggy slits. "When they moving you?"

Dwayne stepped back. "I don't know."

Draping an arm around his neck like he was being friendly, Buster squeezed the vice against Dwayne's windpipe and stepped him into the doorframe. "I haven't seen any treats, Sweet Pea," he whispered. "You know how I love me some Doritos." He increased the pressure. "Or the tuna. Good protein."

Dwayne coughed. He couldn't breathe. The guard would have a tough time seeing inside the doorframe, if he was even watching the monitors. "Espie doesn't have a driver's license. She can't get here." The words squeaked out. On his recorded phone call, he hadn't been able to discuss whether she'd found the goods and sold them, but he'd been clear he needed money. Now.

Buster laughed, released his hold, and shoved Dwayne. "That ain't my problem."

Dwayne massaged his neck. It felt like his windpipe was crushed.

* * *

At her office computer, Vivi hammered the keyboard. Their friend Anne had written again, pressing for an update on the burglary, the innocuous note triggering Vivi's anger over Anne's previous suggestion she should own a gun.

> *Dear Anne,*
>
> *About your last message, if I owned a gun, the burglar would have it now, and it would be stashed, ready for some nefarious use, along with the gun with which he would have killed Ben if the wheel of fortune had spun differently.*

Her ever-present, English-teacher editing forced her to slow down as the banging method of typing produced mistakes.

> *Our burglar was arraigned today. He was already on probation for burglary and grand theft! Our ADA thinks the case should be resolved without a trial, but a bass player Ben knows, a probation officer, told him that black offenders opt for the trial.*

When Ben came into the office, he rested his hands on her shoulders and massaged them. Or tried to. He may as well have tried to massage a boulder. She minimized the message.

"Any response from Art?"

"Not yet."

His lips compressed in a line of disappointment.

"He's probably in Vermont, don't you think?" Art and his wife usually went to his in-laws for Thanksgiving. Cold comfort. How hard was it to respond to an e-mail?

"What was that part about owning a gun?" Ben asked. "Do you think we should buy one?"

"That's a private email."

"It's just to Anne." He sighed.

Unlike her, Ben might let Anne's reaction go, like that, with an exhalation, or he might be pissed. She didn't know. He was less stubborn but more volatile than she was.

"Private, huh?" A teasing smile softened his face. "Are you telling Anne your plans to run off with the hot yoga teacher?"

"How did you guess?"

Ben tugged an earlobe, his face solemn again. "Is it a good thing or a bad thing our ADA is black?"

Vivi's fingernails clicked on the keys. As soon as they'd gotten off the phone with Assistant District Attorney Cheryl Smith, they'd googled her and up popped a photo of a beautiful black woman with cropped hair, full lips, and big eyes.

"If race factors into the equation at all, it will be that as a woman of color, she'll be working twice as hard for convictions."

"I hope you're right."

"What do you think, that she'd side with a criminal because he's black?" Vivi turned away from him and tapped up the email. "Do you mind?"

When Ben left, Vivi scanned the text. *So namby pamby.* Why couldn't she speak her truth, voice her anger, and allow the chips to fall where they may?

She thought of Winn's long fingers on the center of his chest, the *anahata* chakra. When he'd spoken of his wife's death, he'd pressed his fingers there. A wince had crossed his face, replaced almost as quickly by a kind smile. The pain of his wife's death lived in him, beat with his heart. This fourth chakra represented the fundamental truths that connected life, including death and pain. And through them, or maybe with them, joy.

Vivi deleted the message and stared at the blinking cursor. The blank screen like the universe. After Winn had touched his chest, she'd stared at him on the other side of the café table, desire welling in her in a way she hadn't felt since her teens. What she used to call the "hot gushies." If, at that second, he'd proposed they blow the joint, she wondered if she would have left with him. Done something wild and crazy.

Instead Winn had reached for his coffee mug and said, "It's easy to mistake feelings for reality."

Was he speaking about the hormonal surge inside her? Could he sense it?

"In fact," Winn said, "they are point zero, zero, zero, zero, zero one percent of it."

He'd sipped his coffee. "We're standing, or in our case, sitting," he said with a smile, "on the miracle of the earth, spinning in an orbit in a galaxy, a tiny speck of a vast universe. That awesomeness is reality."

"Awesomeness?" Vivi arched her brows.

He carefully placed his empty mug on the table. "Yes. *Awesomeness.*"

And like that, his sex appeal vanished as though the word *awesomeness* possessed magic. Or maybe the word acted more like Toto, tugging aside the curtain to expose the Wizard of Oz.

How could she have a crush on a guy who used the word *awesomeness*? Winn stretched, still lean and appealing, but his man bun suddenly ridiculous, and the lotus blossom design on his tee pretentious.

Vivi rattled the ergonomic keyboard with bouncing fingers. Should she concentrate on the ninety-nine-point-nine percent that was *awesomeness* or compose a different message to Anne and release feelings that seemed pretty damned real to her?

Hadn't another yogi said, "If you think you can do something to better the world, why aren't you doing it?"

But did it better the world to challenge Anne's beliefs?

On the other hand, what about *satya*—truth? Hadn't Winn himself said yogic truth embodied the good, bad and ugly?

But then again, wasn't *satya* a restraint?

In frustration, her hands bounced higher, printing random letters across the Word document: kaaekjekddaadejkedddjslssa.

A single word—the password *Luna* on an alarm system, the abracadabra of *awesomeness*—whisked one reality into another. The power of words overwhelmed her. But she couldn't remain in this *padangushthasana*-like state, balancing on the tips of five toes. She wasn't a guru. She wasn't even a good yogini. She would have to choose. Rein in her anger or express it, come what may.

Chapter Twenty-Nine: Vicodin

WEDNESDAY - afternoon, a week since the burglary

"I don't like Vicodin." Jessika lolled on the grass, itchy against her pale skin. Her neck rested in the crease between Rico's triceps and chest. Rico's body heat was saving her ass from freezing. Shouts and whistles from an after-school soccer game echoed off the buildings, but out here in front, they had the yard to themselves. The peace sign wall sheltered them from a cold breeze coming off the ocean a mile away.

Rico snaked his arm around her shoulder. "You should've taken two, like me. Then you'd be chill, like no worries."

Clouds scudded across the gray sky. She cuddled closer to his body. "I feel like a melted Gummy Worm. Gimme crystal any day."

"Are you still crashing at your mom's?"

Jessika tried to read the question. Was he trying to find out if she was back with Brenden or if her mom was out of town? "I spent last night at Espie's," she lied.

"So your mom's home?"

Jessika pulled away, and a fissure of cold slid between their bodies. "There's nothing you'd want in there."

Floating on the Vicodin, she thought back to entering her mom's garage, utility sink in the corner and stored camping equipment on the shelves, including expensive sleeping bags. So, she'd been comfy, mostly—except for the three new moving boxes stacked beside the shelves, her plush unicorn perched on top.

"Bubby." She'd clutched the unicorn's soft white fur to her body.

Across the lid of the top box, her mom had scrawled "Jessica" with a black sharpie as though she thought the girl she once knew might magically return. The combo of hugging Bubby, knowing her mom had packed up her stuff (but not given it away), and seeing her name the way her mom spelled it had gotten to her. Settled in a sleeping bag, she cuddled Bubby as she slept, wearing flannel PJs she'd dug from the boxes.

"Did she report you?" Rico's voice drifted to her.

"A neighbor saw the light in the garage."

The truth was she'd been rousted, but she was lying about the contents of the garage. There was a lot of stuff Rico might want, like a new drill in a case with a battery charger and set of drill bits.

The cop who showed up knew her. Knew that she'd lived here before her mom kicked her out. Knew she was barely out of high school. He'd let her pull on clothes from the boxes. He wasn't interested in doing more than shooing her off the property.

She'd run back into the garage to snatch Bubby.

The cop shook his head. "You can't take that."

"It's mine."

He waggled his head.

She laid Bubby on a mound of unearthed clothes, petting his softness, tears welling in her eyes. Then she'd spun around, hurried past the officer, and hopped on her bike, glad at least that she'd already stuffed a few items from the boxes into her pack. The previous two nights, she'd been at the shelter.

Now here she was with Rico stretched beside her. "Did you and Dwayne have a thing?" he asked.

"No way. I just told him about the gun 'cuz I was pissed my mom kicked me out."

"Why did you tell him?"

And not me hung on the end of Rico's question. "I've known Dwayne since first grade," she lied. But then, because Rico might be useful, she added, "I told you about the kids taking Dwayne's pack."

Rico snorted. "Oh, yeah, that was productive." He waited a beat. "Did your mom replace her handgun?"

"Dude, I told you she alarmed the house. And the cop who kicked me out said he'd tell my mom to change the garage code." Something about those boxes and Bubby on top of them—like he was waiting for her—made her feel protective.

"Did Brenden finish the tile on that house down the street?" Rico asked.

It was hard to shrug lying down. "They were supposed to go back after the Thanksgiving weekend but his boss pulled him off that job."

In spite of the fuzzy buffer of the Vicodin, Jessika felt bad about that. Brenden was a stand-up guy, a lot better than her dad, who deserted her, took her brother, and started a new family. A lot better than her stepdad and her jerky stepbrothers. All fortunately gone, too.

"The contractor might still be working there," she said. "We could walk by and see if there are any trucks in the driveway."

Jessika snuggled closer and traced a finger along his neck tattoo. She needed a win. Brenden wasn't texting, and her mom was probably busy changing the garage code. She wiggled her phone out of her pocket and held it above them. "Smile."

Rico made a face, but she snapped the shot anyway and put the phone away without checking the photo. "Know what I've been thinking?" she whispered in his ear.

"Uh-oh."

She tugged his earlobe. "Why *uh-oh*?"

"'Cuz anytime you start *thinking*, it's dangerous. Look at what you've already got me into."

"Oh, like it was my idea to get high?" She rolled on top of Rico and straddled his lap.

"That's not what I was talking about."

She playfully slapped his face. Rico put a hand to his stubble. "Hey, you're harshing my mellow here."

"Oh, like you weren't just thinking about ripping off my mom." She slapped his other cheek.

Rico grabbed her wrist and flipped her under him. He pinned her arms against the grass. "Good thing you're a chick."

"You sure about that?"

"Now you mention it…." His hand slithered under the bottom of her skirt.

"You know we are on a school campus." Not like she cared, but it might distract him. She tipped her head back toward the buildings. "A teacher could walk around that corner any time."

Rico flopped back down beside her. His shoes barely extended past her UGGs. Since he wasn't much bigger than she was, two pills must've taken him for a loop. "So what's this big idea you have?" he asked.

A door in the peace wall snicked open and slammed shut. Jessika rolled her eyes to see a chubby woman in a powder blue pantsuit. The woman pushed up her glasses and looked over at them. Holding a leather briefcase in front of her, she strode across the grass.

The woman, older than her mom, stopped. The wind tousled shoulder-length curls. "What are you kids doing here?"

"Just hangin' out." She tried to keep her voice neutral, but like her mom said, it always came out sounding like backtalk. "Enjoying the nice grass."

The woman clutched the briefcase like a shield. "There's a park about two blocks from here. I suggest you enjoy the grass over there."

Behind the woman, the sun shone weakly. Jess squinted. "Isn't this a *public* school?"

"*Public* doesn't mean anything goes," the woman said, nodding toward a sign: NO SKATEBOARDING. NO LOITERING. VISITORS MUST SIGN IN AT THE MAIN OFFICE.

Rico struggled to his feet. He reached down his hand for hers. "Come on, Jess. Let's go."

He pulled her up, and she brushed off the back of her damp skirt. She smiled at the woman. "Have a nice day."

"You too, sweetheart." The woman parroted Jessika's tone.

Giggling, she latched on to Rico's hand and towed him down the sidewalk. "Why waste our time chasing after Dwayne's score? Brenden told me that no one took the money." She released Rico's hand and skipped ahead of him, making her skirt swish. "Let's check out that house. If workers are there, those people will still have a stash of cash."

She grabbed the pole of a speed bump sign and swung around it. "Single story," she sang. "No dog. No alarm."

Rico lunged out and caught the tail of her denim jacket. "Stop!"

She spun around, pulling away from his hold. "What?" Compared to Brenden, Rico was so shrimpy. Broad shoulders, but no butt. He wasn't her type at all. His Impala, parked around the corner, was cool, and usually she could persuade him to do stuff, mainly, she thought, because he wanted to get a little.

"You know Troy?" Rico asked. "That guy Dwayne used to hang with?" Rico stayed put on the sidewalk. "I ran into him downtown."

"The junkie?" She leaned outward and twirled around the pole. The combo of Vicodin and dizzy made her feel like a shaken can of Coke. Above her, the clouds feathered into angel wings. "I thought he was in jail."

"His parents bailed him. He's going back to rehab on Monday."

She sang Amy Winehouse's rehab song.

Rico didn't smile.

"Well, so what?" She stopped spinning and nodded toward the driveway of the yellow house. The CRV had been pulled to the side to make room for a white truck. It wasn't the one Brenden's boss drove, but with the metal boxes for locking up tools, it clearly belonged to a worker. She'd thought Rico was looking for a score, but he didn't even glance over.

"Troy saw Dwayne in jail. He's been charged with two other burglaries on Scenic Drive."

"Oh."

"Yeah, right, *oh*. I don't want to get up in Dwayne's shit and give him a reason to cop a plea. Rat me out."

"He wouldn't do that."

Rico crossed his arms over his chest and smirked. "You obviously don't know Dwayne."

That was true enough. In high school, she'd bought drugs from his older brother Wesley. She'd met Dwayne through him. Bought a phone from him. Partied a couple of times with him and Espie. She tipped her head toward the house. "I know this. He wouldn't be afraid to go in there again."

Rico breezed by her. "You're right." He stopped and turned. "But at this moment, Dwayne's in jail. And you know what he's thinking about?" He narrowed his eyes. "What he has all day to think about? All night too?"

She licked her lips. "Espie?"

Rico didn't laugh. "He's thinking about three strikes. Prison time. With more added if they find that gun. And any second now, those kids could show it to their parents. If that isn't already why it's gone. Asking me, Dwayne's gonna be pretty damn incentivized."

"Troy told you all that?" But she was talking to the back of Rico's flannel shirt. He wasn't going to help break into the house. "Well, I know where the gun is," she blurted.

He wheeled around. His face flushed. "You do, huh? After fucking breaking into that apartment, *now* you know where the gun is."

"I didn't know until *after* the weekend." She raked the chapped skin of her lip with her teeth. She hadn't meant to tell Rico this. She knew it would piss him off. How pissed was hard to gauge with his eyes glassy and his movements slowed from the drugs. "Those kids we chased took it to the other one's house," she explained quickly. "I followed them."

* * *

Inside the yellow house, the phone rang. Vivi carried the receiver away from the new worker, sealing the grout in their bathroom.

Cheryl Smith, the assistant district attorney, identified herself, her voice confident and reassuring. "I just wanted to call and see if you have any questions about the prelim."

"Not really." At their front window, Vivi pushed back the open curtains even more. A brown towhee was chirping, updating his mate on the ground of safety and danger. In Vivi's peripheral vision, black hair and thin bare legs stuffed into UGGs disappeared around the corner. *The bike girl?*

"How to dress?" she asked Cheryl. It seemed superficial, but the girl's skirt had flapped the question into her mind.

"Nice casual," Cheryl said. "You won't be called to say anything, but the judge will notice you. You'll be making a first impression, and as they say, you never receive a second chance for that."

The towhee on the ground whirred toward the roof, the sudden movement making her tug the curtain's fabric. The sight of the girl—or maybe Cheryl Smith's call—had put her on edge. "Will Dwayne's brother be there?"

The lawyer didn't answer. Anxiety percolating through her, Vivi searched the outside view for what had sent the bird flying but the predator remained concealed.

"Friends or family can show up." The ADA's tone shifted from confident to cautionary.

"Dwayne's brother could be in the room with us?"

"I haven't checked on his release date." A note of apology. "If something like that should occur, be mindful and don't interact. If anyone follows you to the parking lot or harasses you, return to the courthouse."

Along the fabric of the curtain, Vivi's fingers stopped moving. *A convicted felon might follow them? Threaten them?*

"Or get in your car if it's closer."

Chapter Thirty: Threat Assessment

THURSDAY - afternoon

At school, Marshall couldn't concentrate. He kept thinking about the gun—the crazy chick who wanted it and James' curiosity about the pack and statistics about accidental shootings....

When the final bell rang, he ditched Rocky and hurried home. He went directly to his bedroom, sliding open the closet door. He lifted out his guitar case. The gun was exactly where he'd left it. Relief flooded him.

He stretched out on his comforter. At this time of day, sun slanted through the window right onto his bed, the warmth mellow. Staring at the ceiling, he rested his head in his hands. His hair draped over and around his fingers. It was way past haircut time, but he liked it this way. Maybe he'd grow his hair long like Rocky's.

He was supposed to be on his Thursday errands, taking the list and money his dad had left for him, pedaling to the supermarket, and bringing home stuff they needed in the side saddles. After that, he was supposed to fill the red plastic container with a gallon of gas at the corner station. It needed to be mixed with special oil and put into the leaf blower so he could clean up the gold and red maple leaves turning gray in their yard. The chores needed to be done, but the sunshine made him lazy. The ebb from the adrenaline rush tired him. He closed his eyes.

The bedroom door cracked open. Marshall bolted upright. "James?" How could he not have heard his steps in the hallway? His brother walked like a baby elephant.

The gap in the doorway widened. Marshall held his breath, thinking about the guy in the Impala and the crazy chick. He rolled off the bed and crouched.

The door swung slowly into the room.

Marshall rolled his weight into the balls of his feet, ready to spring.

James edged into the room and hesitated. "What are you doing here?"

Marshall stood and shook out his fists. "I thought you went to Scotty's."

"Nah, Scotty's here with me."

Marshall bent forward. Peeking over James' shoulder, Scotty frowned at him and then looked away. "What were you guys gonna do in here?" Marshall asked. Scotty had an X-box with all the best stuff. James went to Scotty's. Scotty never came to their house.

"Let's go, man," Scotty said.

Marshall shoved aside his brother. "No, you wait." He stepped up to Scotty. "I want you to tell me what you are doing here."

"Nothing." Scotty cowered, his pasty skin even whiter than usual, his freckles dark. He was an okay kid; he just spent way too much time playing video games.

Marshall moved closer, toe-to-toe.

Shrinking back, palms against the wall, Scotty barely reached the top of Marshall's nose. "I don't know anything," he squeaked. "James said he had something to show me."

"Get out of here!" Marshall's voice cracked like it sometimes did, but Scotty scrammed down the hall, the front door banging behind him.

Turning into the bedroom, Marshall dove at his brother. "You little shit!"

James slid back over his rumpled bedspread and launched a foot toward Marshall's gut.

Marshall latched onto James' checkered canvas shoe. It slipped off, and Marshall stumbled backward. He chucked the shoe at his brother. James squatted down, and the shoe ricocheted, leaving a black smudge on the wall.

"I'm gonna tell Dad," James said.

"Like hell you are." Marshall lunged and pinned his little brother against the mattress.

Tears welled in James' eyes. And then Marshall saw it. A bruise splotched the back of his jawbone. Marshall yanked James' shirt collar away from the bruise. He relaxed his grip and touched the bluish mark. "Who did that?"

James jerked upright, shrugging his shirt back into place.

Marshall grabbed the hem and yanked it up. Another bruise spotted James' rib. "What the fuck, James?"

James tugged his shirt back into place. Leaning against the wall, he hid his face in crossed arms. His shoulders shook.

"Was it Finn?"

A sniffle escaped, but James didn't answer. It didn't matter. Marshall knew it was that little bastard Finn who'd been testing James and pushing at him since the start of the school year—flicking his ears, calling him Lames.

"Did you punch him back?"

The crying stopped, but James didn't lift his head. He mumbled into his shirtsleeve.

"What did you say?" Marshall asked.

"It's your fault." James stayed curled tight.

"My fault?"

"He was getting back 'cuz you jumped him."

Marshall placed his hand on his brother's back. It rose and fell, the jerky breaths smoothing out.

There was truth in what James said and only one solution. "You have to stand up for yourself, James," Marshall said softly.

Chapter Thirty-One: House of Justice

THURSDAY - earlier, morning

T he architect of the Playa Maria County Courthouse had given the gray concrete building a sweeping entrance of broad stairs and walls of windows, achieving a sense of grandeur in a single story. Cold wind off the ocean gusted up the steps and snapped the flags on the poles.

Vivi and Ben passed nervously through security into an echoing hallway. The wide, unheated hall wrapped around interior courtrooms. They followed the hall to courtroom two.

Deep shadows fell over the benches lining the inner side of the hallway. Normally Vivi would have preferred to sit with a view of the world, but she settled on a seat with her back to the wall of windows, where morning sun provided a touch of warmth.

Ben sat beside her, drumming on his thighs. He'd been too anxious to eat, and food wasn't permitted in the courtroom. Vivi gnawed her lip with worry—about Ben, about the hearing, about Dwayne's brother showing up fresh from prison.

Dozens of people congregated in the hallway, waiting for one of the three sets of double doors to open. She sorted the crowd. Attorneys—the men in suits and the women in dark skirts and blazers—gathered in clustered conversations, briefcases or folders in hand. Those appearing before the judge, mostly young and minorities in ill-fitting suits, paced or sat and twitched. The middle-aged people in nice casual clothes must be relatives, witnesses, or victims.

After Vivi had told Ben about Cheryl's call, he had researched "What to wear to court." Not black—too austere and negative. Not red—too aggressive. She'd chosen a pink-and-black checked skirt and jacket, a teacher outfit. Ben had settled on khakis with a dove gray polo shirt.

Ben put an arm around her shoulders. He nudged her toward a young black man coming through the security checkpoint. "Dwayne's brother?"

A spider crawled up her spine. The man was the right age but short and dark, not at all like Dwayne. He loaded items into a gray plastic tub to run through the screening machine.

"I don't know why Cheryl didn't check his release date." Anxiety frayed the edges of Ben's words.

The man emerged on the other side of security and collected his belt and keys. His olive-colored jeans and black long-sleeved thermal-knit shirt were form-fitting and stylish. He lifted his head and scowled at them as though he could feel their inspection. She averted her eyes, embarrassed. Was he glowering because they'd been watching him, or was there greater malice?

His black high-top athletic shoes padded toward them. The shoes squeaked to a stop next to the double doors into the first courtroom. The young man ran his finger down the posted docket.

He spun around. His steely gaze zoned right in on them. Moving in their direction, he stopped at the entrance to courtroom two. He traced his finger down the docket thumbtacked to the corkboard, then took up a post leaning against the concrete interior wall. He was going into the same courtroom.

Vivi reminded herself to breathe. The hallway was dotted with police officers. If he was Dwayne's brother, what could he do?

He took a mobile phone from his pocket and busied himself with texting.

Beyond the checkpoint, Cheryl Smith appeared in the foyer. The internet photo hadn't captured her striking appearance. Cheryl had decked out her broad-shouldered, athletic build in black slacks and an ivory silk blouse. She passed through security and approached them as though she had a homing device.

Of course, Vivi figured, the process wasn't that hard. The Assistant DA probably knew all the lawyers and half the criminals on sight. A middle-aged white couple gawking at her was a big clue. Before reaching them, Cheryl stopped in the hallway to confer with a sheriff's deputy. Ben stared as if willing Cheryl over to them. He shot a glance at the young man leaning against the wall, who pushed off and ambled down the hall to the restroom.

Cheryl Smith strode toward them. They stood to shake her hand.

Ben launched right in. "Without the gun, isn't there a chance Dwayne will be released?"

The bailiff swung open the door to courtroom two. They hung back as a cluster of people entered. A couple of cops also remained in the corridor.

"He's not going anywhere." Cheryl tapped out each word. A young woman scurried into the courtroom, a dolphin wrist tattoo peeking from her blazer when she caught the door. Cheryl held it for them. "He violated his probation, and while Dwayne was in jail, they linked him to additional burglaries."

The three of them turned toward advancing footsteps, staying in the hallway to let the young man pass. Cheryl's face revealed nothing.

"Dwayne's brother?" Ben whispered.

"Wesley is a taller, even lighter version of Dwayne. He's out, by the way."

Now she tells us? Vivi had tossed around in bed, twisting the sheets, worrying about the brother showing up. She clenched a fist.

"Look," Cheryl said, glancing at the crescent marks Vivi's nails had dug into her palm. "I'm not expecting anyone on Dwayne's behalf. If Wesley had ever been the kind of brother to show up for him, Dwayne might have had half a chance." She shook her head. "His mom is a piece of work, too."

Cheryl motioned Ben and Vivi forward into the courtroom. Vivi's heart raced. Ben's jaw tightened.

Chapter Thirty-Two: Prelim

THURSDAY - a short time later

I n his jail clothes, Dwayne Williams lounged at the defense table with a female lawyer. His small ears lay close to his skull, his cheeks and jaw planed in strong angles. Objectively, Vivi thought, Dwayne was good-looking—not strikingly handsome, but well-built with regular features. He dipped his head, twisting a lock of hair.

She and Ben slid into the spectators' seats as Cheryl moved down the aisle and through the bar. At the prosecutor's table, she joined a man in a blue dress shirt that strained around bulky shoulders.

Other people were scattered in the gallery: the woman with the wrist tattoo, an elderly bald guy, an Indian man, and a person who might be his son. A man with an open notepad. *A reporter?* Two people who looked like a couple. *Other crime victims?* The black guy they'd seen in the hall.

"All rise." The bailiff called the court to session.

The lanky judge stepped up to his dais, framed by the flags of the United States of America and the State of California. He scanned his realm with an open, friendly face. Ben had googled the judge, too. The Honorable Judge Horowitz previously worked in Juvenile Court, which made Ben worry he'd be soft.

"On the other hand, he might already know Dwayne," Vivi had said.

In front of the dais, a tired-looking clerk hunched over a keyboard, and a court reporter perched over her machine, fingers poised to go.

Cheryl identified herself for the court. Vivi startled when she also introduced her and Ben. Dwayne's head pivoted. His eyes cut right at them. Her heart jumped. What if they did decide just to let him go? Ben took her hand.

The judge met their eyes, smiled, and thanked them for coming, welcoming them as though they had arrived at his home for a barbecue. Her body relaxed a fraction against the hard wood bench.

The defense attorney stood with a straight backbone, her chin lifted in a pugnacious manner, silver hair catching the courtroom light. She introduced herself as Shawna Morrison.

As casually as if he were fetching coffee, the bailiff walked out to the hallway to call the first witness, one of the deputies who'd remained outside the courtroom where she could banter with her colleagues. She was sworn in as Deputy Sheriff Kay Carpenter.

Cheryl asked the deputy questions about a burglary that occurred on October 15th, one of the new charges brought against Dwayne while he was in jail. She extracted straightforward information. A laptop, Nintendo, and jewelry had been taken. The jewelry box had been dusted for prints.

Vivi scribbled on the legal pad she'd brought: *Prints! How can Dwayne wiggle out of that?*

Ben nodded at the message.

When it was Shawna Morrison's turn to question Deputy Carpenter, the defense attorney took her time approaching the witness box. "Was any DNA evidence collected from the scene?"

"No."

The defense attorney waited, but the deputy did not elaborate.

"That will be all."

The attorney pivoted as though she'd made a triumphant point, but why would they need DNA if they had prints? Vivi reminded herself the hearing was simply to weigh whether there was enough evidence to hold Dwayne. Right now, as far as she could see, fingerprints should bury him.

Ben took the legal pad from her lap and wrote in his usual caps: DEFENSE ATTORNEY HAS WEAK CASE! The pen dug into the paper.

The judge asked about the next witness. This time, Cheryl stood, passed through the bar, marched down the aisle, and checked the hallway. She returned with another deputy, introduced as Mathew Montez, who looked fresh-faced like he'd have trouble growing a beard. In the witness stand, prompted by Cheryl, the deputy painted the outline of the second burglary with which Dwayne was charged.

Mr. Carmona, the victim, was carrying in cat food from his car. He heard a noise upstairs and went to check on his cat.

"Mort, right?" Cheryl asked with a smile.

"Yes, ma'am." The deputy blushed to have included the detail in his report.

Vivi scrawled a note: *Dwayne gets caught a lot!*

Ben scribbled back: NOT REALLY. HE'S AT IT 24/7. ITS HIS JOB!!

She inserted the apostrophe in "its."

The sheriff's deputy continued the story. When Mr. Carmona peeked into his bedroom—the master—he heard a rustle that he thought originated from his housemate's room, so he entered that room instead. Something clumped against the house, so he opened the window in his housemate's room. A thin Hispanic male, about five-foot-six, was dangling from the window of Mr. Carmona's master bedroom. In the backyard, another young man, a light-skinned African American, about six feet tall, yelled at Mr. Carmona, "Don't do anything. I have a gun."

Vivi widened her eyes at Ben. He wrote on the legal pad: GUN!!! And underlined it twice, for good measure. Deputy Montez's testimony bolstered the idea Dwayne had been armed even if the gun in their burglary never materialized.

Dwayne was picking at a tooth with a thumbnail. Casual like he'd polished off a burger. How, Vivi wondered, had he traveled from being someone's precious baby to being a gun-toting thief?

In yoga, Winn taught that their practice wasn't to obtain some lofty goal, but to remember "the self we were born with, the pure self, carried inside of everyone, connecting us all." Could there be anything left in Dwayne as delicate as the curl of his ear?

Led by Cheryl, Deputy Montez fleshed out his tale. When he was first called to the scene, he noticed a drink container on the street's retaining wall. The condensation on the forty-four-ounce cup indicated a recent purchase. He followed up a hunch by talking to the person on duty at a nearby convenience store. That person was a Mr. Patel, the owner.

Deputy Montez glanced toward the Indian man among the spectators, across the aisle from Vivi and one row back. Mr. Patel sat upright and attentive, dignified in dark slacks and a white shirt. "Mr. Patel later identified Dwayne Williams from a six-pack of photos."

"And you obtained the store's security video?" Cheryl prompted.

Vivi's attention snapped back to the deputy.

"Yes, it showed an Hispanic man, matching the description of the second perpetrator, purchasing a forty-four-ounce drink." The deputy went on to add that the video quality was grainy, and the suspect wore a cap, so at the present time, the second suspect remained unidentified.

"However, Mr. Patel's son…." Deputy Montez's voice rose. He nodded toward the man beside Mr. Patel, "…was flattening boxes and saw two young men, one black, one Hispanic, running through the back lot of the store shortly after the time of the burglary. The Hispanic man was hobbling like he'd hurt his leg."

Confidence surged in Vivi. What could the defense do except try for the lowest sentence?

"The straw and cup have been sent for DNA testing?" Cheryl asked.

"Yes. They are being processed."

On that triumphant note, the assistant district attorney strode to the prosecution's table and swept into her seat.

Excited, Vivi looked at Ben and then at Dwayne. Dwayne remained slouched and staring forward. He cracked his neck.

Attorney Shawna Morrison levered herself up to question the deputy, slowly approaching the witness stand, imbuing the act with gravitas. She thanked Deputy Montez for serving the community and appearing in court, but followed the niceties with: "What is the distance from the *upstairs* bedroom window of Mr. Carmona's housemate to the back of the yard?"

Lifting his head, the young deputy eyed the attorney. "I'm not sure."

"Your estimation?"

"Maybe thirty feet."

The lawyer asked for the court's indulgence and took ten long strides from the witness stand through the bar and up the corridor until she passed them.

The judge said, "Let the record show that Defense Attorney Morrison has paced off a distance of approximately thirty feet."

Like Cheryl's flourish with the cat's name, this all seemed for show. Maybe lawyers couldn't help themselves.

Shawna Morrison returned to her post in front of the witness box. "And at what time of day did this incident take place?"

"Late afternoon."

"Seven minutes past five?"

The deputy didn't respond.

"That's the time noted on the report."

"Okay," the deputy answered. His boyish face flushed.

"And what was the date?"

"November 7th."

"After we had changed from daylight savings time?"

"Yes."

"So, it was dusk." Her tone suggested this was a fact.

"Not really," the deputy said, as though she'd asked a question.

He sounded rattled. Vivi wondered if this might be Deputy Montez's first occasion to testify.

Shawna Morrison didn't react at all. "Mr. Carmona says the man in his yard claimed to have a gun, but could he actually see a gun?"

The deputy's face hardened. "I don't know, counselor."

"Was there any sign of forced entry?"

"The screen had been popped. It was on the ground."

"Was the room in disarray?"

"No."

"Was anything taken?"

"Nothing Mr. Carmona could immediately identify."

"Thank you. That will be all."

Vivi glanced at Ben. His mouth tightened into a thin line, and his eyes pinched.

Cheryl said something to the deputy on his way past her table. After he swung through the doors of the courtroom, Deputy Sheriff Hashimoto immediately entered. As the next witness, he outlined the burglary of Vivi and Ben's house, adding bits of information new to Vivi. The tow truck driver had sent the police on a search down the fire road, but they'd eventually nabbed Dwayne because a person had called about a guy cutting through his back yard.

After Cheryl finished leading Deputy Hashimoto through a recount of their burglary, Defense Attorney Morrison focused her questions on the gun. How long had law enforcement officers searched? Where had they searched?

Both the Playa Maria County Sheriff's Office and the city police had put in a lot of man-hours poking into places she and Ben had not even considered, such as parked cars and storm drains.

"So after that thorough search, no gun was found?" Shawna Morrison asked.

"That's correct."

LOT ABOUT THE GUN, Ben wrote.

She penned back: *The gun seems to be the lawyer's primary concern—not innocence. She's going for lesser charges.*

"Did you discuss the gun with Ben Russo?" Shawna Morrison asked.

Vivi startled. Beside her, Ben stiffened.

"Briefly," Hashimoto said.

The lawyer asked Deputy Hashimoto about an orange tip on the gun.

"The witness did not see an orange tip," the deputy reported.

Vivi scrawled: *What is this orange tip stuff?*

Ben shrugged.

The defense attorney shot her next question at the deputy. "Did you suggest to Mr. Russo that the gun was a semi-automatic?"

At the word *suggest*, Vivi's chest tightened. The word carried connotations of *placed the idea in his head.* She swallowed and turned to Ben, but his focus was riveted on the deputy.

"No," Hashimoto said.

After Hashimoto was released, yet another deputy was summoned from the hallway. Vivi shifted. *What an incredible amount of time and manpower being given to one burglar.*

She turned Ben's wrist so she could see his watch, wondering if they would finish in time for lunch.

The new deputy testified that Dwayne had been apprehended and held in his patrol car. Prompted by Cheryl, he described Dwayne as "drenched in sweat." According to the deputy, Dwayne had asked what he was being charged with, and then of his own volition, said, "Robbery?"

The deputy's testimony was brief. When he was dismissed, a Dr. Tara Miller was called. The woman with the dolphin tattoo scooted from the end of a pew and passed through the bar, a dark blue skirt swishing from wide hips, a tailored blazer flaring from her narrow waist. She wore her dark hair in a severe twist, a style Vivi had used in her early days of teaching to make herself look older.

Cheryl emphasized that the woman was *Doctor* Tara Miller. Cheryl didn't have to tease out the good doctor's testimony. It sounded well-rehearsed. When Dwayne was arrested, a detective had suggested that Tara run the prints from the October burglary through AFIS, the automatic fingerprint identification system. She'd received a hit. They belonged to Dwayne Williams.

When Shawna Morrison took her run at Dr. Tara Miller, her first question was, "How old are you?"

Dr. Miller looked up at the judge. He nodded for her to answer.

"Twenty-eight."

"And your first job, *Doctor*, is as a fingerprint analyst?"

Without the slightest trace of rudeness, the lawyer had managed to slide a hint of disdain into the question, asking without asking what type of PhD was stuck analyzing fingerprints.

Frowning, the young woman glanced up at the judge again, not doing herself any favors. "Yes."

"And how long have you worked for the County of Playa Maria?"

Dr. Miller flushed like a schoolgirl. "Four months."

"Thank you. That will be all."

The defense attorney was doing her job, but Vivi disliked the seemingly unnecessary attack on the young doctor.

The fingerprint expert was the final witness. The judge motioned both lawyers to the bench. They conferred, the attorneys talking and thumbing their mobile phones, probably checking their calendars. When they returned to their tables, the judge pronounced that Dwayne Williams would continue to be held with the bail of $25,000 set at his arraignment. His present incarceration would count toward time served. The judge thanked them all, including Dwayne, for coming.

With Ben behind her, Vivi walked up the corridor, her legs stiff from sitting. The hallway was still chilly, the gloom settling over her like a fog. She slid her sleeves back and rubbed her goose bumps, the pad and pen clutched in one hand. "How do you think it went?" she asked Ben.

"Good."

Her stomach rumbled. "Are you hungry?"

"I'll be okay," he said. "I want to talk to Cheryl."

After a couple of minutes, the Assistant District Attorney pushed through the doors, the black man following. Vivi watched him continue toward the exit, wondering why he'd been in the courtroom.

"The evidence seems overwhelming," Ben said to Cheryl. "The fingerprints on the jewelry case at the first crime scene?"

Cheryl bobbed her head in agreement. "That's good. Very good. But my guess is Dwayne's attorney will get him to plead guilty to that charge."

"Why's that?" Vivi asked.

"She won't want the case with straight-up physical evidence rolled in with the other charges. If she can get her way, she'll have the three cases dealt with separately."

"Less damning?" Ben asked.

"Yes."

"But how about the DNA evidence in the Carmona case?" he persisted.

Cheryl sighed. "We won't see those results for a loooonnng time. Burglary ranks pretty low on the totem pole. And that evidence won't link Dwayne to the crime. His pal had the drink." The attorney glanced down. "I like your shoes, Vivi. Very retro chic."

"Thanks. Naots." She smiled thinly. The brand was expensive, but she wouldn't have expected the simple Mary Jane style to capture Cheryl's eye.

Ben shifted impatiently. "Is Attorney Morrison a public defender?"

Cheryl shook her head, swinging heavy onyx earrings. "The County doesn't have enough public defenders." Her gaze drifted down the shadowy hallway. "Ms. Morrison was contracted from a private firm. I've seen her in action. She's solid. Very competent."

"The county must pay a fortune for a private attorney," Ben said. "Wouldn't it be cost-effective to employ more public defenders?"

"Yeah, you'd think."

"But the Carmona case is pretty strong, isn't it?" Vivi pressed. "The one with the accomplice?"

Cheryl hitched her briefcase a fraction as though uncomfortable from the weight dangling at the end of her arm. "The weak link is that Carmona came home to find the accomplice hanging from the window. Nothing was stolen. The screen was off the window, but we don't have any evidence of actual entry, other than the victim thought he heard someone in the house."

"How does that change things?" Ben asked.

"We have no lead on this other kid, and we can't place Dwayne in the house. We can't even place the other guy *inside the house*. The defense will argue for that charge to be reduced to attempted burglary."

"So we're screwed." Ben threw both hands into the air in an I-surrender gesture.

"No," Cheryl said. "We still have a good case."

Ben shifted again, his face weary. "If this goes to trial, how will the jurors sort through this? A four-way stop is enough to paralyze most people."

"Have faith."

"Don't you think that deputy screwed up saying he wasn't sure Mr.

Carmona could see the gun?"

"That wasn't optimal."

In spite of Cheryl's reassurances, anxiety coursed through Vivi. "Why did Dwayne's lawyer ask Hashimoto so many questions about the gun?" What had seemed a slam dunk in the courtroom now rolled like a loose ball. "About the orange tip?"

"Federal law requires toy guns to have orange tips."

"It was a real gun," Ben said.

The prosecutor drew a deep breath. "As I explained, the prelim isn't a trial." Even though irritation tinged Cheryl's voice, she assumed a tone meant to tamp down feelings, a soothing, calming tone Vivi had used a thousand times in the classroom. "A prelim is just an opportunity to weigh the evidence so the judge can consider the charges and decide if there's enough to hold the defendant. Obviously, we had enough evidence. Dwayne's been returned to jail. And because of the gun, our office has pushed to elevate the burglary charge to robbery. The defense just tipped their hand a bit, is all."

Vivi's stomach pinwheeled. She sensed where the defense was going. "The defense is going to discredit Ben?"

"I think they will paint him as..." Cheryl searched for the right word, "...excitable."

Ben's eyes stretched wide. "Like I made up the gun?"

"More like you saw something, but it wasn't a gun. At least not a real gun—that Hashimoto planted the idea of a semi-automatic in your head."

"It didn't have an orange tip." Ben's voice rose, the acoustics of the cavernous hallway amplifying it.

"What about our neighbor?" Vivi asked. "Didn't he see the gun?"

Cheryl shook her head. "The dumpster blocked his view."

The cold in the hallway reached Vivi's core. "How about the apprentice at Big Al's Ironworks?"

"We haven't been able to locate him. Unlike the private firm hired for the defense, we can't just hire a PI and bill the county."

Vivi latched onto Ben's hand to keep him grounded.

"They're going to emphasize how you kept chasing the perpetrator after he supposedly drew a weapon," Cheryl said, "and why would a person do that."

"It wasn't because I made up the gun or it was a toy!" Ben's voice echoed in the hallway. Stragglers from the courtrooms turned.

"The defense will portray that as abnormal behavior." Cheryl peered down the hall again. "There was another burglary on Scenic—apparently Dwayne's route—that did involve the theft of a handgun."

Hope surged through Vivi.

"Unfortunately, there was zero evidence from that scene. The victim herself floated the idea her daughter might have taken it."

"Why bring it up if it doesn't help us?"

Cheryl held a palm up toward Ben. "Mr. Russo, you'll have to work on that. Don't feed their narrative that you're excitable."

"But—"

"No *but*." Cheryl closed her palm so the index finger stood alone. "Remember the private investigator I mentioned?"

Sickness swirled in Vivi's gut. This was not going well. They both waited for the shoe to drop.

"Assault, Ben?" Cheryl lifted her eyebrows.

"His son was an out-of-control drug addict." Anger flamed through Vivi like a bygone hot flash.

Ben looked down at the floor. "I just lost it." He slowly raised his head. "It was after his third go at rehab." His voice was barely audible. "I let Art come over for dinner."

"He was stealing money from Ben's wallet!"

This was not fair, sticking an ice pick into Ben's most private and painful spot, going after the victim. The respect she'd felt for the criminal justice system leaked out of her.

Injustice usually spurred Ben into action, but he stood still. "I should have known better." His voice was sad, subdued, like Cheryl had punctured his underbelly and deflated him.

"Fool me once, huh?" Cheryl said briskly. "Believe me, though, the defense was happy to share that tidbit with me."

For a moment Vivi hated it all—lawyers, courts, the whole shebang—the machinations had nothing to do with truth. What parent didn't want to believe in his child? And then for Ben to be betrayed by Art again. Yeah, Ben had shoved Art out the door, and Art had stumbled off the step, dislocating his shoulder, but underlying Ben's action was a broken heart. Shards of dreams for his son.

The event had happened years ago but their relationship had never healed. Art, she thought, was too ashamed of the way he'd been. Trust had been destroyed.

In the end, when Art cooled down and decided not to testify, the charges had been dropped. But the private investigator had managed to pick up the scent.

"Will you excuse me?" It wasn't really a question. "I need to confer about another case." Cheryl turned away. "Contact me if you have any other questions. I'll keep you posted about developments." Cheryl beat a retreat down the marble floor to where she joined the camaraderie of a police officer and another lawyer.

Ben's eyes smoldered. "Do you feel abandoned?"

"We've always been on our own. The District Attorney's job is to prosecute criminals, not defend victims." The truth of her words, the fact of the matter, did not prevent a rime of bitterness.

* * *

Ben wailed on his drum kit, the safest retreat for his frustration. He didn't have Vivi's way with words or the temperament for yoga. He bashed the cymbals.

His kit had no extensions—no cowbells or fru-fru stuff—and at one point or another he'd broken all the breakables.

"More Ringo Starr than Ginger Baker," he'd told Vivi when they met.

Physical drumming with no fuss. "No finesse," some would say.

It beat away the disappointment he'd been from the get-go. A mother who didn't like pregnancy and childbirth and vowed "never to do that again." All the expectation landed on his solitary shoulders.

He'd been quick and athletic, but his father considered him too small to excel in sports. A scholar might have pleased them, but he'd brought home B's and C's, preferring to smoke dope and catch music at the Electric Factory.

He'd gone off to a state-system university. His parents pinned their hopes on his good looks, thinking he might marry up as his father had done. Instead, he gave them Lynn and Art. Whatever rebellion he'd intended, they'd had the last laugh; marriage and a baby had killed the silly notion he'd be a drummer.

Chapter Thirty-Three: River House

SATURDAY - morning

Cuffed to a table, Dwayne sprawled in a chair, moldering. His legs spread wide in gray sweatpants. He winged his thighs back and forth. The peels here at River House were substantially more comfy than jail threads. A person could air out his nut sack.

He twisted strands of hair. Where was his visitor?

The County hadn't wasted any time. Right after his prelim, they had moved him—like now that was settled, he could start his waiting game. The downside: they'd bused him out with the crazy Harrison Adams, but at least he didn't have to share a bunk with him. The upside: the morning in court and the quick move put distance between him and Buster.

Dwayne plucked at his shirt, a green-and-white striped Henley, minus buttons.

They'd assured him the visitor was not a cop, and they would have said if it was his lawyer. Plus, he wasn't in the right room for that. He was in a room with a row of cubicles, staring at a window with a speak-through in it—no phones here—the cheapest type of set-up. His leg jiggled. Maybe his visitor was Espie.

On the other side of the scratched "glass," the guard at the entrance to the room looked bored. Amplified mumbles came from another cubicle, but Dwayne couldn't make out the conversation.

To pass the time, he mulled over his encounter the day before with the new Christian leader at River House.

"What happened to Lavonne?" he'd asked her.

"She had a hip replacement. I'm Melissa. I'll be filling in until she's back on her feet."

"I'll pray for her," he'd said. That had been good. He smiled now, thinking about it.

Melissa nodded, pulled out a chair, and sat. "Uh-huh." She tucked a knee-length black skirt under her. She didn't wear much make-up and had her hair skimmed back in a ponytail, her white blouse buttoned up tight.

Blue eyes, shiny as a rock of crystal, regarded him. She was no fool. He'd looked down at the stainless-steel table. "I've been locked up for five days. Gave me time to think." Scratching at his shoulder, he'd rolled his eyes up toward the Christian Youth Leader. "I don't wanna do all day and a night in prison."

Melissa tapped the tabletop. Her stare drilled into him, as though God had given her some superpower, a regular Professor X reading his secrets. "Wise choice."

He hadn't been able to crab anything out of her tone. She planted both pale palms on the tabletop—no jewelry except for a gold wedding band. *Married to some cheapskate.*

Leaning toward her, he said with sincerity: "I want to get back in with God."

"*Get back in with?*" Her upper lip twitched like she wanted to smile.

"You know, like go to the prayer meetings."

"We'll see."

He was pondering whether he should see any hope in Melissa's remark when movement roused him. Espie shimmied across the room. He tried to stand. The leash to the bolted chair snapped him back.

He leaned close to the metal slats of the speak-through. "Hey, babe." His insides lifted. He hadn't known how good it would feel to see her. "What's up with the shirt?"

Espie's full lips pouted. She wiggled into her chair. "They made me put it on 'to cover myself.'"

"What were you wearing?"

She rolled her eyes. "A tee." She bent forward and tweaked out the neck opening of the gray sweatshirt.

Glitter spread across her chest, and the cross he'd given her dangled down into a pink V-neck.

"Sit down," the guard barked.

Plopping back into her chair, Espie swiveled and waved at the guard, flashing him a flirty smile. Espie's hand in the air was little and pudgy like a baby's. When those hands slid down Dwayne's body, they felt like she was brushing him with innocence.

His sweatpants stirred. "Damn, girl." He slipped his hand down to his cock, leaned back, and looked down the row of cubicles. "Did your aunt bring you?"

"Yeah, she hadda come. She's my legal guardian." Espie dipped her chin toward the door. "She's right over there."

The aunt hung back with the correctional officer on duty and turned her head away. She was dark-skinned and dressed in old lady jeans. It was hard to see her as Espie's blood. The excitement under his hand fizzled. In the chain of cubicles with people coming and going, it would have been hard to rub one out anyway.

"Do you have money?"

Espie lowered her eyelids, painted with green shadow and swooping eyeliner. "Twenty."

"That's all?"

Her head snapped up. "Hey! That's food right outta your baby's mouth, motherfucker."

If he'd been on the other side of the glass, he would have slapped her. But even if he did, she would back talk. Espie was the type where you could knock her down, but she'd spring up like a blow-up toy. Tugging the cuff chain, he crossed his arms over his chest. "You didn't get my present?"

"Someone stole it."

"Stole it!" Across the room the guard and Espie's aunt stopped chatting. He lowered his voice. "What the fuck?"

"For reals?" Espie barked a laugh. "It was in the garbage, *pendejo*. You steal outta your grandma's purse. Why you think someone wouldn't take stuff from a dumpster?"

His leg bounced uncontrollably.

"I thought Jessika must've took it," Espie said. "She's the one—"

"Shhhhhh." He slapped the glass. They might not tape here, but the speak-through amplified their voices.

Espie pulled back. "You didn't have to do that. I know they're recording." *Oh my God she's a dumbass.* He wished he could slip through the glass.

Her lip plumped under a biting tooth. She leaned close and whispered. "Babe, only your jacket was there, but I ran into Jessika right on that street." She turned her head and pressed the side of her face against the glass. "See this?"

Her features distorted like in an arcade mirror. Little dried scabs traced the bottom of her cheek.

"Away from the glass!" the officer said.

Espie whipped around and gave the guard another smile. His face creased, and he stepped in their direction. But the aunt said something that seemed to calm him down.

Probably saying how sorry she was for Espie's behavior—kissing white authority's ass when he'd send her back to Mexico given half a chance.

Dwayne pulled on his ear. "You jumped Jessika?"

"Got her good." The glow made Espie's eyes turn gold, like a cat's. "But Jessika swears a couple of kids took it."

"Little kids?"

"Nuh uh, like tweeners." Her nails rapped on the glass to command his attention. "At first, I didn't believe her, but then I was thinking she was on her way to—"

"Shhhhhh."

"Anyway, Jess seemed to be going there, not leaving. But check this out." Her voice was excited. "Two old people came along and broke us up."

He leaned forward. "A short guy and a skinny lady with silver hair?"

Espie gawked at him. "Yeah. How did you know?"

He grunted. If those two were that close to where he'd stashed the gun, maybe it was a good thing the kids took it.

"I texted Jess," Espie said. "We're cool now. She says that spot is like the kids' hangout."

"Does she know what the kids did with it?"

Espie chewed off her lip gloss and inspected the room. "She didn't tell me."

"Did you ask?"

She wouldn't look at him.

"I need more than twenty." He jiggled his foot, his jail sandal tapping the linoleum. "That first call to you cost, and since you didn't do nothin', the price went up to fifty."

Anxiety pounded his head. The situation was out of control. Buster was over in County, but he knew people, and here at River inmates had too much freedom.

"Fifty?" Espie said. "That's crazy."

"Crazy is what could happen to me."

"Over fifty bucks?"

He rubbed his jawline with a fist. He'd done plenty for less. "The guy who fronted me is going up for murder. He don't care."

Espie looked from one side wall to the other and then back over her shoulder, as though searching for a clock. "I left a photo of Tanisha for you. I made the dress she's wearing," Espie said. "And don't be a hater with that stupid *is-she-mine*."

He wished Espie would stop twisting around. She was chattering about the dress she made with help from the aunt and something called bric-a-brac and how great it turned out and maybe she could be a fashion designer. "Look!"

She barely glanced at him.

"That necklace has diamonds on it."

Her fingers gripped the cross under her shirt. "Seriously? The only fucking thing you've ever given me?"

He needed to regain control. "Lean on Rico. If he don't have money, he can get some."

"Rico? I thought you didn't like him anymore."

He slapped the glass. "Listen!"

The guard started across the room toward them.

Espie used her charm smile that cut little dimples in each cheek. Her face glowed, as if the guard's pasty, old white ass amped her up. She turned back to Dwayne.

"Rico has motivation to help. Feel me?"

"But that guy you owe is over there, and you're over here." Espie waved both hands back and forth in the air. "How does that work?"

Espie was a stupid bitch. "Didn't you see inmates? On work duties? Walking around free to deliver a beat down. Minimum."

Espie opened her mouth to respond, but the guard hovered.

"Tell Rico to deposit money at the jail. For Buster Jones. Today."

"But—"

"Want Tanisha to have a daddy?" he hissed. "Just do it."

He tipped his chin and eyed the guard. If one of Buster's posse went for him over here, no fat-ass white guard was gonna ride to his rescue.

Chapter Thirty-Four: Pawned

SATURDAY - afternoon

Someone pounded the front door, and Marshall almost dropped the cups in his hands. Normal people rang the bell. It had to be Rocky. "I'm coming!" He put away the cups and rolled the dishwasher rack into place, bumping the door shut with his leg.

The front door banged open. Marshall's heart jumped. Even Rocky wouldn't just barge in. Marshall turned the corner from the kitchen and collided with his friend. "What the fuck, dude?"

Rocky was gulping, his eyes bugged so he looked like a goldfish. He didn't speak, which freaked Marshall out. He backed Rocky into a chair at the kitchen table. "Is your mom okay?"

Rocky's head bobbled. "Yeah." That fact seemed to calm him. He yanked up the high socks below his long shorts, then tucked his hair behind an ear. "But I went to the pawnshop."

"Okay…." Marshall tried to follow. "Want some water?"

"Yeah."

He filled a glass, still warm from the dishwasher. "Were you running?"

"I think the pawnbroker called the cops."

Cops. This was not good. Shaking, Marshall handed him the glass. "Dude, this is all like…." Marshall sailed a hand over his head. "Start at the beginning."

Rocky chugged the water and thumped the empty glass onto the table.

"You know that backpack?" Sweat trickled down his temple.

"Well, duh. Not that far back."

"I took the ring out of it."

Marshall plopped into a chair across from Rocky. "What ring?"

"Before I gave you the pack, I found a ring."

"So you took it to a pawnshop?" Marshall's voice cracked and pitched higher. He hated when that happened. It made him sound like a scared kid.

Rocky dragged a flannel sleeve across his forehead.

"What happened?" Marshall rolled his hand in an impatient, keep-going gesture, not something he remembered ever doing with Rocky, who usually blurted stuff out.

"The guy at the pawnshop asked for ID."

"Why?"

"I guess you need to be eighteen."

"The guy called the cops for that?"

"Not exactly. The guy asked what I had. I thought he was interested, even if I wasn't eighteen."

"And?" Marshall couldn't get air past his throat. He tapped the saltshaker on the kitchen table.

"And I showed him the ring."

"Then he called the cops?"

"No, he held the ring in his fingers and studied it like maybe to see if it was real gold."

"Was it?"

Rocky grabbed the pepper shaker and drummed the table. "No, that wasn't the problem. He asked me where I got it."

"And?" Now that Rocky was rapping the table too, it was seriously annoying, like they were caught in a hippie drum circle. Marshall slid the saltshaker to the center of the table and grabbed Rocky's wrist to stop the noise. He lined the glass pepper shaker up with its hula-dance partner.

"I told the guy I found it."

"And?"

"He gave me this stink eye like he didn't believe me. So, I told him about the dumpster—"

"Oh, fool. And the gun?"

"I'm not that stupid, but—"

"But!"

"But he took the ring and went in his office." Rocky teetered back and forth in his chair. "I could see him through the window, and when he picked up the phone, I jammed."

"Shit."

"Yeah," Rocky agreed.

"How do you know it was the cops he called?"

"Seriously, dude, you think he was calling his mom?"

"But you never gave the guy ID. He doesn't know your name."

"No, but there were video cameras."

Marshall tried to collect his thoughts. "We have to tell my dad. All of it. About the gun, too. Maybe give it to the police."

Rocky's eyes blinked, shiny now. "Bro, I'm sorry I got you into all this."

Without answering, Marshall headed toward the bedroom. He'd like to hit Rocky. He'd like to knock his own head into a wall for listening to him, for not doing something sooner. Marshall slid open his closet door, banging it against the frame. He wiggled his beat-up black guitar case from the corner, hefting it over a pile of shoes.

"You changed the hiding place?" Rocky said from behind him. "Good idea."

"I caught James getting ready to show it to Scotty."

Marshall placed the case on his rumpled bed. Something wasn't right. There'd been no thump. When he snapped open the silver clasps, his hands shook.

"What's wrong?"

His heart revved. He lifted the lid and patted the dark blue pack. It smashed flat. No gun.

Chapter Thirty-Five: Satya

SATURDAY - afternoon

Seated in full *virasana*, Vivi spun her wedding ring on her finger, her way to let Winn know she was married without making a big deal out of it. She'd take it off later if the diamond rolled and pinched her skin.

With her calves folded back, her sitz bones sank between her thighs. Why did they call such a surrendering position *hero's pose*? Was it because a true hero sat to ponder? Could a hero who had vanquished his foes afford a floor-bound position?

Eyes lowered, she waited for Winn to enter the room. He'd put on his music, an *om shanti, shanti, shanti* peace mantra. Students were still arriving, unrolling their mats and chatting.

Winn's footfalls crossed the wooden floor. In spite of herself, Vivi lifted her head.

The gentle padding halted beside her, along with a whiff of an essential oil she couldn't name. Winn squatted, balanced on his toes, knees spread apart, a smile aimed at her face. The smile tightened. "Nice ring," he whispered.

Heat rose up her neck.

"Lucky guy." He stood and bowed to her.

She bowed back, her heart relieved and sad.

At the front of the room, Winn lowered into a half lotus. The class quieted. The energy around them grounded. "Today I'm going to talk about *satya*, one of five *yamas* or restraints."

She knew them all. *Ahimsa*, non-violence, most teachers mentioned at some point, but she'd only ever heard one teacher mention *brahmacharya*, sexual restraint. That went farther than the average gym-yoga participant wanted.

Two of the other restraints would be good ones for Dwayne, she thought bitterly. *Asteya* had to do with not stealing, and *aparigraha* was more or less thou shalt not covet.

"*Satya* is about truth," Winn said.

The word *satya* sifted down into the room with the dust motes. But she didn't feel like a vessel open to catch truth. She felt untruthful, not having mentioned her husband to Winn, and not having told Ben her secret. Her heart chakra, the *anahata* chakra, was full, but the *vishudda* chakra, the throat chakra, clamped shut like a floodgate. It had been that way since she could remember. A shy child by nature intimidated by older brothers.

"In Western culture, we often think truth is *speaking our mind*. We have to get on Twitter right now and voice our opinion. Truth is aggressive. But in the practice of yoga, *satya* is a restraint, more like the Buddhist concept of Right Speech. It pairs with the first *yama, ahimsa,* the practice of nonviolence. *Satya* is not about being right. It's about being peaceful."

The curls of Vivi's ears caught the calming waves of his speech, words that carried more than their meaning. Inside each ear, three tiny bones quivered, like magic tossed by a witch doctor, sailing a message along a secret canal that delivered codes even to those who lay dying, abandoned by other senses.

Vivi's shoulders dropped. She exhaled audibly.

After a long pause, Winn said, "Breathe in."

The inhalation of forty students sounded like air soughing through grass. Like home.

"Ommmmmmmmmmm."

She rode the vibration of the word like a magic carpet up into a place of nothing but *satya*.

* * *

Carrying a folder from the second alarm company, Ben patrolled in front of the living room window. He willed Vivi to return from yoga. He wanted to tell her the news. *Big news. Exciting news.* The call from the Sheriff's Office. It had come as soon as he got home from the appointment.

But with no school in session, the street remained empty. Crows strutted up and down the middle of it. The day was quiet. *Too quiet. Like the day before Thanksgiving.* Uneasy, he rolled the folder and beat a clave rhythm on his palm. They needed to get an alarm installed.

He'd liked this second alarm company rep. No hard sell. This rep agreed that all they needed was something to scare off a burglar.

"But the other company wasn't misleading you." Behind his metal desk, the rep had touched a bald circle on the crown of his head like it was his go-to spot. "Burglars do return. They've already scoped out the place, and they expect their victims to replace items. And your thief was interrupted, so he didn't nab everything he wanted in the first go-round."

"He's been arrested."

The man's hand returned to the quarter-sized bare patch as if to check whether the hair was still missing. "These guys typically aren't lone wolves. And often, they're not too bright. I wouldn't be surprised if he has a whole posse of friends who know about your place." He placed both palms flat on his desk as though to indicate everything was on the table. He wasn't trying to scare Ben, just give him the facts.

Mulling over those facts, Ben paced. He didn't want to leave the house empty when the street was so quiet. He never used to think about things like this. It irritated him that now he did. He checked his phone to see if Vivi had texted. A text from Art filled the screen.

He scanned it eagerly: *Glad you didn't get shot! Sorry about the late response. The news landed differently for me than it would for most.*

That was it.

The brevity stung.

And what did Art mean? Did it land differently because of Art's run-ins with the law? Because of their tense relationship? Because Art was half black?

184

The text didn't manage to kill Ben's excitement about the latest development. The Sheriff's Department had received a call from the downtown pawnshop. They had a ring that matched the description he'd given. Some kid had brought it in—said he found it—but scrammed as soon as the pawnshop owner picked up the phone.

He took a position at the window, peering out from the widest angle. Where was she? Maybe chatting with the good-looking yoga teacher? Could Vivi really be interested in someone wearing a man bun?

He left a note on the entrance floor where she couldn't miss it. When he opened the front door, the crows flapped up, cawing. He paused by his car, giving Vivi one last chance to turn the corner before he left the house unoccupied. Unprotected.

* * *

Stretched on the floor in *shivasana*, corpse pose, Vivi peeked at the clock.

"I want to return to the idea from the beginning of the class," Winn said. "*Satya.*"

Normally she would be happy for an extended class, but today Ben would be home from seeing the second alarm guy and eager to give her a report. Agitation fought her attempt to relax.

"While we do our final meditation, I'd like you first to think of all the things today that have been less than satisfying," Winn said.

Right now less-than-satisfying is this class running late.

She could leave, but getting up in the middle of *shivasana* was the height of yogic rudeness.

Winn gave them time to think. It didn't require effort. She wanted to get home to Ben, who'd been nice enough to go to this appointment alone so she didn't have to miss yoga. Resentment of Dwayne Williams and the fallout from his burglary bubbled up.

"Now," Winn continued, "think of the parts of your life that are content. The parts that make you feel safe and satisfied."

In spite of the burglary, this was easy too. *Safe* had been compromised, but

185

she and Ben enjoyed so much privilege—a comfortable house, retirement benefits, good health. They had no debt. They lived in Playa Maria.

"Now, think of those things that bring you joy. Pure bliss. Complete happiness."

Luna sprinting down the hallway, ears back, sliding around the corner on the wood floor. She almost giggled at the image. Good books. Her raised flowerbeds. The hummingbirds sipping from the deep purple Mexican sage. In the spring, riots of color danced in the breeze, tall pink and red opium poppies among Peruvian lilies and blue love-in-the-mist, the flowers her gift of beauty to the world.

"All of this together," Winn said, "frustrations, satisfactions, and joy, all of it, is your *satya*."

Sat. Chit. Ananda. Truth. Consciousness. Bliss. She was stuck at *satya*, unable, in spite of all her privilege, to bundle life in a comfortable way. More yoga practice was needed. Much more.

Chapter Thirty-Six: Plea Deal

SATURDAY - afternoon

Across from Dwayne, Shawna Morrison, in her gray suit and tie, sat staring at him. The *agreement*, as the defense attorney called it, was eight years, serving eighty-five percent of the time unless he did something stupid in custody.

"Credit for time served," Morrison added. "We good?" One strong drum on the table for each word.

She froze the two tapping fingers, waiting for his answer. He was surprised she worked on Saturdays, but then she wasn't from County.

After a minute, she bent down and lifted her briefcase onto the table.

He eyed the black leather, mint condition. Expensive. "How much time is that?"

"Six years and two hundred ninety-two days minus the ones you've served." She said the numbers without using her phone calculator or opening her case to check notes. "A little time off for good behavior if you can hack it."

He rubbed his chin and swallowed. *Almost seven years.* Even if he played the game with good behavior, he'd see at least five. He ran his fingernails up his neck a few times.

"It's a good deal." Her eyes were like black dimes, the pupil and eye color all the same, making them hard to read. "They have solid cases. If you go to trial, you never know what will happen." She pursed her lips and tapped the briefcase once with her pointer finger. "If you take that route, a trial that is, the DA will file the gun charges." The single finger tapped the leather again. "They don't have the gun, so it will come down to your word against the resident's, but he's a credible witness." One more tap. "Plus, there is another person who saw the gun."

"I thought he wasn't gonna testify."

The black eyes stayed locked on his. "They haven't produced him, but things can change. If they locate him, he can be compelled to testify." Another single strong tap like she was putting in a nail. "So, are we good?"

She didn't blink or flinch. There was only that one tapping finger.

He nodded.

"Smart choice." She said it like she was telling her dog, "Good boy."

She studied his face. "There's public sentiment now in favor of lighter sentencing for non-violent offenders. All that changes when you add a gun to the equation." Picking up her briefcase, she rose from the chair. "Of course, I could bill a lot more hours if we went to trial." One corner of her mouth lifted as though she considered smiling at the joke, but she didn't.

As soon as the guard deposited Dwayne back in the communal area, Harrison Adams bee-lined toward him.

Dwayne froze. Adams had been in County. Adams knew Buster.

Eyes wide and teeth clicking, the crazy blocked his path, but his hands remained occupied with jacking up the waistband of his sweats. "What did your lawyer offer?"

Dwayne didn't answer. Could Adams be reporting to Buster? Adams was crazy, but smart to have pieced together what had happened. Maybe he'd been released to pick up the yard and had seen Morrison enter the facility. He knew from court she was his lawyer. The rest, Dwayne supposed, was guesswork.

Adams hoisted his pants so the gray cloth outlined his dick. "You're a stupid motherfucker." Adams sniffed. When he let go of the waistband, the sweats fell around his hips as if the elastic was shot.

Other inmates lounging on busted-down sofas raised their heads to watch the show. Dwayne stepped forward, and Adams stepped back, lifting his hands into a *Don't Shoot*, as though afraid he'd touch him.

"You never done any real time, so you think you're going to laze around here until POOF," Adams made explosions with his hands, "some miracle happens, and you get out and go home, or some other insane Hollywood fantasy."

Dwayne stamped one foot forward, and Adams jumped back. "The only insane here is you."

"Don't push your luck, son." The teeth clicked faster, and Adams's eyes blinked several times. "You stand right there and let me school you."

Dwayne wanted to shove him out of the way, but the release programs depended on good behavior. His whole possible sentence depended on good behavior. He feinted to his left and then moved right, but Adams copied his movements exactly and jumped in front of him again. He was one springy son-of-a-bitch.

One of the watchers snickered.

"That attorney, she's the best friend you have in the world," Adams said like he was a professor or something. "Whatever she offered today, that's the best deal you're gonna get." He wagged a finger.

"What the fuck do you know?" Dwayne dodged, faster this time, and brushed by Adams.

The crazy leapt aside, swiping wildly at his green and white top. "You touched me," he shrieked. "You stupid fuckin' little faggot." He fled across the room to the sink and yanked out one paper towel after another.

Dwayne went to his bunk and propped a magazine in front of his face for camouflage. Adams was howling. Nobody paid him any mind. Jails were the new mental institutions.

He thought about the agreement he'd made, but as the attorney said, *things can change.* The deal wasn't done until he agreed to it in court.

If he took the deal, he'd be shipped to San Quentin. That's how it'd worked with Wesley.

At that idea, he dropped the magazine onto his chest. He'd never been outside Playa Maria County except once when his mama took him and Wesley on the train to see her sister in San Francisco. He bit at a fingernail.

Before they'd even taken off their jackets, his mom and Aunt Francine got up in each other's faces about Grammy Rice's house. His mom said the house was her inheritance, and how was she supposed to support two boys, already becoming teens. Francine said his Grammy Rice wasn't dead, and his mom should have thought about all of that before she ran off with a piece of white trash and had kids. His mom called Francine "high and mighty," and Francine called her a "pathetic mooch."

San Francisco had been gray and cold. San Quentin was up there somewhere. He propped the magazine back in front of his face as a screen.

He could make things change. If he asked for a trial, he could stay in Playa Maria. For now. While he was here, Espie could visit. He might run into peeps from the 'hood like Troy. With a trial, the court would have to work with the schedules of the lawyers and all those witnesses. Then, jury selection. The process could take months. He could end up like Buster, ticking off his sentence in County.

Buster. Dwayne turned his finger and chewed the full arc of the nail. If he didn't pay Buster, he'd be better off at San Quentin. Espie had to come through for him. Get some money or get Rico to get some money.

If she did, things would be cool even if they moved him to County to wait for a trial. On the other hand, if he took the deal and went to San Quentin like Wesley, guys from all over funneled together for processing. There were suicides and stabbings.

When the judge asked how he pled, he could say not guilty. That would wipe the smart look off Morrison's face. He smirked.

She'd get over it. That was her job.

With a trial, someone on the jury could be soft, and his lawyer was tough. She could play up how young he was. What a difficult home life he'd had—no dad, moving from place to place, his older brother a bad role model. Like Morrison said, all more billable hours for her.

He nodded to himself. It was a good plan.

As long as Espie came through for him.

All this *fretting,* as Grammy Rice called it, mattered only if he stayed locked up. There was another way to change things.

He'd see what happened tomorrow. See if he could persuade the new

Christian counselor—Melissa—to take him to the church program. He was in bad need of "communion." Jonesing for it. Hidden behind the magazine, he chuckled at his cleverness.

Chapter Thirty-Seven: Pursuit

SATURDAY - afternoon

Espie pushed the stroller along the sidewalk, worrying about Dwayne and then cussing him in her head. What had the cabrón done for her? Her fingers strayed to the cross around her neck. A present. But mostly it was just do this, do that. "Get money," he'd said this morning. Like that was easy. She wasn't a thief like him.

But she didn't want him to die.

Espie hadn't worked out the details of her plan, but Jessika had told her where the gun had gone, right down to the address—saying she had 'more lucrative things' to pursue. Then the *puta* had laughed, saying, "So what you gonna do, go steal it?"

Not her. But maybe Rico. She'd only come to check out the house, a small place, the yard covered with dead leaves. If Rico went in there and got the gun and sold it, that would be a twofer. They'd get money for Buster and make sure the gun couldn't be found. No gun, no robbery. No assault with a deadly weapon. No extra sentence.

Dwayne had said Rico would be *motivated* to help. Dwayne had something on him.

She was bending over to check on Tanisha when two boys barreled out of the house. The one in the lead yelled over his shoulder, "We have to find James!"

"Holy crap," the second one said. "James took the gun?"

Espie was only thirty feet away, but she was sure they hadn't seen her in any real way. She was just part of the scenery, like the cars parked along the curb. It was surreal to her the way she'd come to scope out where the gun was, and here they were, springing down the steps, screaming about it.

The one with long blond hair threw his skateboard onto the sidewalk and rolled ahead, away from her.

Espie blinked. This was epic karma.

For a few seconds, Espie pushed the stroller as fast as she could, thinking the boys would lead her to the gun. Somewhere with a kid? Named James? When they got there, she'd text Rico.

But no way could she keep up. For one thing, the right front wheel wobbled. She stopped to catch her breath and flipped back the pink flannel blanket to check on Tanisha. Dark curly lashes rested on round cheeks, her little chest rising and falling peacefully under the dress Espie had sewed herself with ruffles at the shoulder seams. Espie's heart swelled. Her baby didn't know nothing. *Lucky little princesa.*

The temperature dropped as a dark cloud traveled across the sun. She whipped the cover back over the small face. Jessika and Dwayne had told her to get an abortion. She couldn't imagine not having Tanisha. Plus she would burn in hell.

A block ahead, the skater looked back, then disappeared down a side street. Espie shivered in a chilly gust. The other kid continued straight ahead. His tee-shirt flamed neon red, so if he kept going forward, she'd be able to track him. For a while.

She resumed pushing, the stroller rattling, the bad wheel veering crazily to the right at unexpected moments. *Fucking Dwayne.* Why did she even bother? Especially when he trash-talked that Tanisha wasn't his. She hadn't even been with anyone before him—well, one guy, that didn't count because she'd been drunk at a party and didn't know his name. When she'd tripped back downstairs, this older girl had latched onto her like they knew each other. "You went upstairs with him?" Her eyes narrowed. "You better get yourself tested, girl." She'd handed Espie a red party cup. "I'm Jessika."

The wheel froze sideways and almost tipped over the stroller. Espie

193

reached down and banged the wheel into alignment. She'd begged her aunt to take Tanisha, but she wouldn't, no matter how important Espie said it was and that it was too cold out for the baby. Her aunt *had to* go to work, couldn't call in sick. Espie knew she had sick days. She just didn't want to use them. Said she'd already done plenty taking Espie to River House.

Up ahead, the red shirt turned a corner. Espie galloped forward. If she could keep the boy in sight, she could call Rico to come help her. Follow the kid to the gun. But if he took another turn after this one, she was screwed.

If she and Rico got that gun, they could get at least fifty for it. Maybe a hundred. Dwayne said guns pulled good money. If she got extra, she'd use it to buy a better stroller at Goodwill. Maybe she'd use the whole thing for a stroller. Let Dwayne fuck himself.

"Hey!"

Espie stopped. With the rattle of the stroller, she hadn't even noticed the clatter of the skateboard coming from the side street. The skater ollied to a stop. They stood at a remodeled corner house, a McMansion crowding its lot, the lawn bright green.

She looked away from the boy toward the house, the American Dream. The yard even had a white fence. As a kid, she'd imagined herself in a nice house like this.

When she turned back, the longhaired kid inspected her and then the baby carriage. She'd seen that flipbook of expressions a thousand times. It said: That *your* baby? You're, like, only fifteen. But then almost as fast, the faces softened. Because there was a baby girl in the stroller. *La pequeña princesa.*

"Have you seen a kid around here?" Sweat filmed the skater's face. "He's about this tall." The boy held a hand at his nose. "Eleven years old. Brown hair. A little chubby. Maybe all upset."

"No. Sorry." *Cool.* She had a description of the kid with the gun—James.

The skater shot off without saying thanks. Espie flicked back Tanisha's flannel cloth. Pink lips puckered in and out, and her tiny fist curled next to them like people came into the world for two things—to eat and to fight. Espie pulled out her phone and called Rico. No answer. She texted. No response.

Espie tucked the cover back over Tanisha's head, inhaling deeply the sweet smells of baby shampoo and talcum powder. Her aunt told her she dusted the baby like she was putting powdered sugar on *sopaipillas*.

Espie smiled. When she had Tanisha with her, people who wouldn't normally trust her in a million years stopped and talked to her. If she found the kid—James—he might talk to her.

The two boys obviously thought he was in the neighborhood. She just needed some good luck to run into him and for Rico to pick up his cell.

She glanced at the dark clouds, held the necklace's cross in her hand for a moment, and pushed the stroller forward.

* * *

In front of Marshall, Scotty shivered in the doorway of his house, his freckles dark against his pale face. He didn't invite Marshall and Rocky inside, and in spite of everything, Marshall felt sorry for James' nerdy friend. A December gloom surrounded them, tangible as fog, and the kid didn't have any shoes on. His white toes gripped the threshold. "I don't know where he is," Scotty whined.

"When's the last time you saw him?" Marshall's insides whirled, but he tried to keep his voice gentle, not to freak out Scotty.

The kid swallowed and shook his head. "I haven't seen him." He crossed thin arms over his tee shirt and huddled in on himself.

"Not at all today?"

"Not since you kicked us out of your room."

"Do you know Finn?" Marshall asked.

Scotty's freckled nose wrinkled. "Yeah."

"Do you know where he lives?"

Scotty shivered and rubbed his bare arms. "Yeah. But James wouldn't go over there. Finn's a jerk."

"Get your shoes and jacket."

"Say what? I'm not going to Finn's house. He doesn't like me either."

Marshall clutched a handful of Scotty's shirt and pushed him back into the house. "Go put on some friggin' clothes unless you want me to drag you into the street the way you are." He stepped up onto the threshold so Scotty couldn't close and lock the door.

"I'm grounded. My dad will kill me if I go out." Scotty backed toward a staircase. "Why not use Google Maps? I'll tell you the cross street and describe the house."

"My phone doesn't have Google Maps." Marshall feigned a charge. Scotty ran up the staircase. As soon as a door slammed, Marshall knew his mistake. He raced up the steps and tried the knob.

"You're trespassing," Scotty shouted through the barrier. "I'm calling my dad."

"Listen," Marshall coaxed. "Did James tell you what he was gonna show you?" Silence emanated from the other side of the door. "It was a gun," Marshall said. "Now it's gone. I don't know what James is planning to do, but this is serious."

"It's all your fault," Scotty croaked, the clog of crying in his voice. "Why'd you have a gun?"

Marshall rattled the knob. He glanced down the stairwell but couldn't see Rocky. "Come on, Scotty. Please. At least tell me where Finn lives."

"Go down Del Amo west." Scotty sniffled. "You know the new houses past Tranquillo Street?"

"Yeah."

"Finn lives there. The second house on Del Amo. Greenish. Red door."

Marshall flew down the stairs. The front door didn't shut all the way, but he didn't stop. Running dead on, he bailed past Rocky. Blood throbbed in his ears and head. If he stopped to call his dad, if he took the time to explain this to anyone, it could be too late.

Chapter Thirty-Eight: Old Wounds

SATURDAY - afternoon

When Vivi swung open the front door, the legal paper on the floor fluttered. Ben had written in his usual all caps: GONE TO SHERIFFS OFFICE. POSSIBLE GOOD NEWS.

Her heart lifted for a second before cool air drafted down the entryway, carrying a foreign smell. She jerked up her head. Broken glass glinted on the kitchen tile. Adrenaline kicked her body into full alert. She crept toward the shattered kitchen door, her ears pricked for any sound. A towhee chirped a warning to its partner.

A creak from the bedroom. She whirled, then froze, her heart pounding. An airplane passed over the house, followed by silence. The towhee again, more insistent. Danger was near.

A rustle in the trees beyond the smashed door.

A black creature leapt to the back porch, jolting her heart. *Luna.* Her cat sniffed at the huge hole in the door. This thief had used none of Dwayne's finesse. He'd broken the glass with a rock or a hammer.

"No, Luna!" She stamped her foot to scare the cat away from the jagged shards. Luna sprang back into the yard.

Perfume hung in the air. Her pulse throbbed in her skull.

Ben would have waited for her before leaving. She was only a half hour late. This break-in had just happened, as if someone had been watching the house.

Vivi grabbed the landline phone and backed toward the front door. Moving off the porch steps into full view of the street, she angrily punched in 9-1-1. A gust of cold air lifted her hair. She blurted her name and address and found herself saying that another thief had been—might still be—in their house.

"A woman, I think."

Ben's car turned the corner as the dispatcher reassured her someone would be there and to stay outside. Ben pulled into the driveway and climbed from the CRV. Sirens shrilled in the distance before he reached her.

"What's going on?"

She grabbed at his sleeve and yanked him away from the house. "Don't go in!"

No one ran out the front door. If the burglar fled out the back, she'd be caged, as Dwayne had been.

"Someone broke into the house."

They both spun toward three sheriff's cars, converging at the corner and squealing onto Beverly Lane. The deputies slammed out of the vehicles, weapons drawn, and she threw her hands in the air, her heart launching off her fingertips.

"We're the homeowners," Ben called.

A deputy hurried over, the other two hanging back to cover him. The cops were at least six feet tall, barrel-chested, and clean-cut with bullish necks above crisp uniforms, like a distinct breed of people. The one near them was tanned as if he spent his time off surfing. A red splotch that looked permanent bridged his nose.

The deputies paused long enough for Vivi to confirm the burglary could be in progress, and the two other exits from the house would pen the thief in the backyard. The gates into the yard were locked from the back side.

"Wait over there." The tanned deputy gestured to the farthest sheriff's vehicle. "Behind the engine compartment."

Crossing the street, they ducked behind the cruiser. Vivi nestled against the metal, warm from the engine. Gray clouds sagged with moisture, and the air smelled oxygenated. It was going to rain soon.

Ben grasped her hand. "I moved the money again. There's no way the thief will find it."

He meant to reassure her, she thought, and his hand was warm and strong. She squeezed it. The sunburnt deputy remained outside, hunkered behind the juniper, gun out, watching the escape routes.

They always said television wasn't realistic, but the scene resembled what she had seen on TV, with one deputy pushing the door open, shouting, "Police!" and rapidly sliding in as the other covered his entrance.

"I think it's a girl," she said to Ben, her voice shaky.

"Why do you think that?"

"I smelled perfume."

Her eyes strained toward the house, but she couldn't see or hear anything from inside.

This time, would the thief dig through her cedar chest, tossing through the memorabilia of her life down to her secret at the bottom?

Walking a dark collie, a neighbor turned the corner. The sheriff's deputy motioned her back. Instead, she moved behind a Speed Bump sign as though the slim metal pole could offer protection. "What's going on?" she called.

Without answering, Vivi waved her away.

The woman glanced at the uniform again, the drawn gun. She made kissing noises to her dog and retreated, but stopped to watch the action over the corner house's fence.

The two deputies emerged from the house, the one in the lead shaking his head. "All clear." He sounded disappointed.

The deputy behind the bush joined his colleagues on the walkway. She and Ben crossed Beverly Lane to the group.

"Too late," one of the officers from the house said. "Weren't you burglarized right before Thanksgiving?"

"Yeah," Ben said. "I'm the guy who chased the thief—Dwayne Williams? He's in custody now."

"Good job." The deputy let his command presence drop. "He's a regular...." He stopped himself and cocked one thick eyebrow.

His tag said Zepeda. He was thicker through the legs and chest than the sunburnt deputy, like a guy who preferred pumping iron over riding waves.

Vivi considered her idea of a girl but didn't speak. Last time, when she'd voiced her concerns about Brenden, the tile guy's helper, her judgment had left a sick feeling in her stomach that maybe she'd jumped to a conclusion and falsely accused.

One deputy took off in his squad car, but Zepeda stayed behind to walk through the house and to take a report. The surfer cop tagged along as if he were bored and had nothing better to do.

They assembled in the bedroom, where mounds of scattered clothing littered the floor. The papers and trinkets from Ben's drawer strewed over the maple floor, the photo album for Art flipped again to the thirteen-year-old at his birthday party, blissfully unaware of the bad choices he'd make, the turn his life would take.

Ben reached down and snapped the book shut.

"The digital camera is gone," he said, scanning the mess. "A Canon Elph. A couple hundred new."

While Zepeda jotted it down, Vivi slid into the closet. The cedar chest remained closed. Relief washed over her. Now, she wondered, would she finally throw away the girlie magazines—the *Chopper* with her leaning naked over a cherried hog, a *Gallery* with her on the cover, a *Hustler* featuring her in a birth-control ad?

Thank God that part of her life occurred before the age of the internet, a decade before she became a teacher. And yet she held on to the magazines with some strange mixture of vanity and rationalization to remember she'd once been nineteen and beautiful. But it was more than that. The magazines were evidence of a colorful chapter in her life when pimps strolled Sunset Boulevard in purple jumpsuits and cocaine-powdered shiny surfaces. She'd liked the spirit behind her short streak of wildness, the escape from the oppressiveness of a small town and a family full of men.

But like any good story, it had a dark side.

She turned quickly to see what the two deputies were doing. They stood with their backs to her, Zepeda with his legs apart and arms folded, the surfer relaxing into one leg, as Ben recounted the former burglary. The two cops listened, their heads subtly bobbing. "There might be a connection," Ben said.

"Probably," Zepeda said.

She sat on top of the chest as though guarding her secret. Most likely, the incident in her past had never been reported. The photographer paid her in cash and didn't have her real name. On the other hand, he could have provided the cops with photos revealing her in minute detail. It would have been easy for them to track her down, she thought, but they never did.

She watched the scene outside the closet door as if from a great distance. "I guess you're pretty familiar with Dwayne Williams."

"Oh yeah," Zepeda said. "And his mother, and his brother. I had the pleasure of re-arresting Dwayne in jail for two other burglaries."

Zepeda clicked his pen and pivoted toward her. His professional mask slid down over his face as though he'd said too much. His eyes hardened, and his jaw squared. "You okay in there?"

"Just collecting myself."

"Take your time. This kind of thing can be quite a shock. To have it happen twice could send anyone spinning."

Spinning.

A whole other universe out there—every day—swirled around them. Vivi had never once considered their neighborhood a bad one. It was a diverse part of Playa Maria, to be sure, part of what they liked about it. They lived on a street that flooded at intervals with parents and schoolchildren and then fell silent. On weekends, people walked by with their dogs, headed to the school's sports fields.

Then this other reality crashed into their lives like an asteroid.

Back in the seventies, in Hollywood—surrounded by coke users and photographers who dabbled in porn—crime hadn't surprised her. She'd somehow fooled herself into believing that was another life, that the cedar wood under her butt safely segregated her from it.

Zepeda tapped his pen on his notepad like a conductor gathering everyone's attention. He flushed a little as though embarrassed by his previous departure from decorum.

The sunburned deputy announced that he better "get back to protecting the good citizens of Playa Maria County" and moseyed off down the hall.

"Do you see anything else that was taken?" Zepeda asked, all business now.

She rose and moved through the bedroom to look in the bathroom. Items from the medicine cabinet were spilled into the sink. She inspected what was there and what remained on the shelves. "The burglar took some old prescription bottles," she said, "but I'm not sure what was in them."

She glanced at Ben.

He shrugged. "Darvon, maybe?"

She returned to the closet as though drawn to its darkness.

"Anything from in there?" Zepeda asked.

"No."

As Ben escorted the deputy to the office, she sank back onto the chest. If the thief had dug inside it, she would have scored a bottle of Quaaludes. Were they potent after so many years? The photographer had offered one to her on his palm. "This will help you relax."

That it did. Woozy, she'd walked to the set—a bed decked out in red velvet and gold braid, covered with furry pillows. Maybe he'd slipped her something more with her water, or maybe at one hundred and ten pounds, no more was necessary. She'd woken up in the dim, stale room with stickiness between her thighs. Groggy, she'd reached down to see if she'd gotten her period. But it wasn't blood.

She didn't remember having sex.

Quiet had surrounded her, the photo studio windowless and soundproofed against the traffic on Hollywood Boulevard. The room was stuffy with residual heat from the mounted studio lights. The photographer had left her there to let herself out, apparently unworried she would report anything. *Did I agree to have sex? With a balding old overweight guy?*

But even if she hadn't consented, who would believe her anyway? She had been willingly naked and alone with him. Had taken the Quaalude voluntarily. Her family, for sure, would blame her for putting herself in that situation. And the police? She was a teenage model, while the photographer bragged about the famous people he knew, borne out by signed headshots of celebrities in his studio.

Pulling on her panties, she found her sundress draped over a chair back. She slipped it on, shivering in spite of the heat. She picked up her bag from the corner and slung it over her shoulder.

Her fingers trailed over the counters. At least she used birth control pills, so there was that. But what if the fucker gave her a venereal disease? She snapped up the bottle of pills and stuffed it into her purse, then dumped in dollar bills and coins and a heavy gold ring with a blue sapphire stone from a small ceramic dish. Her hand hesitated at a bulky camera. She swiped it to the floor. It bounced harmlessly on the shag carpet. She pushed over the lamp poles. Nothing crashed or broke in a way commensurate with her rage.

Opening the door out into his office, she blinked against bright sun slanting through the blinds. Her pink flip-flops were parked beside the door. She slid them on, muffled traffic noise seeping through the exterior door, locked no doubt from the outside. The office smelled like stale cigarettes and burnt coffee. Girlie magazines and invoices littered the desk.

Jittery, she stalked the room's perimeter, looking for something that would hurt him. But there was nothing—no lovely photo of his family, no award, no fancy Mont Blanc pen. She yanked out his desk drawer and slid forward the plastic tray of office junk. In the back rolled a fat wad of rubber-banded bills.

Jamming the roll into her bag, she'd fled into the bright Hollywood morning. Her pussy hurt as she walked, the lips burning.

Had the sex been rough? How had she remained unconscious?

In her apartment, she'd counted the money, hands shaking—five hundred and forty dollars in hundreds and twenties. And three dollars and forty-seven cents from inside the studio.

She sat on the toilet seat and inspected herself with a hand mirror, her vaginal lips inflamed and red, but she didn't seem otherwise injured.

She put all the evidence—the pills, the ring, the money—in a white cardboard box that had once contained a gift mug. Like an inoperable cancer, the box had traveled with her through her life.

"What are you doing in here?" Ben leaned through the doorway. "Are you all right?"

She nodded, but he inspected her—a person didn't sit in a dark closet for five minutes doing nothing. He sat down beside her. "What's going on?"

"I'll tell you later."

He scrubbed his forehead with his palms, weary. "Do you want to see what the thief did to the office?"

A frisson of guilt shivered through her as though *the thief* meant her.

In the office, the drawers of the desk hung open—office supplies thrown so that pens and pencils had rolled to the far walls, as though the burglar were crazed—digging for something—file folders yanked out en masse and dumped. To do all of this before Vivi got home, the burglar must have entered as soon as Ben left.

"Looks like the thief was after something," Zepeda said.

"Money."

"In previous burglaries, Dwayne did have an accomplice," Vivi said. "In court, the deputy who testified about the Carmona burglary described a thin Hispanic guy dangling from a window."

And the girl on the bike had told her about some guy ducking down in a car around the corner.

She froze. The girl on the bike—Jessika—circling around on the street the day they were first burglarized, chatting with Vivi, as though to distract her or get information. Then, when she and Ben had tried to track down the gun, they'd run into her in the middle of a brawl. And Vivi had seen her coming from a house off Del Amo. Frank, the tile guy, had told Ben that Brenden lived on Del Amo.

"What's going on, Vivi?"

Zepeda stopped taking notes and peered at her over Ben's shoulder.

They trailed her into the kitchen. She sniffed the air. Spicy, but definitely not a man's cologne. *Like orange blossoms and cinnamon.*

Zepeda studied her.

"I have a suspect," she said.

Chapter Thirty-Nine: Panic

SATURDAY - late afternoon

Marshall stabbed the doorbell over and over, his attention shifting back and forth from the door to the street. Rocky should appear from his search of the side street.

Marshall squinted toward the gray sky. A raindrop caught on his eyelashes.

Finn yanked open the door. His pinched rat face scowled at Marshall. "What do you want?"

Hatred roiled in Marshall's gut. His fists clenched. He detested this scrawny little punk, trying to look tough with his shaved head. Finn was the kind who caused trouble and then blamed it on someone like James. "Is my brother here?"

Finn squinted past Marshall to Rocky, rolling up behind him on the walkway.

"I haven't done anything to that retard." Finn slammed the door. The deadbolt clunked into place.

Marshall hammered on the door. "He has a gun! He's gonna kill you!"

A big window a few feet from the door slid open an inch. "A gun?"

Marshall tromped across the porch and put his nose to the screen to peer inside. Finn backed away. "What did you do to him this time?"

"I didn't do anything." Finn's voice quavered.

"Tell me, or I'll let him do it."

"Some guys pantsed him is all. And James held his dick and cried like a baby."

The window opening was too narrow and Finn too far away, or Marshall would have punched him through the screen. "And what, you announced it to the world?"

"I didn't do anything. The other guys pulled his pants off."

With his fingers in a tight spear, Marshall jabbed at the screen. The impact hurt like hell. "And what were you doing the whole time?"

"I took a picture. So what?"

"You little punk." Marshall chopped at the screen with the edge of his hand. "I hope he does shoot you."

"I didn't put it on Instagram." Finn's voice took on a pleading whine. "Tell him that. Tell him I didn't do it."

"I hope he kills you and your whole fucking family."

The window slammed shut.

Rocky's hand clamped Marshall's shoulder to calm him. "Count to three."

Marshall reeled about. "This isn't some fucking joke, Rocky!"

"I know it isn't." Rocky cradled his skateboard. "I want to pound the piss out of him myself." Rocky put the skateboard on top of his head like he meant to use it as an umbrella. A few raindrops pattered on the deck. "But look at the bright side. Finn's alive. James hasn't shot him. Yet."

Marshall shuddered. Now that he'd seen Finn was okay, he pulled out his phone.

"Yi-up. What's up?" his dad said. "Why aren't you home? Where's your brother?"

His father's voice wrapped him like a strong arm around his shoulder.

"Dad…." Marshall's voice broke.

"Shelby, what's wrong?"

Shelby. No one had called him by that name since his mom died. The single word slipped behind a guarded door, and Marshall choked a sob.

"Where are you?" his dad's deep voice edged with panic. "I'm on my way. Just tell me, Shelby. I'll be there."

* * *

Cool air whipped by Jessika's face as she pedaled her bike toward Rico's. The pack on her back swished, the pills rattling inside their containers. Rico would like those.

Her heartbeat throbbed in her temples. She was panting like she was about to orgasm. She'd shoplifted before. She'd been the lookout for Rico when he'd gone to search the kid's apartment for the gun. But she'd never done a burglary on her own. It was a complete high, even if she didn't find the money.

She should have gone after the gun again instead of throwing that bone to Espie. But the bitch was her friend. And desperate.

It would be fun to show Rico the photos she'd taken of her first job—the epic explosion of glass on the floor.

A siren shrilled, and her heart jumped. The piercing noise grew louder. She twisted around on her bike to see. The cruiser racing toward her didn't slow down. It wasn't coming after her; it was headed to the house.

She stood to pump faster, her UGG boots slipping on the too-narrow pedals, her body swaying. She careened around the corner into a quiet neighborhood. Other sirens screamed into the peace of the lawns and trees. In a front yard, a mother with two small children was tying birthday balloons onto a mailbox, barely lifting her head at the wailing police cars. The trouble was over there, somewhere else, not her problem. The mother's biggest concern seemed to be securing the balloons. The little boy fired at Jessika with a finger gun.

Jessika relaxed on the bike seat. "Whose birthday?"

The woman smiled and rested her hand on the smaller child's head. The breeze gusted golden hair away from a shiny tiara. "This one's."

Stirring the grass with the bottom of her pink princess dress, the girl waved a wand at Jessika and sang, "Make a wish! Make a wish!" She was too little to care if it rained on her birthday.

"Peace on earth!" Jess laughed. She rolled by and rounded the next corner, the wind hitting her, pushing her back.

* * *

Marshall, his dad, and Rocky piled into the seat of the old pickup truck. Crammed against his father's shoulder, on the little middle section where James usually had to sit, Marshall tried to tell his dad the whole story, but it came out in jumbled stutters. Rocky leaned over from riding shotgun and inserted bits of information, which didn't help. His dad drove with one hand. With the other he squeezed Marshall tighter.

The truck swung into a parking lot of an official building with flags flapping on a pole in front. Playa Maria County Sheriff's Office—a new greenish stucco building. An officer exited the glass front door.

Springing from the truck, his dad left the door yawning and ran toward the man.

The officer halted. Put a hand on his weapon.

When Rocky and Marshall spilled from the truck, the deputy let his hand drop.

They raced to Marshall's dad, who was already talking. Marshall was sure a person did not report an emergency this way. But the sheriff's deputy listened, trying to absorb facts that rolled from his father's mouth like dice skittering on a sidewalk.

The deputy kept a calm face even as rain speckled the shoulder creases of his uniform. Hashimoto, his tag said, kept trying to get his father to slow down and put the pieces in order. "Where did your son get this gun?"

"We found it!" Rocky yelled. His eyes were wide and wild. "In a dumpster."

The deputy turned toward Rocky. "Around Thanksgiving?"

"Yup!" Rocky danced from foot to foot. "The day before."

"Why does that matter?" His dad's voice broke. "My boy, my son, has disappeared, and he has a gun." Silhouetted against the dark sky, his father's body was tight, his arm gestures emphatic. He looked like a figure in a graphic novel, all sharp black ink lines. "He's only eleven years old, and he has a gun."

And it's my fault. A sour taste pitched up in Marshall's throat. He barely reached the bushes before he bent over and heaved his morning Pop-Tarts. Rain sprinkled the back of his neck.

Beside him, Rocky doubled over, puking too. When Rocky straightened, his face was white. "Sorry," he said, swiping at his mouth. "Sympathy chunks. Happens every time."

* * *

Drops speckled the blue canvas of the stroller top. Espie stopped and turned up her face. A drop of moisture hit her eyeball. The sky had bruised into purple, but blue fringed the distance with the sun peeking out. Maybe she'd see a rainbow. Then she could draw a cross on the ground and make a wish. *Get the gun. Get some money.*

She tried to turn the corner, but the front wheel of the stroller stuck sideways. Tipping up the front of the stroller, she banged it down to straighten the wheel. It stayed stuck. Kicking at the wheel, she jammed the stroller around the corner.

Tanisha whimpered. Espie brushed aside the blanket. Big dark eyes stared back, and then the baby's face squeezed like she was trying to poop. Sometimes moving the stroller back and forth calmed Tanisha. Espie gave the handles a gentle push. The front wheel rocked like it would fall off, and the baby's cry gained momentum along with the rain.

Scooping up the pink bundle, Espie snuggled the baby against her shoulder. Tanisha mouthed the fabric of her sweatshirt, searching for food, and milk released in Espie's breasts. She liked how her breasts plumped with motherhood, big and full, and now that her nipples had gotten used to it, she liked nursing. But the leaks were embarrassing. She wouldn't be able to take off her hoodie now without someone seeing the circle of wetness.

Espie bounced the crying baby, and the flannel fell away from her head. Raindrops sprinkled Tanisha's face. She wailed. Covering the baby, Espie arranged her in one arm and grabbed the handle of the stroller.

Down the block a big tree grew at the corner of a yard. She dragged the stroller behind her tipped onto its back wheels, stopping every couple of steps to hitch the baby up her torso. Tanisha's tiny voice cranked into full indignation. Espie gave the stroller one last angry jerk. "Fucking piece of shit."

Under the protection of the branches and remaining leaves, she shushed the baby. "There, there, sweet pum'kin." The yard's fence stood on top of a retaining wall. A two-inch ledge stuck out, and Espie perched her bottom on it. Pushing her sneakers onto the sidewalk, she braced her back against the fence. Hunched over, she used one hand to bunch the light gray hoodie and her shirt up her body.

She was tugging at her bra cup when the kid rounded the corner. He hunkered against the rain, the gun tucked under an armpit.

* * *

Rico was between jobs so Jessika wasn't surprised to see his Impala out front. Asphalt ran right up to the splintered door of what looked like a converted motel unit. But at this end of the apartments, Rico's side windows viewed one of the streams that ran through Playa Maria. On normal days, his crib was kinda nice, but today the trees down in the gulley whished in the wind in a spooky way. Rain spattered the pavement.

Jessika leaned her bike against the stucco. Shivering, she rapped on the door. The walkway for the upstairs apartments shielded her. Footsteps pounded on the concrete over her head. She watched the window to see if Rico would check through the blinds before opening the door. He did. A quick flash.

Near her, a gangbanger thumped down the stairwell, wearing chinos and a wife-beater undershirt in spite of the weather. She gave him a smile, but he scowled at her and strolled by, rolling his tatted shoulders. He ducked into a maroon sedan.

When Rico opened the door, he wasn't wearing shoes. The dry warmth of the room blasted out at Jessika. From behind Rico's body, slender arms circled his bare chest. A girl's chin rested on his shoulder, and false eyelashes batted at Jess over Rico's tattoo of a cross with RIP for someone named Shorty.

The girl grinned at her. "Who the fuck are you?"

"Whaddaya want, Jess?" Rico asked.

"I just wanna come in." She patted the pack. "Remember that yellow house?"

He frowned at her. "You're crazy, you know that?"

"Wanna see what I got?"

"We're a little busy here." Rico arced a hand over his shoulder into the girl's mane of dark curls. Her cheek nuzzled his neck.

The girl stepped from behind Rico, naked except for a lacy red thong. Bending over her purse on the floor, the girl mooned Jessika before springing up with a Bic lighter. She pulled a little glass pipe from the dresser.

The lighter snicked, and craving coursed through Jessika's body. No. Fuck. This was a need, like a wild animal inside, clawing at her body. Rico's new friend turned away as the lighter snapped again.

A slight showercurtain smell puffed out of the room as Rico shut the door in her face. Jessika pounded on the splintered wood. "We could do a three-way," she bellowed.

"Get a life!"

Jess bit her lip and stood for a moment under the shelter of the overhead walkway, eyeing the maroon sedan. She trotted across the parking lot. The gangbanger's head shot up as she swung into the car.

"Why don't you make yourself at home?" The guy held a pencil, and for a second, she thought he might jab her.

Ignoring the sarcasm, she unhooked one arm from her pack and swung it to her side. She licked her lips and inched her damp skirt up her thigh. "Wanna party?" She glanced at his lap and back to his face. He had little wrinkles around his eyes and below his ears—definitely older than she'd thought. But he was pretty ripped. Her gaze returned to his lap. A white envelope rested on his thigh. On the corner of it, the guy had printed: diapers, dish soap, rice.

He frowned at her bare thigh and then into her face. "Get outta my car." He didn't sound mean, but he sounded like he meant it. He looked over his shoulder. He had a teardrop tat under his eye. "My wife and baby are right up there."

"I'll get down, and you can drive around the corner."

His eyes narrowed. "I've been where you are, *chica*, and this I know." He pointed at her. "I can't help you. Now get the fuck outta my car."

"But it's raining."

"I noticed."

She didn't move. He sighed, opened his door, and slid out. When he circled around the back of the car, Jessika hopped out. "Loser," she hissed, shrugging her arm back through the strap of the pack. She wiggled everything into place as she strolled across the lot to her bike, trying for casual, like she wasn't getting drenched. The car door slammed.

It sucked to be back in the rain, but she was only a few blocks from Del Amo. Unlike Rico, Brenden had a steady job. He often worked on Saturday. She wormed her cell phone out of her jacket pocket and called his landline to make sure. The phone was a relic from the old couple who owned the place and lived in the front house. They were traveling around China now. They were gone a lot, part of why they charged Brenden a low rent. They liked having him around, bringing in their mail, and keeping an eye on the place.

Brenden hadn't even recorded a greeting on the machine, but if he was home, he'd answer it eventually. She counted the rings. At nineteen, she disconnected.

By the time she reached his rental, her skirt was clinging to her skin. From under a red Adirondack chair, she fished Brenden's spare key.

Inside, Jessika took off her pack and tossed it onto the couch facing the door. She wormed out of her wet Levi's jacket and toed off her UGGs. Her teeth chattered. She slid the skirt down her legs into a mound by the shoes.

Padding into the bathroom, she trailed droplets on the wide pine planks. She dried her hair but left it sticking up all over and went into Brenden's bedroom, peeling off her damp shirt on the way. Still shivering, she tossed it on the floor and tipped one of Brenden's flannel shirts from a hanger. It hung almost to her knees. She slid off her thong and rummaged through the drawers, but Brenden had removed her clothes.

Sliding on a pair of his boxers, Jessika inspected herself in the mirror—blue and white checks sticking out below a plaid of mocha and green—smeared mascara around her eyes. *Very stylin'*. She retrieved her phone from her jacket, snapped a selfie, and tucked the cell into the pocket of the flannel shirt.

In the kitchenette, she put on a kettle of water. She stood on tiptoe to find her box of peppermint tea, but it was gone too. Brenden must have thrown it out. She chewed a fingernail. When did he become such a dick?

She went back to the bathroom and shoved around the contents of the drawers. All her stuff was gone. Even her toothbrush. She snorted. Well, if Brenden thought he'd cleared her out, he was in for a surprise.

The kettle shrieked. In the kitchen, she pawed around on the shelf and found an old box of black tea.

Tucking her legs under her, she settled on the couch, a steaming mug between her palms. Shifting the mug to one hand, she shook the contents of the pack onto the nubby fabric. She spread out the loot. One pendant was kinda cool, the large red and black glass beads glinting in the lamp's light.

Footsteps. Her head reared up. She put down the mug. Brenden must have finished his job early. Construction was like that, especially during the rainy season. She bulldozed the junk back toward the mouth of the pack. Brenden would not be cool with this at all. The pendant clasp caught in the couch's weave.

She jerked at the hook to get it free.

The knock on the door froze her. *Not Brenden.*

She tumbled over the arm of the couch and hid behind it. People talked outside the door, one voice female, the other mega-manly. The two people weren't Brenden's parents. His mom had a precise voice that grated on her nerves. And the homeowners were in China.

Jessika slid from behind the end of the couch and crossed the room in a crouch to below the window. If they peeked through the openings in the blinds, she'd be out of their line of sight.

"I think she's here." The woman's voice sounded familiar. "That's her bike."

"We don't have a search warrant."

Police. Jessika pressed against the wall and dug fingernails into her palm. She had to sit tight. Wait for them to leave. Like he said, they didn't have a warrant.

Steps approached the window. Jessika backed tight against the wall. Without seeing, she knew one of them was looking through the slats right above her.

The manly voice commanded the woman away from the window. "That's a dangerous thing to do."

But the woman tapped on the glass. "Look!"

Jessika shrank against the wall.

"On the couch," the woman said. "Under the lamp." The clicks on the window quickened. "That's my necklace."

The woman from the house!

"Step away from the window." He spoke some more, and his radio crackled back at him.

He was calling for backup. This problem was not going to disappear.

"Isn't that probable cause?" the woman prodded. "Plain view?"

Jessika chewed the nail of her index finger, thinking about the angle from the window and if there was a way to escape across the open room to the bedroom without being seen. Maybe—if the woman had obeyed the cop's order—but she seemed a little obsessed. Like when she broke up the fight between her and Espie.

What was the woman even doing here? If the cop had brought her, no doubt he would have told her to stay in the car.

"Are you sure it's yours?"

"Yes," the woman said. "A local artist made it. You can't buy something like that at CVS."

The deputy's radio crackled again. *Fuck, fuck, fuck.* Jessika sprinted to the bedroom.

"I heard movement inside." *The woman's voice, but away from the window now.*

The backpack full of incriminating evidence sat right on the couch. But it was Brenden's crib. She could say she found it there. *Yeah, right.*

Jessika slid open the bedroom window. Dead flies rested in the track. She frantically worked at the corner of the screen, blocked with a crust of built-up dirt. Slamming her palm against the aluminum frame, she knocked out one corner.

Her heart pounded like she'd been tweaking. She pushed with her full weight against the screen, but it stuck in place. She banged along its bottom, starting to sweat under the weight of Brenden's flannel shirt. The other corner popped free. When she pushed at the screen, it bent and flew into a strip of shriveled grass, hitting the back fence. Using her hands for leverage, she hopped to get her butt onto the window ledge. The metal window track cut through the thin fabric of Brenden's boxers.

The front door banged open. "Jessika! You in here?"

Brenden! She dropped out the window, her phone falling next to the window screen. Sweeping her hands through the blades of grass—prickly from years of drought—she scooped up her phone, then hesitated. It was full of incriminating photos. But Dwayne had sold it to her for twenty bucks—she'd never get another deal like that—and her whole life was on it. She jammed it back into the shirt pocket.

In front of her, the back fence blocked her way. To her right, the side fence would force her down a narrow corridor. And to her left, the deputy peeked around the corner of the granny unit. He told her to stay right there, but there was a crack in his voice, a fissure where he was seeing a small, young girl wearing boxer shorts—a sliver of opportunity.

Backup couldn't have already arrived. Jessika tore to the right, the grass needle-sharp on her bare feet, flicking water up her calves. At the front of the side passage, the woman stepped into her path. Head down, Jessika charged her.

But her target moved, simply turned to the side. As Jessika flew past, the woman pushed on her back—hard. She stumbled forward, hands outstretched. Her palms skidded over a stepping stone. The cop rounded the front corner of the house, wrenched her arms behind her, and cuffed her.

He stood, panting. "Good job," he said to the woman. The fracture of kindness, gone. Above her, the woman flashed him a quick smile.

"But don't ever do that again," the deputy said.

The silvery-haired woman looked down at Jessika. Jessika remembered how the lady had yanked her off Espie—stronger and tougher than a person would guess. The way she'd swung her out of the path of Espie's charge.

Pressed against the ground, the boxer shorts sponged up coldness. Grit pebbled Jessika's knees, and the arches of her feet cramped. The cop left her there to eat dirt. Jessika twisted her head away from the woman, who should plant a victorious shoe on her back. That's what she would do.

Brenden's work boots tromped up behind the deputy's legs. Her UGG boots plopped down in front of her face. Her jacket and skirt were crammed into them. Brenden asked if the sheriff's deputy was taking her to jail. He sounded like he didn't give a shit.

* * *

Tugging her bra and sweatshirt into place, Espie turned as the boy neared. His head was down, but of course, it was that kid James. He came toward her, his shoulders rounded, brown hair falling over his forehead, wet canvas shoes slapping the sidewalk. An old No Fear tee-shirt plastered against his chubby body, the gun pinned between an arm and his chest.

He stomped by her, like she was nothing, even though she sat with a baby in her arms. A normal person would at least give her a corner of the eye. His body, shorter than hers, was shivering all over.

"Hey!" she yelled at his back.

He didn't slow down. The barrel of the gun stuck out from the flab under his arm. *Dwayne's gun.*

Jumping up, she bounded forward, losing some of her grip on Tanisha. The baby squealed at the sudden movement. Espie bounded forward, grabbed the barrel with one hand, and yanked. The metal was slippery, and the kid fiercely hung on to the grip.

The boy spun, his head springing up. He blinked at her. "Leave me alone." The gun dangled in his hand.

She jacked Tanisha back onto her hip. "That's mine." She grabbed at the gun again and jerked the slick barrel down, so it pointed at the sidewalk.

The boy pulled away from her.

Outside the tree's drip line, fat raindrops spat on the concrete. The baby choked on sobs, her head uncovered and cold splashing her face.

The kid shook his head. "No, it isn't." His eyes squinted at her. "You're only like fourteen."

"Fifteen." She lunged and tugged at the barrel again, but the stupid little kid wasn't letting go. "It's my boyfriend's."

"Oh, yeah?" The boy's voice snarked with attitude. "How'd *he* get it?"

Tonto de culo. She jerked the barrel down hard, but she couldn't put everything into it with Tanisha in her other arm. Even with the tug she gave, the baby's blanket-wrapped legs flew out from her hip.

The boy yanked back hard this time, stronger than she had imagined. The barrel popped free of her grasp. The gun came up. Ducking, she twisted away, curling her body over Tanisha. A blast cracked through the gentle thrum of rain.

The force slammed into her side. Her arms gripped Tanisha's shoulders and neck. Under the hoodie, warmth trickled down the inside of her shirt. In spite of searing pain, she clung to Tanisha's tiny body. Blood oozed from the pink blanket.

She stared. The blood must be hers. Her gaze trailed down the spatter of blood on her hoodie. But it didn't match the burning throb along her side. Nothing made sense. There was a hole in the flannel blanket. And the baby had gone still.

She shook Tanisha. Nothing. Silence.

Espie clutched her limp baby and howled in horror.

* * *

When Deputy Zepeda pulled the cruiser to the curb, relief surged through Vivi. She was home, and Ben was waiting on the sidewalk. She hadn't even climbed out before Ben was leaning inside the vehicle, offering her a hand, and thanking Deputy Zepeda.

"Are you all right?" Ben asked.

"We got her!"

Ben eyed the empty back seat.

"Back-up took her to the county jail."

Ben bent toward the patrol car like he wanted to discuss the whole matter, but Zepeda said, "Yup, off to County. Your wife's a trooper." There was a burst of chatter on the vehicle's radio. As soon as she closed the door, the car zoomed off.

A truck from a glass company occupied their driveway. Ben hadn't wasted any time. As they headed toward the house, she started to pour out the story about the trip to Brenden's. In the kitchen, a glazier was taking measurements of the door. She stopped talking.

"I assumed the same kind of door would be fine," Ben said.

She smiled. He'd probably gotten the best deal, too.

The worker, a slender man, hooked his tape measure to a leather belt, finishing up. He wore a crisp dress shirt, which made him seem precise, a good quality for someone measuring the fit of a door. Ben introduced him, and she shook his hand. The glazier stretched a clipboard toward Ben.

The ebb of adrenaline left her like a sea creature without its shell—soft, vulnerable, exposed.

The kitchen floor had been swept, minuscule bits of glass and dust tracing the arcs of the broom. Emily Dickinson's poem "The Bustle in a House" arrived, full-blown, in her head with its sweet lines *The Sweeping up the Heart/And putting Love away.*

She'd selected that poem for the programs at her mother's memorial. But was love something you could put away? Even her brother's death from so long ago could rear up and bite her.

Could a person put anything *away*?

Cold, wet air funneled through the broken door. It wasn't just the glass that was shattered. A hole had punched through an invisible barrier in herself.

The worker nodded toward the opening. "Do you have some plywood?"

"Yeah," Ben said, placing his hand on the small of her back. She wiped her eyes with a forefinger.

"It's a hell of a thing to have your home broken into."

When the glazier left, she finished telling Ben about going to Brenden's place, how Jessika had been there with the stolen goods, and how she'd helped to catch her.

"I'm not the only crime fighter in this house."

She smiled wearily. She'd acted with agency—*Tarzan, not Jane*—but it wasn't how she'd imagined. It was exhilarating, but sad.

"In all this excitement, I didn't have a chance to tell you the good news." Ben reached for something on the butcher block table. "The Sheriff's Office had lots of photos and let me take this one."

"Your wedding ring!"

"A kid brought it into the downtown pawnshop. Said he found it."

"No doubt he did."

"You don't sound very happy."

Staring at the hole in the door, she thought of the weight of two possible trials—Dwayne's, then maybe the girl's—and Ben, on the stand, grilled about pushing Art down the steps.

What would it all be worth in the end? When they went to their grave, what vestigial grace would remain?

"I'm not."

"We'll get through this." He stood behind her and massaged her shoulders, unyielding as concrete.

* * *

Marshall wiped the vomit from his mouth and returned to his father's side. The deputy's shoulder radio popped with the dry voice of a dispatcher, rattling code. Deputy Hashimoto shot his dad a sharp look. Without explanation, the deputy pivoted and run-walked to his vehicle, but his expression had betrayed everything.

His dad sprinted toward the truck. Marshall ran to catch up. Rocky was at his heels. They piled onto the seat.

When the cruiser shrilled out of the parking lot, lights flashing, the truck careened behind it. They rode in frozen silence, following the sheriff's vehicle, all suspended in fear of where they must be headed.

Several blocks from the station, the sheriff's cruiser skidded to a stop behind other cruisers and emergency vehicles on the scene. But his dad rocketed his truck down the center of the road, right to the circle of activity, as though he meant to mow down the officers. He slammed on his brakes, his truck in the middle of the street. Cruisers kept arriving until the street was choked with them, the last ones parking sideways to make a roadblock. Patrol officers from the city of Playa Maria, County Sheriff's Deputies, and California Highway Patrol swarmed the area.

Marshall had thought the worst moment in his life, forever, would be the afternoon his father sat between him and James on the couch and explained their mother wasn't coming home. She'd gone to Heaven. He had hated Heaven like it was a body snatcher. A villain.

This was worse.

Two cops restrained his father, ordering him to kneel, but his dad didn't listen.

Hashimoto yelled at him and Rocky to get back into their truck, but they scrambled onto the hood to see better, the metal thundering under them.

James sat on the sidewalk with a deputy asking him, loud enough for them to hear, "Nothing else crazy, right?" The deputy's hands frisked over James' body. "No other gun or knife?" James didn't look up at Marshall or even at the deputy.

"James!" Marshall yelled. "We're here." He leapt down from the hood.

A deputy seized him. "Get into the car! Before you get hurt."

Right in front of Marshall, straining toward James, his dad struggled to escape from the two uniforms. "He's my son! That's my boy!" The two men forced him to his knees. "Sir, put your hands behind your back," one of them ordered. His dad struggled to rise. They pushed him back to his knees, wrenched his arms back, and cuffed him.

"Dad!" he screamed. He wanted to run to him and to James, but Hashimoto grabbed him by the shoulder, guided him to the nearest patrol car and into the back seat. Somehow Rocky was already there. Hashimoto cracked the window, so they could have air. There was no escape. No door handle.

Water sheeted down the window. Marshall pressed close to the small opening. Rocky scooted across the hard plastic, squishing against him so he could peer over his shoulder.

His dad shrugged at the officers and put a foot forward to stand up.

The deputy who had cuffed him pushed him again. "Down!"

While his father was on his knees, the other deputy said in a "good cop" voice. "We have to secure the scene. We have a fatality here." He continued calmly. "The sooner we sort this mess out, the sooner you can be with your son."

Officers and deputies surrounding the scene had weapons drawn, not just handguns, but assault rifles. So much adrenaline spurted through Marshall that he thought he might puke again. *A fatality! Someone is dead!* He screamed through the crack in the window, "Listen to him, Daddy!"

The circle of bodies opened a bit. Inside it, his brother stared at smashed leaves on the sidewalk. James looked so lifeless, Marshall wondered if he had been shot, too. But beside James, a girl lay on the sidewalk, her back propped against a retaining wall, the side of her gray hoodie splattered with blood. But she wasn't dead. She was whimpering like a wounded animal, "My baby. My *princesa*."

Rocky crushed against him. "Oh my God, dude. I know her."

A baby's dead? Marshall's head swam. A female highway patrol officer rose from beside the girl, and a paramedic squatted down, uncapping a syringe. He couldn't see a baby, but a little blanket rested behind another paramedic who was bent over and turned away from Marshall, facing the house. Past the retaining wall, fence, and lawn, a middle-aged couple stood on a protected porch, clutching each other. A deputy beside them took notes.

Law enforcement officers, guns drawn, expanded outward. Far up the block, past the sideways patrol cars, where two cops were unspooling crime scene tape, a cluster of people gathered under umbrellas.

A gurney with the girl on it rushed by Marshall. A tiny pink bootie loosened from the back of one of the paramedic's boots and lay crushed in the street. A male officer used a gloved hand to pick it up and turned abruptly. Marshall choked a sob. His brother had killed a baby? It had to be an accident.

A deputy hoisted James to his feet. James' wrists were cuffed. His head lolled like he was drunk. His legs collapsed like those of a blow-up Gumby who'd lost air. The deputy kept him upright.

Marshall shouted through the cracked window. "I'm sorry! James, I'm sorry." James didn't turn. Frantically he scanned the scene for his father, but he had disappeared.

He twisted toward Rocky. "This is your fault!"

Rocky bowed his head into both hands, then collapsed face down on the hard seat. "Oh my God."

Marshall lifted a fist to hit him, but Rocky's back rose and fell as he cried, and Marshall's hand landed open and gentle on his friend's spine. Rocky's breath waved in and out, like a wash of sorrow, the saddest song in the world.

Chapter Forty: Aftermath

SATURDAY - early evening

"What's going on, Vivi?" Ben resettled on the kitchen stool across from her; his forehead wrinkled, the dark eyes intent on hers. She swallowed. No one could be more loyal, more protective, than Ben. He loved her completely. "Winn, my yoga teacher, is offering a retreat. I want to go."

Ben sucked in a breath. Then his body relaxed as though relieved that was all. "When is the retreat?"

"In one week."

"That's impossible." He waved his hand toward the hole in the door. "What about this? What about the trial?" He stood and paced.

"The ADA assured us a trial was unlikely, that a plea deal was being worked out."

"A police buddy from the gym told me guys like Dwayne don't take plea deals. They go for the trial."

"The retreat is in Sayulita."

"Mexico! You think you're going to Mexico? In one week? You can't even get a ticket now."

"We'll see." She walked toward the office.

Ben bustled in front of her. "I'm so much better at figuring out travel stuff."

He was. He had bookmarks for airline and travel sites and within minutes found a flight to Puerto Vallarta.

Outside, a hummingbird glinted through a slice of light in the cloudy dusk. It lit on its branch. She leaned over Ben, nuzzling the side of his face. After a moment of silence, she said, "The universe is saying I ought to go."

"You're a key witness, Vivi."

She snapped straight, hands flying out. "So, my life is supposed to revolve around a trial that we don't even know is going to happen?"

Ben's face flushed. "This trip is more important to you than getting the shithead who tried to kill me?"

She squeezed her eyes shut, weary to the core. These last few months had been too much—unexpected retirement, her mother's death, two burglaries. When she opened her eyes, the hummingbird took flight. Its little heart pounded over a thousand times a minute so he could flit about in constant search of fuel. People admired his grace, but it required an endless, circular, supreme effort. Nothing was easy.

"I'll call Cheryl," she said, "and tell her that if there's going to be a trial, I won't be available that week. I got the impression the court constantly rearranges its calendar based on people's schedules."

Ben looked back at the screen. "This fare is not nothing. And how much is the retreat?"

"I have a secret stash of money—five hundred forty-three dollars and forty-seven cents—that I want to get rid of."

She backed up a bit as Ben swung around in the chair. "A *secret* stash?"

"It's a long story. I'll tell you when we go for our walk." *When we're both moving in the same direction.*

"I don't have any secrets from you."

"This goes way back to before I met you." And it stretched back, even farther than the rape, to her childhood, when to ward off the feeling of being left out by her father and brothers, she'd constructed the myth she didn't care if she was included. She'd excluded them right back, held her secret close, her own little pearl.

Ben was clicking on a computer page to book the flight. A wave of tenderness flooded her. If she only managed to ask for something, Ben might grouse, but in the end, he supported her. But she'd been brought up in a family with nothing to give and had developed a habit of not asking.

Ben looked up from the online form. "When's your birthday?" he asked, teasing.

She ruffled his dark curls.

"I don't want you to go to this retreat, but if you have to…." Ben lifted a sad-clown face toward her.

"Maybe you should take a trip, too."

He shook his head. "Someone has to hold down the fort."

"We could have the alarm system by then."

"Where would I go?"

"Santa Barbara?"

"That would be too much for Art," he said. "And his wife."

"You wouldn't have to stay with them. Treat yourself to a nice hotel. Eat at a fine restaurant," she said, meaning the one Art managed.

He didn't dismiss the idea outright, a hopeful sign.

"I need to start smaller," he said. "Maybe FaceTime?"

"That's a great idea."

The shrill of the telephone made her heart jump. She snatched up the phone. Assistant District Attorney Cheryl Smith, calling on a Saturday. Vivi didn't want the *Ganesha* energy of another obstacle. Why was the damned elephant deity so popular, anyway?

"Did you hear we were burglarized again?" she asked, guessing at the ADA's motive for calling.

"Are you and Ben okay?" Cheryl sounded surprised.

"Yes. Fine. They arrested the person—the girl on the bike I saw at our first burglary. Jessika Fitzgerald."

"Interestinger and interestinger."

Cheryl had obviously called about another matter. Vivi hazarded another guess. "Did you reach a deal?" Ben pressed near so he could hear.

"We were very close, but all that is up in the air now with our latest developments."

"What happened with the plea deal?"

"Don't worry about that. This is better news."

Ben reached for the handset, but she held on to it. "I'm putting you on speakerphone."

"Good," Cheryl said. "First, remember that drink cup the officer found near the Carmona burglary? On the retaining wall?"

"Tell me they got DNA results," Ben said.

"Yup." The lawyer sounded gleeful. "A known local. Ricardo Ballesteros. Goes by Rico."

"So maybe he'll flip?" Ben asked.

"Or maybe his arrest will incentivize Dwayne. But there's more." Cheryl's voice pitched toward the exuberance of an infomercial. "We have a lead on the gun."

"You found it?" Ben asked.

"Maybe." The guarded answer danced a victory lap. "There was a shooting today. A gun was retrieved from the scene. Its serial number matched that of a handgun taken in a burglary several months ago. Owner one Eileen Fitzgerald."

"Dwayne was the burglar?" Ben asked.

"*Fitzgerald?* Same as the girl Jessika?" Vivi's mind raced.

"The address of that burglary was off Scenic Drive—Dwayne's bus route." Smug satisfaction honeyed the attorney's voice.

"But the shooting?" Vivi prompted. "How did the gun end up there?"

"The brother of the kid involved in the shooting said he found it."

"A kid?" Her heart felt like a hunk of lead. "The shooting involved a kid?"

The lawyer didn't seem to hear. "Deputy Hashimoto reported that the brother of the shooter and his friend say they got it out of a dumpster. Guess where?"

An ocean swell, a whoosh, filled Vivi. *A child. A gun. A shooting.*

Chapter Forty-One: Epiphany

SUNDAY - morning

On the way to the church, Dwayne scanned the road. Sun lit up the two narrow lanes, everything bright after yesterday's rain. Three other dressed-up inmates rode in the van with him, all silent. Dwayne's shirt pinched under his armpits, which were sweating because he didn't have any deodorant.

"Beggars can't be choosers," Melissa had told him as he slid the hangers on the single rack of clothes. River House had a limited supply of donated items for people like him with no civvies except what they'd been arrested in.

Two of the guys in the van looked old enough to die—stringy hair, teeth missing from drug use, their skin crusty from living outdoors, wearing freebies like him. But the third one was duded up in a nice suit like he'd been arrested for cheating on his taxes. None of them were cuffed. He could understand why Melissa had chosen the other three for the field trip, but why him? Must've won a lottery. He'd lobbied to go, but seriously?

He chewed the side of a finger. Not a word from Espie. He was glad to be away from River House with a group where none of them looked like a possible enforcer for Buster.

Melissa sat up front with the correctional officer, an old guy who probably couldn't run fifty yards. Probably hadn't drawn his handgun since training.

That was all good. But through the dividing screen, out through the front window, stretched fields, flat open country, muddy from rain. He chewed his finger, working his teeth up to a hangnail.

Maybe he didn't need to run. If Espie got the gun from those kids, things could be cool. They'd get some money for Buster, and the guy he'd burglarized could scream all he wanted, they wouldn't be able to prove the gun at trial. But that all rested on a big "if." And while a trial presented the possibility he'd get off, it also meant he could get a heavy sentence.

On the other hand, the plea agreement meant six years, straight up.

The bare landscape stretched glumly before him. Six years, if Buster didn't have someone stick him before he shipped out to San Quentin.

The seat bounced him as the bus traveled the rough road. Right now, he had no idea how things would go. He hadn't heard about the gun, about the money, about anything.

When his brother Wesley had rabbited, a friend had been waiting in a car. It had been a dope escape except for holing up at the friend's crib. They got picked up two hours later.

The church, in the distance, rose into view—a small white building with a steeple. There wasn't going to be any big crowd. He looked back over the open stretch of land.

He wouldn't make Wesley's mistake, although he understood why his brother had made it. The thought of going to his grammy's retirement apartment or sneaking into Espie's room tugged with a force like gravity. It was like a person had a built-in Navi system programmed to Go Home. But if he even made it as far as town, he couldn't go to any place resembling home, not to Espie's aunt's house, his grammy's apartment, or his mom's dumpy garage unit. He'd check out the homeless encampments. Anonymous places. Miserable, damp places. Without a blanket or even a dollar bill and only one way to get stuff.

He rocked against one of the junkie inmates. The man stared down at hands cupped in his lap. He showed no reaction to their shoulders colliding.

When Wesley made his escape, he must have been about eighteen, his age now. Wesley had chillaxed afterward. Ordering pizza. The Round Table pizza with four meats, no doubt. His mouth watered.

The van entered the church parking lot. Old dented American cars and two big, dirty trucks sat in the lot. They could provide some cover.

The families heading toward the double doors looked like migrants. What had he expected? Of course it would be a church that worked with the down-and-out. The kind of place that held Nar-Anon meetings. A church that welcomed outlaws at its service.

They pulled up near the entrance. A family climbed the concrete steps. The father in a flapping overcoat stopped and squinted at the van. His wife, bundled in a colorful sweater, waited on the landing and turned to see why her husband wasn't following her. One by one, three boys, their hair wetly combed, and all of them in black pants and white shirts, followed suit. It was like watching dominoes fall, oldest to youngest, like Wesley and him. He'd followed Wesley's lead for what seemed like his whole fucked-up life.

The officer and Melissa climbed out of the van, Melissa's face rigid. In her black slacks and practical shoes, she might be more of a threat than the correctional officer. The two of them disappeared from Dwayne's line of sight. His body tensed. If he bolted, would any of the other inmates take off with him? The druggies weren't sprinting anywhere, and Mr. Corporate had no need to run.

Watching the van, the father guided his family into the church, one hand on the youngest boy's head, the other on the woman's back. A twinge of a lost feeling ran through Dwayne and lodged in his throat.

The van door slid open with a bang. Melissa stood there, her body positioned to block a dash down the sidewalk toward the fields. The officer had probably taken up a position behind her, near the back of the van, ready for trouble.

Dwayne flicked his hand at the other inmates. "Age before beauty." His pulse accelerated.

The ancient addicts stumbled out, the second one unsteady, dropping to one knee. Melissa stayed on guard, not reaching to help him.

"Single file alongside the van," she snapped.

Inside the van, the man in the suit hesitated. He smirked at Dwayne. "The Lord worketh in mysterious ways." He ducked through the opening and stepped down.

"All right, Dwayne." Melissa sounded bitchy.

Stooped over, he moved to the van's doorway. The three inmates were lined up like grade school kids. Below him, Melissa's ice-blue eyes watched. She would be in front of him. The van behind him. The row of inmates beside him. The guard on the other side—old, but standing erect, with a no-nonsense vibe. Once he stepped down, he'd be caged in.

The sun shone, but to the north rain clouds bruised the sky. Wind whipped up into his face as he scanned the flat exposed countryside.

As a fifteen-year-old kid, he'd considered Wesley's rabbit parole epic. Wesley had laughed about it and bragged like he'd scored a Super Bowl touchdown.

Framed in the van's doorway, Dwayne faced a solitary bare tree. He rubbed at his goatee. Seriously, though, Wesley had made a bonehead move.

"Don't even think about it." Melissa brushed back her blazer to reveal a shoulder holster.

He snorted. "That's not very Christian." He mimicked the words and tone of Steverson at the county jail.

"God proposes, man disposes," she said.

"You think a gun makes you God?" He hopped down and took his place in line. The van door slammed behind him.

"That's rich," Melissa said, "coming from you."

He took a final survey of the barren, muddy fields and followed the others toward the church door. Melissa and her gun loomed a short distance behind him. Why hadn't Espie gotten in touch with him or deposited some money? But he knew the answer, had known the answer before he'd sent her on the mission. *Because she's unreliable.*

He mounted the church steps, each one compressing his decision. It rode heavy on his back like a monkey. At least he'd kept his mouth shut about his escape plan. No one could razz him for not following through. He grunted. He'd be going into prison when Wesley was getting out.

In the warmth of the entranceway, a little girl handed him a program. A lacy white dress left her skinny arms exposed, and goose bumps dotted her flesh. Tied back with lavender ribbons, long hair as dark as Tanisha's sprang down her back. She had big black eyes like his baby girl. "Welcome to the All Ne-nom-a-tion-al Church." The girl smiled, showing off missing front teeth.

He smiled back. Damn, she was cute.

At the back of the church, he slid into a pew with the three inmates. The guard and Melissa sandwiched them.

The little girl skipped up the aisle, her white dress flouncing. She snuggled into a seat against her father. He draped an arm around her and pulled her closer. Maybe when Tanisha got older, she'd be an angel like that. When he got out of prison, he could be that father, with a little girl happy against his side.

Warmth spread through his center like melted chocolate. The cross and altar shimmered. He blinked his eyes and shook his head. "Don't be a pussy," Wesley's voice said.

The girl twisted in her pew, stared at him, and grinned, all the love and happiness in the whole world right there between her two missing teeth.

Chapter Forty-Two: All Over Again

MONDAY - late morning

Cars and trucks filled every space in the parking lot at Baker's Guns. Eileen Fitzgerald got her Miata turned around and drove out to the street. If you wanted knowledgeable help and a decent selection, Baker's Guns was the place to come, even if it was located in a sketchy neighborhood. She squeezed into a spot at the curb.

Gun retorts popped. The store did what it could to muffle them, but the noise penetrated the walls of the enclosed gallery.

Eileen remained in her leather seat, glancing up and down the short street. It was packed with vehicles, and she felt lucky to have found a spot. No one seemed deterred by the two guys who'd been robbed. If gangsters did cruise the area, they wouldn't pick her as a target, anyway. With their machismo, they'd expect her to have a puny revolver, not worth the trouble.

Still, when Eileen got out of the car, she hustled for the store's entrance, the ends of her untied raincoat sash flying behind her.

Pop. Pause. *Pop.* One gun, then a moment later, another answering. Inside the store, through the big bulletproof windows behind the counter, shooters aimed at their suspended targets. With their ear protectors, their backs intent and posed, the men looked like science fiction creatures.

Eileen inhaled deeply. She liked the smell of this place—the oil and gunpowder. Forget musk; *this* was a manly scent. If single guys should go to Whole Foods to meet women, single women should come here to meet

232

guys.

The owner stood across the room in the back with a bald man. The man's voice rose in anger. "You should be responsible!"

Eileen's gaze remained on the confrontation. The owner had helped Eileen in the past. She'd checked out his left hand, but like all the good ones, he was taken. The bald man looked like an asshole, poking a finger at the owner's chest. The owner waved the big guy toward his office, but the man wouldn't budge.

She meandered over to a glass display of Glocks to let the salesman know she was looking, that she had not come to admire the mounted animal-head decor. Near her, two guys took down an assault rifle from the wall racks. They talked softly in Spanish. She moved over to a glass case of handguns in the middle of the room. The only other woman in the place was pulling a magazine from a semi-automatic.

"Ten rounds?" The woman arched a penciled brow.

"This is California," the salesman said.

Up close, Eileen could tell the woman's hair was dyed black, like her daughter Jessica's—a harsh look. The woman had crow's feet and sun-damaged skin. Tattoos covering her arms disappeared under a Rolling Stones tank top and reappeared as snips of color above the neckline. How could she not be freezing? She was the kind of woman Eileen imagined usually shopped at Baker's—not a woman like her dressed in slacks and pearls.

The woman swiped aside her black leather jacket lying on the case so Eileen could view the merchandise, but the angry voice at the back of the store pulled Eileen's attention from the display.

"You are liable!" The bald man knocked away the arm, trying to sweep him into the office.

The woman and the clerk swiveled toward the argument, too. The clerk pulled a cell phone from his pocket and held it in the air. "Boss?" he asked.

"Not yet." The owner's focus remained on the heavy-set man in front of him. "Listen, Al," he said, "you were parked on the street. Public property. If you had parked in our lot...we have security cameras back there and make routine sweeps." The owner crossed his arms tightly over his black polo shirt. "Never had any problem."

Eileen strode to the front window and glanced anxiously at her car on the street. The two men who'd been admiring the assault rifles sauntered out the back exit. She considered moving her car into the space they'd vacate.

This man, Al, must have been one of the guys who got robbed. She'd seen the headline but had barely skimmed the article.

The street looked quiet. And what were the chances of the same crime happening twice? Eileen strolled back to the counter. In the back of the room, the owner tried to lay a hand on Al's shoulder.

Al shrugged away. His face flushed all the way up and over his bald crown. "That boy's arm will never be the same. He's a musician. How's he supposed to make a living with a bad arm?"

"It's a police matter." The owner's voice held a sincere tone of sympathy.

"They're not doing jack," Al said.

"What a surprise," the raven-haired woman muttered.

Eileen disregarded the comment. The police who'd responded to her burglary had been professional enough. They had not sugarcoated the situation, informing her straight up that once the burglar left the premises, there wasn't much chance he'd be caught. It had taken her a week to mention Jessica, even though her daughter had been stealing from her since age fifteen and had just broken into the garage while she was gone for Thanksgiving. God knows which of her low-life friends Jessica might have brought with her. Thank God nothing important was missing.

Eileen perused the guns under the glass, but the argument in the back was hard to ignore.

The man behind the counter gave Eileen a curious once over. The other woman resumed what she'd been doing, snapping the magazine back into place and asking, "So even though you sell this handgun as ten rounds, it will hold a larger capacity?"

"Yes. We just can't sell you one."

She smirked, arched an eyebrow at Eileen, and handed the gun back to the salesman. She rapped on the top of the glass. "Are all of these guns used?"

"We say 'pre-owned'—maybe used, maybe not." The clerk smiled. He had a smooth face—a little bland for Eileen's taste—but a fit body packed into outdoorsman clothes.

The woman nodded knowingly. Her dark eyes shifted toward Eileen. "Want me to help you out, hon?"

Eileen stiffened, taken aback, but then said, "That would be great. I need protection. Woman living alone, you know, and my house was broken into."

"Nobody's gonna break into my place." The woman chipped at dark blue polish on her fingernail, then tapped the glass again. "Let's see this six-shooter." Her eyes cut toward Eileen, and Eileen nodded.

"Name's Squirt," she said.

Eileen tried to maintain a neutral face and introduced herself.

The clerk lifted a Smith & Wesson from the cabinet and snapped open the chamber. "This model actually takes five bullets."

The owner of the store breezed behind them, ushering the bald man toward the front door. "Al, I'm truly sorry about what happened," he said. "It must be frustrating. I'm with you; I don't know how the police could be so clueless when the incident happened in broad daylight. They even have a description of the car."

"Makes you wonder if they're trying." Al shook his head. With his anger dissipated, sadness hung on him like a blanket.

Squirt, the salesman, and Eileen watched the owner and Al move to the door. When they both exited, Eileen sighed in relief.

"What's that about?" Squirt asked, as if hoping to pick up a juicy bit of gossip.

The sales clerk shrugged. "Out on the street, some thugs tried to jack Al's guns."

"Why didn't Al just shoot them?"

"He and the guy who got shot—his son-in-law, I think—had their firearms locked in the back of their truck."

Squirt snorted. "That there was a mistake. Somebody comes for me, they're dead meat."

The clerk cleared his throat. He extended the Smith & Wesson to Eileen.

Eileen gripped the gun to gauge its heft. "This is sort of what I'm after."

Cold air gusted through the front door. The owner slid behind the display to wait on Eileen, and the clerk edged closer to Squirt.

The owner's hazel eyes softened as they moved to Eileen, the display case light catching the green in his irises. "How does that feel?" His voice was brisk, upbeat, getting back to business.

"Maybe a little bigger than I want. I have small hands." She rested the handgun on the glass and extended her soft palm so he could see its size.

"The smaller the gun," he cautioned, "the bigger the kick."

Snickering, Squirt turned toward them, holding a cannon. "Size matters."

Eileen angled away from her and studied the handguns on display. "I'm looking for something to replace my pistol," she said. "It was stolen in a burglary."

Chapter Forty-Three: Inside

MONDAY - late morning

"Good morning." Attorney Shawna Morrison's voice didn't sound like there was anything good about it. She seated herself across from Dwayne. She didn't bother putting her briefcase on the table.

Dwayne changed his mind about Morrison's eyes. They didn't look like black dimes; they looked like dark tunnels you could crawl through and never find any light at the end.

"They have the gun," she said.

"What?" He lowered his eyelids to cover his panic. Thoughts skittered. He should've run when he had the chance, should've taken off across that muddy field.

Morrison tugged her blazer, ironing out a tiny wrinkle over her white shirt. "My advice, as your legal counsel, is to try to get the same plea agreement, relying on the fact no one wants to tie up resources in a lengthy trial."

He stopped moving. San Quentin would be nothing like kicking it here in River House. "The gun doesn't have any prints," he blurted.

The lawyer lifted her eyebrows. "None of yours. That's correct."

He realized his mistake and leaned back, arms tight over his chest. His heart was jumping. "It's circumstantial evidence."

Morrison cleared her throat. "There are people on Death Row because of *circumstantial evidence*."

"How do they know it's the gun?"

"Stolen in October from an address near Scenic." The black eyes drilled him.

She checked her watch.

"How'd they get it?" he asked.

"It was used in a fatal shooting."

He shot upright. "Who was killed?" His heart felt like it could vault over his arms. "A girl?"

The attorney kept her eyes leveled at him like gun barrels. "A young woman was injured. An Esperanza Mendoza. Know her?"

Dizziness made his head woozy. No wonder he hadn't heard from Espie. "If she was *injured*," he croaked, "who was killed?"

"This is the reason we *cannot* go to trial." The attorney bit off each word and kept her eyes locked on him. "Before, we might have been able to create some uncertainty about the weapon. But now." She sliced a hand across the air. "Public sentiment will be against you, too. It couldn't be worse."

He cut through the jumble of her words: "Who died?"

"A baby."

"A baby?" He collapsed back into the metal chair. "Like whose baby?"

"The young woman's baby."

His baby. Tanisha.

"Are you okay?" the attorney asked. "Should I call an officer?"

"Take the deal." The words came out strangled.

"Agreement," she said. "Not deal."

Tears pooled in his eyes. He whipped his head away. "I'll take the deal." *Tanisha.* Nothing in his life had ever gone right.

He stood up, his head swimming. Grammy Rice's voice said, "Take responsibility." Wes's voice reverbed even louder. *Man up.*

"There's nothing left for me here," he said. The statement came out hard and cold, and he felt proud for holding it together.

Chapter Forty-Four: On the Mat

MONDAY - late morning

Seated in full lotus, Vivi let her eyelids lower. Every time she became quiet, the shooting haunted her. It didn't involve just a kid. A baby had been killed.

What if's attacked her, arrows flying up from her core. *What if they'd come home five minutes later from the grocery store? What if Ben had not chased the thief?* She knew from her brother's death that this assault of guilt had an endless supply of ammunition. *What if her brother had worn his neon vest? What if he'd been an inch to the left? An inch to the right?*

What if she'd left the quaalude in the photographer's fleshy palm?

What if there'd been no gun? A different narrative.

Winn was prattling away. "Today I'd like to share the story of Krishna, a beautiful god with a blue body and long-flowing black hair adorned with a peacock feather. Now, you don't have to believe in these deities," he said lightly. "I interpret them as archetypal representations of the energies we embody."

Archetypal representations? Her eyes sprang open. Winn shimmered like a deity himself, in a turquoise tank-top, long limbs tanned.

He looked at her. She hastily closed her eyes, squeezing a tear from below her lashes. It trickled down her cheek.

Once Winn's single word *awesomeness* had chased away her lust. Now the words *archetypal representations* dangled before her like a rope. She could grab it and swing to safety on the chest-thumping power of such words.

But was Ben right? Was it meaningless to say *unsheltered* rather than *homeless*? Did words alter a single fact? Wasn't that Shakespeare's point with *a rose by any other name*?

Yet, yoga argued—Winn argued—that if you changed the words, the narrative, you changed yourself and in turn, the world.

"When Krishna was a little boy," Winn was saying, "he was naughty. One day, his older brothers went to pick fruit. Krishna was supposed to stay home, but he followed them."

The floor under Vivi's mat pressed into her buttocks, but the high windows allowed in fresh Playa Maria air and a rattle of palm fronds. Why was Winn talking about Krishna being naughty?

She shook her head. Even if they were both headed to Mexico in a week, she was married, and Winn knew it. But hadn't he once flashed those dimples and said, "I'm a yoga teacher. Not a saint."

"Krishna's brothers climbed the trees to pick the ripest, juiciest fruit and told their little brother not to eat it until they were home where the harvest could be equally divided," Winn said. "But Krishna loved this fruit, and his hands twirled like a helicopter propeller picking it up and stuffing it into his mouth."

Vivi envisioned cherries, her mouth watering. But little Krishna reminded her of Dwayne—taking, disregarding others' efforts, not caring what was fair.

But what was fair? Had life been fair to him with a murdered father, a negligent mother, and a criminal brother?

"When his brothers saw what Krishna had done," Winn continued, "they called their mother to punish him. She came and demanded that Krishna open his mouth.

"But Krishna's mouth was packed with fruit and dirt; he couldn't speak. Finally, he mumbled, 'Do you really want to look?'

"When his mother insisted, Krishna opened wide, and his mother peered down his throat. Inside Krishna, was not just fruit, but the mother staring down Krishna's throat, and Krishna and her, again and again, and the mud, and all earth, and beyond that the stars and the whole universe."

Winn stopped talking.

That's it? Vivi peeked from below her lowered lids. His eyes were closed now, his hands in Anjali mudra. *What archetypal energy is that?*

Lotus pose hiked his shorts along his inner thighs. Vivi averted her eyes and spied on the other members of the class, sitting serenely, seemingly unperturbed by Winn or their thoughts. She tried to tap into their peacefulness, their communal breath, but instead dove into a collective pool of sadness. Another tear drizzled down her cheek.

If she looked inside Dwayne, she wondered, would she, like Krishna's mother, gaze at herself, and the woman from whom he'd stolen the gun, and the child who had used it, and the dead baby—the one she and Ben had, in horror, read about—and then Dwayne, and herself, and the woman, and the child, and the dead baby, all connected and repeated into infinity?

"Let's open our practice with the universal sound of *om*."

Winn led the first chant with the ancient three sounds—aaaaahh, oooooo, mmmmmm. The past, the present, the future.

Vivi's spirit rode the vibration. It took her to Dwayne and Ben and Big Al and Jessika—through the earthly events of the last few weeks—out into gossamer purple haze, past the sun and moon. Out where her own sweet mother swirled as molecules through the cosmos. Riding the magic carpet of the word *om*, she ventured into morning.

A Note from the Author

Several years ago, my husband and I interrupted a burglar in our home. Screaming for help, my husband chased the young man down the street while I frantically dialed 9-1-1. The thief stopped, pulled a gun, and aimed it at my husband's head.

This real-life event provided the seed for this novel. The thief ditched the handgun, which was never recovered. I wanted to explore what could have happened to the gun and how lives could have been altered as a result. I had no intention of delving into issues of race. However, the burglar in our house was African American. I considered making the thief in my story white, avoiding pushback, and ducking any discussion of race and social justice. But something about that choice seemed cowardly back when I started the book (several years ago) and seems cowardly now.

After the burglar's arrest, preliminary hearing, and trial, my husband and I were able to read the pre-sentencing report. I drew on this information to create Dwayne Williams, my fictional character, trying to make him more sympathetic and certainly less damaged and dangerous than the real person in our house.

I hired a sensitivity reader to help me avoid the pitfall of stereotyping. If Dwayne still reads as a stereotype, the fault lies in my lack of imagination or perhaps in our collective, oversimplified view of young male African Americans.

Acknowledgements

As much as we envision the writer alone, plugging away in solitude, no book arrives to the reader's hands without assists. In my case, there are so many that I fear leaving out people who deserve my gratitude. First, there's my husband, Daniel Friedman, for making the space for me to write, reading over drafts, and giving me brutally honest feedback. Many thanks to Steve Fabian, Esq. for indispensable help with legal tidbits and to Sergeant Adam Plantinga of the San Francisco PD for thoughtfully answering my crime-scene questions. I recommend his two non-fiction books, 400 Things Cops Know and Police Craft, to anyone who wants engaging reads about the nature of police work. Props to my sensitivity reader, Jennifer Younger, for her candid and kind reading of One Gun. And many thanks to Edgar-nominated author, Susan Bickford, for stepping up, early on, to blurb the book, and to Anthony, Barry and Macavity-winning author James Ziskin for eloquently taking on the task. My Drop-In Writing friend, the Agatha Award winning G.M. Malliet, voluntarily endorsed the book, and fellow Santa Cruz writer, Peggy Townsend added her accolades. I fully appreciate the value of time. Thank you all for giving yours to me. Hats off to my Capitola Book Café critique group and my Guppies critique group, especially Elizabeth Mayes, and my beta readers who gave so generously of their time: Margie Bunting, Lynda West Scott, and Debra Roberts. A deep bow of gratitude to Mary Feliz, who voluntarily read the book when I was ready to pitch it into the flames, and gave suggestions on ways to salvage it. And finally, thank you to Level Best Books and editor Shawn Reilly Simmons, who almost brought me to tears with the simple statement, "You are a very good writer."

Now my book travels into the world where a whole new set of people deserve acknowledgment—the librarians and booksellers who deliver it to your hands, readers who finish the creative process in their imaginations, and fans who pass along the book to someone else. Thank you all!

Crime Writer - Chapter One

Please enjoy this preview of the upcoming novel *CRIME WRITER* by Vinnie Hansen

Day 1 – early evening

Heat from the Mobile Data Transmitter radiated onto Zoey Kozinski's arm. The interior of the patrol car cooked, muggy and close. September brought the hottest weather to the central coast of California, anxiety about fires growing as the oak leaves curled and undergrowth crisped. Thankfully, Officer Austin kept the windows of the patrol car open even as the sun started to set.

"Must be boiling with your vest."

"Better to sweat than bleed." Austin's profile was sharp angles, pointed nose, strong chin.

"How much does that thing weigh?" Zoey already knew, but the officer didn't seem talkative. She needed to crack the façade and dig out some grist to apply to Officer Horne, the character in her book. Her stalled, barely-started book.

"Six pounds."

Officer Austin rolled along Scenic Drive, a main thoroughfare through Playa Maria County. Zoey wished they could listen to music, something to go with driving on a sultry evening, maybe Ella Fitzgerald's "Summertime." Instead, the radio spat information, filling awkward silence. Zoey jotted down that a list of stolen cars was tucked on the left side of his dash. She'd chosen a night shift, hoping for a modicum of action, but nothing on the radio stirred Austin's interest.

"How do you feel about ride-alongs?" She flipped her legal pad, and the printed-out opening pages of her manuscript winged to the floor. All two of them. A whopping three hundred ten words. She bent down to retrieve them.

"It's part of our Community Policing." Austin kept his focus forward. "To increase civilian awareness of what police work entails."

She didn't bother to write down the canned response.

Austin must be a rookie to receive the crappy assignment of hauling a ride-along, but he didn't look like one. Silver highlighted his short hair. Older than her fictional Officer Horne. Her protagonist Horne should be young, freshly free of his training wheels, a more credible character to rush toward a terrible mistake after witnessing the shooting of a fellow officer.

In the margin of the legal pad, she scribbled: *A hot-head. Temper-hubris. Too eager to prove himself?*

Then she wrote *Stan* and put a question mark after it. The name of the murdered officer in her manuscript had appeared in a magician's puff of smoke, typed by her fingers before she was conscious of a choice. Not a common name for guys of her generation, the lost kids born between Generation X and the Millennials. The name had merit—easy to pronounce, but not overly used. Why had it popped into her head?

She slipped her pen through her tangle of red hair and scratched her scalp.

Austin shot her a glance, maybe thinking she didn't know she was using the ink end.

"Writing off the top of your head?"

She smiled slightly. *Witty for a police officer.*

He quirked a brow. "Making headlines?" His tone was dry. No smile. Was he being funny or busting her balls?

Zoey tapped the legal pad. Her next question wasn't on it, but Austin's age and his quips begged for it.

"What did you do before becoming a law enforcement officer?"

Long fingers curled around the wheel, maneuvering the vehicle through the rush-hour clog of Scenic Drive. He scanned the lanes of traffic and sidewalks long enough that she thought he wasn't going to answer.

"I was a teacher."

"Really?" Her voice squeaked with unveiled surprise. Heat rose up her face. With her coloring, there was no playing off a blush. When she was a kid, her Grosse Point classmates had pinned her with the nickname Tomato.

"High-school history." In the parking lot, he'd offered a firm handshake and introduced himself formally as Officer Austin, although he'd added with a trace of humor 'at your service.' Over six feet with ropy muscles, he was a bit old for her, maybe forty-five, but a hottie, nonetheless.

"That's a strange career trajectory."

"Not really. In both jobs, you deal with a lot of young punks."

As part of the outreach program, he probably was not supposed to refer to members of the community as *punks*. She was making progress.

"In policing, I bet you have more flexibility about how you deal with *punks*?"

His lip curled, but he didn't respond.

"So why the career move?"

"In teaching, the more you work, the less you're paid," he said. "Police work offers time-and-a-half for overtime. Ten-hour shifts and four-day work weeks. More money and time for my family."

"Kids?"

"Three."

She felt a twinge of disappointment. Her sex life had been reduced to her Magic Wand, and Austin wasn't wearing a wedding ring, so a bit of fantasy had slipped under her normally guarded door. Since she didn't want a *relationship*, a hot cop could be the ticket. *Married* killed that idea.

And three kids! With the world's exploding population and global climate change, that was self-indulgent. One of her least favorite character flaws—in reality. In fiction, it was a great character flaw.

"My wife's the one who should have made the career move to cop," Austin volunteered. "She's a tiger. Can outshoot me." He waggled his head in admiration.

Another twinge. She had a serious weakness for men who complimented women in absentia.

Zoey touched the cool metal of the AR-15 propped in front of the passenger seat. "This is some serious firepower."

The creases in his uniform lifted infinitesimally, a hint of a shrug. "You should see what they have on the street."

She ran her finger down her list of questions. Nothing so far had gotten the juices flowing. "What kind of handgun do you carry?"

"Smith & Wesson. Officers with more seniority get Berettas. The most senior officers have Glocks." Jealousy tinged his voice. "But if you want a better gun, you can buy one. I'm looking at a Glock."

The crackling voice of dispatch relayed a report of a middle-aged black male dealing drugs in Playa Maria Park.

Austin swung off Scenic onto a street that cut along the seedier edge of downtown, where the homeless population dwarfed the number of university students. He slowed at the park.

Dusk had sifted into darkness, but streetlights illuminated the perimeter of the grass. Young men played basketball on a well-lit court. A lone man leaning against a light pole straightened at the cruiser's arrival. Austin put the windows up, parked the car, and plucked a wood baton from the base of his door. "Remain in the vehicle."

Another patrolman pulled up and joined him. She noted details. *Suspect's dreadlocks glisten in bluish light. Tan pants bag around skinny legs.*

Austin questioned the man while the other officer patted him down and dipped into the pockets of his army-fatigue jacket. With the window closed, Zoey sweated.

In the end, the man bumped away and swaggered toward the basketball court.

Talking together, the officers watched him, then turned in the direction of the vehicle. Austin nodded. The other man laughed. They were talking about her. The inside of the cruiser steamed like a sauna. Austin was letting her marinate in a patina of sweat.

Zoey opened the passenger door, which prompted Austin to step toward the cruiser. Before he plopped into his seat, he thunked his baton into its spot.

"I asked the suspect if we could search him, and he said no," he started before Zoey even asked. "But he has a Search Clause." Austin cleaned his hands with foam sanitizer. "That's a bargain he made for probation. He relinquished his right to probable cause."

She scribbled the information. This was good stuff, strengthening her knowledge of the law.

"But you didn't find anything?"

"Maybe he sold out."

Dry humor. Deadpan delivery. Her favorite. To curtail a blush, she cast her eyes to the pocket of his door.

"Don't most officers these days carry whip-batons?"

He gave her a look.

Amazing eyes—way greener than her own. He yanked the baton from its spot and held it across his lap, the top grazing her thigh.

Phallic symbol, for sure. The air inside the car shifted subtly.

"See all those nicks?" he said. "My T.O. gave this to me, said the riff-raff on the street noticed the dents. They're mostly from getting in and out of the car, but hey," he returned the baton to the door pocket, "they don't know that."

He gave his hand a second squirt of the sanitizer. "I tell you one part of this job I don't like. The grime. You'd have to get up close to appreciate how much that guy…how grubby he was." Austin started the car. "Tell you the truth, I'm more afraid of an accidental needle poke than a gunshot."

"Was he dealing?"

"I imagine." Austin put down the windows. Fresh air rushed into the compartment. "He doesn't have any other means of income."

The radio called Austin to roust a panhandler near the entrance to the freeway. *Civilian complaint.* Austin zoomed back up to Scenic. At the intersection before the freeway entrance, he stopped at a red light with the rest of the traffic. The girl panhandling on the median spotted the cruiser, folded her sign, and meandered down the sidewalk.

Austin turned and rolled along the street across from the girl. In spite of a curvaceous figure packed into tight jeans, with her wavy brown hair hitched into pigtails, she looked all of fifteen. The girl ignored them.

Zoey twisted toward Austin. "Are you going to stop?"

"She's not doing anything illegal now. She didn't even jaywalk." He sped up. "We got her off the median."

"Yup. Sure did." He knew, and she knew, that as soon as they were out of sight, the girl would return to her spot.

How do they negotiate spots? She wrote. *First come, first served?*

If she asked Austin about the girl—did he know her—what was her story—she sensed he'd blow off the questions. The police department had picked the wrong officer to give ride-alongs. Austin lacked a gregarious, empathetic personality.

Zoey tried to unpack how she'd arrived at this conclusion. Maybe because he'd chosen policing over teaching. Police work had to be more frustrating than high school teaching, certainly less rewarding.

She shook her head. *Don't assume.* She asked about the girl.

"Espie Gonzales."

"You know her?"

"Yeah." His forefinger tapped the steering wheel a few times. "She lost her baby in that shooting."

"Oh, that's her." Zoey strained to see the girl disappearing into the darkness. Her tragic case had dominated the front page.

"Hell of a way to start this job." Officer Austin looped around the block back to Scenic Drive. Rush hour traffic had thinned. "I was there earlier when they arrested her piece-of-shit boyfriend, too."

She was sure Officer Austin was not supposed to say that. Zoey chewed on her pen and scribbled an idea: *Stan dies b/c he harbors a secret?* She doodled hashtag symbols on her paper.

Maybe Austin recognized zoning-out behavior from all those past students because he volunteered, "As a mystery writer, you're probably looking for something more exciting. Let's see if I can find a car to pull over."

Within two minutes, he pointed out a white sedan. "Burned-out taillight." He unclipped his seatbelt.

"Why are you doing that?"

"Your car is your coffin. Cop training 101. If someone jumps out of a vehicle, you don't want to be fumbling with a seatbelt."

She unlatched her seatbelt, too. He didn't object.

He called in the license plate, citing the letters phonetically. "Old model white sedan. Make unclear. One male." He concluded the call with their location and lit up the patrol car.

The driver continued along Scenic toward the outskirts of town. Austin tapped his air horn. The silhouetted head, wearing a hat, lifted as though checking the rearview.

The dispatcher reported back on the license plate. No red flags.

Austin used the air horn again. But the white sedan tooled along. The number of businesses thinned. Traffic dwindled.

Muscles jumped in Austin's jaw.

Zoey jotted. *Wants authority obeyed!* No wonder high school kids drove him crazy. *Austin like Camille?* Camille, her mother, was a first-class control freak.

He eyed her notepad and frowned. Closing the windows, he put on the siren and left it on, wailing, but this could hardly be called a chase. They were traveling thirty miles per hour.

"Why isn't he pulling over?"

Austin didn't have an answer, at least not one he could utter with her in the vehicle. Finally, he said, "Could be absorbed in his cell phone."

That was not the reason. She was an eagle at spotting drivers using a device and, in this case, the hat would have accentuated any dip of the head. He was not using his phone, and his actions were sure to piss off a cop, especially this cop—an authoritarian personality with an audience to impress. Zoey planted her Keds against the cruiser's floor and stretched her torso, staring at the car ahead, anxiety percolating up her legs.

"His car could be sound baffled." Austin's voice tightened as he offered the flimsy possibility.

Rationalizing. Even if the driver couldn't hear, he could see the cruiser lights. The situation reminded her of the pursuit of the Bronco carrying O.J.

Simpson up the 405. That day in June 1994, she'd come into the house after smoking a Swisher Sweet cigar with her middle school friend Brett. Her mom was fixated on the television.

Ahead of them, the white sedan left Playa Maria proper. Scenic Drive opened onto coastal highway along the Pacific, an empty stretch of dark two-lane highway. The driver put on his blinker. She sighed in relief. The car crunched onto the steeply-graded gravel shoulder.

Austin pulled in behind it. She slouched down in her seat, taking notes on the pad propped against her thighs. Her heart hammered. A routine traffic stop, but it felt off. *Austin pissed.* She drew an anger emoji. And he had not called for back-up.

Too macho? she wrote.

She shrank in her seat as Austin approached the sedan, his hand on his weapon. She scribbled details. The car's window glided open. The man stuck his head out, glancing back.

At the turn of the driver's head, Austin crouched and drew. A gun muzzle appeared out the window opening.

Three pops split the silence.

Austin collapsed onto the asphalt.

Zoey's stomach lurched. The white car roared to life. Its tires spat gravel and squealed onto the pavement, the back end fishtailing. She opened the passenger door, her pulse throbbing in her head, the world awash in swirling blue and red. Her shoes skidded on the gravel. She caught herself by grabbing the door. With the tilt of the car, the door continued to fly open, whirling her toward the drainage ditch.

Regaining her balance, she crept forward, the night so quiet she could hear the distant whoosh of the ocean. Or was the whoosh inside her head?

Officer Austin lay splayed on the edge of the pavement. He'd landed so the exit wound faced her, the back of his head a bloody pulp.

She swallowed bile and recoiled behind the cruiser. There was no way he was alive.

Her body felt floaty, unreal, tethered only by the pain of pebbles under her knee.

A red sportscar passed headed toward town. The driver slowed. Hope surged in her. Help had arrived. She started to rise on wobbly legs.

The car zoomed off, leaving her.

She forced herself to draw a breath but couldn't get it beyond her throat. Austin had been hit close range with something high caliber. Leaving the cruiser door gaping open, she leaned across the seat divider and grabbed the police radio, her hand shaking wildly. She tried another breath, but air kept going in and out in sharp jags.

The radio would be faster than her cell phone, skirting any telecommunicator and going directly to dispatch. Officers in the area would hear the transmission. She wanted someone to come right now.

The radio suddenly squawked to life in her hands. Her heart slammed her chest.

"555 are you 10-4 on your stop?"

Hell no. Nothing was 10-4. She keyed the mic.

Another set of headlights zoomed toward her. Maybe when she'd gotten out, the killer had spotted her and was returning to take care of loose ends. Her whole body shook. Shrinking down, she identified herself to the dispatcher.

"The ride-along?" the suspicious voice snapped. "Where's Officer Austin?"

"He's been shot!"

An intake of air. A tiny pause.

The car in the opposite lane sped by. A white car! Its bright lights were blinding, the driver in too big of a hurry to be bothered with the odd appearance of a lone police vehicle at the side of the road, overhead lights flashing. Or maybe the driver didn't slow down because he already knew what was there.

"Where are you?" the dispatcher's voice steeled into all business.

Zoey wished she had the dispatcher's nerves, hoped she could get through her report before fainting or puking. Sweat slicked her palm. "Edge of town on the coast highway headed north, about a mile past where Officer Austin called in the stop."

"Help is on the way. Stay put."

As though she were going to do what? Run up the deserted, dark highway? The white car that had sped by flipped a U-ey and roared back toward her, skidding to a stop behind the cruiser.

The sedan's lights remained on bright. Her stomach shriveled. A man strolled toward the cruiser.

Maybe she should run.

About the Author

Vinnie Hansen fled the howling winds of the South Dakota prairie and headed for the California coast the day after high school graduation.

She graduated from the University of California, Irvine (BA) and San Francisco State University (MA) writing programs. She's gone on to pen numerous short stories; Lostart Street, a novel of mystery, murder and moonbeams; and the Carol Sabala mystery series. The seventh installment in the series, Black Beans & Venom, made the finalist list for the Claymore Award as did the opening of One Gun.

Still sane after 27 years of teaching high school English, Vinnie has retired and lives in Santa Cruz, California, with her husband and the requisite cat.

You can visit her website at http://vinniehansen.com or find her on Facebook and Goodreads. A button on the website will allow you to sign up for her quarterly newsletter. Each issue comes with a book recommendation and the opportunity to win an autographed copy.

Finally, authors live and die by reviews. Please consider leaving a short, honest comment about One Gun on Amazon, Goodreads, or any other site that accepts reviews. Thank you for reading!

AUTHOR WEBSITE: https://vinniehansen.com/

Also by Vinnie Hansen

The Carol Sabala Mystery Series:
Murder, Honey
One Tough Cookie
Rotten Dates
Squeezed & Juiced
Death with Dessert
Art, Wine & Bullets
Black Beans & Venom
Smoked Meat (a prequel novella)

Stand-alone Novel:
Lostart Street

Short Stories

Vinnie is the author of over 60 short works. Her stories can be found in: *Santa Cruz Noir; Santa Cruz Weird; Lake Region Review; Porter Gulch Review; Fault Lines; Fishy Business; Hook, Line, and Sinker; Gabba Gabba Hey; The Dark Waves of Winter; Crimeucopia's One More Thing to Worry About, and Let Me Tell You About; Mystery Magazine; Yellow Mama; Mysterical-E; Catamaran Literary Magazine; Indelible; (I Just) Died in Your Arms: Crime Fiction Inspired by One-hit Wonders; Invasive Species; Friend of the Devil,* and more!

www.ingramcontent.com/pod-product-compliance
Lightning Source LLC
Chambersburg PA
CBHW020614110726
47899CB00002B/507